NIGHTSOUL

(RAVEN CURSED BOOK 3)

MCKENZIE HUNTER

McKenzie Hunter

Nightsoul

© 2020, McKenzie Hunter

McKenzieHunter@McKenzieHunter.com

ISBN: 978-1-946457-15-8

ACKNOWLEDGMENT

Every time I publish a book, I'm always humbled by the number of people who make it possible. Thank you to my friends and family for their encouragement and support. Márcia Alexandra, Robyn Mather, Sherrie Simpson Clark, Stacey Mann, you all are wonderful beta readers and I really appreciate you for giving your time and feedback. Elizabeth Bracker, my PA, there are no words to express how much I appreciate everything you do. I am truly grateful.

Meredith Tenant and Therin Knite, thank you for improving my words and helping me tell are better story. Thank you, Orina, for my beautiful cover. I love it.

To my readers, thank you for giving me another chance to entertain you with Erin's story. I hope you enjoy reading it, as much as I enjoyed writing it.

CHAPTER 1

*M*ephisto's placid expression foreshadowed bleaker news. His eyes tracked my glass as it went to my lips for the third time as I waited for him to speak. The liquor hadn't dulled my senses or the cold, hard, irrefutable fact that I had died. *I died.* Mephisto and the Others brought me back to life. That bit of information kept repeating in my head. Dread and curiosity snaked through me. *How did they do that?* Which was more troubling: the dying or the living after death?

He gave me a disapproving leer the fourth time I took a sip. Why was he judging? What was I supposed to do, ignore it while he told me how he, Clayton, Simeon, and Kai brought me back to life without making me a vampire? Even vampires don't technically bring you back to life. You have to feed from them prior to dying and waking up a vamp.

Leaning forward, Mephisto moved the unopened bottle of red wine closer to him. *You're the one who put three bottles on the table.*

I'd finished the first bottle of white before I'd even started with my probing questions and was one glass into the red.

"What are you all?" I asked, my voice low and hesitant.

1

Again, I brought my hand to my neck, feeling for nonexistent vampire bite marks. As if there would be any. When vampires bite, they don't leave evidence, unless they want to. Laving over the area sealed the bite and healed the skin. It's the reason they were able to live in the shadows for so long. There was no evidence of their existence.

"Do you remember the first time you went through the Veil, and what you saw?" Mephisto asked.

Of course I remembered. It was hard to forget such a surreal, heavenly vision. Snow-capped mountains, clear blue water, a soothing breeze. Winged people soaring through the air. Animals: predator and prey living in a harmonious state, neither one the wiser of the hierarchical position. It was peaceful and beautiful. The image initially brought a smile to my face, but somehow the memory was sobering, and I set the glass down without taking another sip. I needed to be totally lucid. No matter how much I wanted to dull it, I *needed* to feel the sharp reality.

"You said that you'd guided me to the nice part of it," I reminded him.

He nodded. "Most of it is nice, but you remember what I said of the residents of the Veil."

"They're stronger," I said.

"And deadlier. Where you don't have gods here, we do"—he stopped for a moment—"the Veil does." Retrieving his glass of wine, he took a sip and sighed. He hadn't touched his food, and I figured he probably wouldn't. Mephisto didn't strike me as a mac and cheese type of man. He was refusing the pinnacle of comfort food. His loss. Noticing me eying his plate, he pushed it toward me.

I may not drink but I'd gorge myself on comfort food.

"The downfall of having power is that people will always desire more, whether it's control or domination. Give them a territory, they will want a city. Give them a city, they'll long for a state, a country, or a nation. For some, that need is unquenchable." He took an indulgent sip, savoring the taste.

"Powerful magical beings never simply acquiesce to civility. Often it requires the threat of consequences and punishment before one can achieve some semblance of it. You've probably seen it here on a smaller scale. I suspect that the Supernatural Task Force exists not because of a superfluous desire, but necessity. Each denizen of the Veil often regulates their own, but then there are those whose actions are so reprehensible they have to be sent to the Abyssus. It's where the most powerful and ruthless denizens are held. Where your mother was eventually sentenced."

I cringed at his use of that title. Technically she was, but I'd prefer "baby host". Yes, baby host worked just fine for me. I waited patiently for him to continue, the familiarity of the word Abyssus going through my mind. But I couldn't place it. Mephisto seemed restrained, doling out just pieces of information and assessing my response. It was going to get worse. I knew it.

"Malific is an Arch-deity and so was her brother, Oedeus, the Lord of the Abyssus. Once a person was sentenced, it was our responsibility to apprehend them. We're the Huntsmen of the Abyssus."

The meaning finally came to me. "Hell," I whispered. "*Abyssus* means hell."

Mephisto barely nodded into the answer. "It's what we called the prison, but I suspect it's quite different than what you're imagining." He gave me a weak smile. "It's not a subterranean dwelling guarded by a fallen angel and where the occupants are tortured. It's similar to your Enclave." He stopped for a moment, choosing his words carefully. "With substantial security measures, mostly magic and fire."

Sounds like hell to me, but go on, Huntsman of Hell. Oedeus was the Lord of Hell and his sister was a hellion, making his job even harder.

3

"Her sentencing wasn't immediate. For over a century she was a terror, flouting the leniency afforded her because of her brother's position," he said, taking a small sip from his glass and exhaling a heavy sigh. "He was too merciful, thinking she would change. He allowed sentimentality and nostalgia to cloud his judgment and his obligations to the Veil. Warnings after warnings he gave her and far too many opportunities.

"After she created the Immortalis and devastated three cities, Oedeus gave his first punishment, enlisting the Caste to exile her army. He assumed it would curb her behavior, discourage her from trying to enlist other gods in her goal to make the Veil a god-rule, an oligarchy. Like Ian, she believed her great power entitled her to rule over others. She lived by the dictum that if you weren't with her, you were against her." His face became pensive. "It didn't dissuade her but incited and spawned retaliation. She created another army and they were…dealt with."

"By you all," I guessed.

He nodded. "It enraged her and she vowed vengeance. Her first act was to break out the occupants of the Abyssus. For nearly three years that's what she did. Oedeus finally recognized Malific was a reprobate and wasn't showing any signs of abandoning her ways. He presented her list of offenses and cruelties to the Warders and she was sentenced."

Before he could continue, his phone vibrated. He pulled it out, looked at it, scowled, and ignored the call. When it immediately vibrated again, he glared at it. "Asher, how can I help you?" he asked in a crisp, tight voice.

I couldn't hear what Asher said but it made Mephisto put a lot of effort into the tight smile. "Yes, I know where Erin is and I'm quite aware that I was the last person she was seen with before she allegedly went missing." His tone was stilted with obligatory politeness.

Mephisto's eyes were steady on mine, mischief playing in

the dark pools. "She is fine. We are having lunch at the moment. I can assure you, Asher, our interests align. I don't want to see her hurt any more than you do. I'll have to ask that you excuse me so we can continue with our meal."

I lobbed a glare in his direction and would have loved to treat Asher to the same for calling Mephisto instead of me. Then it dawned on me that he couldn't. My phone was on the nightstand and I hadn't checked it and was sure it wasn't charged. He'd probably been calling it for days only to have it go to voicemail. That had to be alarming.

I didn't like Mephisto's response and apparently neither did Asher. His reply, whatever it was, made Mephisto's smile vanish and the muscles around his neck distend from his jaw being clenched so tightly.

"You *need* to speak with her? Do you really think she's hurt and I wouldn't disclose that to you?"

Obviously so because after listening for a moment, Mephisto sneered at the phone before placing it on the table. "Erin, apparently my word isn't good enough and the Alpha needs to speak with you. Since I don't want this to escalate to needless violence, it is probably good if you ease his concerns."

He clicked the screen and Asher's voice came over the speaker.

"Mephisto," Asher drawled, "I simply said that I'd like to hear from her and if not, perhaps I need to visit to make sure all is well. She's been missing for three days and her phone has been off for two of them and her neighbors are quite concerned … and, well, it needed to be investigated. Nothing more, nothing less."

Neighbors? Not neighbors—one neighbor. Ms. Harp, president and founder of Team Asher. Your spy and snitch.

I needed to have a conversation with Ms. Harp.

"Asher, Erin's safety when she is with me isn't anything

you have to worry about," Mephisto asserted, his voice now devoid of any pseudo-pleasantness.

"Perhaps, but one must be concerned when she leaves with you and goes missing. It calls into question whether our interests do truly align."

I was getting sick of the dueling niceties. *Just go at it and sling your curses, call each some choice insulting names, and be done with it. While you're at it, why not whip out your man parts, measure them, and see who actually wins this verbal duel?*

"Do I get to take part in this conversation, or do I just sit here and pretend I can't take care of my damn self?" I snipped.

I picked up the phone, took it off speaker, and moved to the opposite side of the kitchen. Mephisto kept a steady eye on me until I turned my back to him.

"What's up, Asher?"

"You tell me. You're the one who's been missing. Are you okay?" he asked, concern heavy in his voice.

No, I'm not okay. I died. How was your day? "Yes. Safe and sound." I sounded sprightlier than I felt.

He responded with a hmmm. "Are you injured?"

"What?" The question spilled out, giving me an opportunity to take creative license with the story.

"Are you injured?" he repeated, impatience in his voice.

"No, not at all," I said. Technically that was true. I was stabbed, had a scar, but I wasn't injured.

"That's not true," he said.

"I call BS on you being able to determine that over the phone."

"If you study a person well enough you can detect changes in modulation and the timbre of their voice. You're holding something back. Tell me, what's wrong?"

"I can't talk right now. I'll be home tomorrow. Let's talk then. Okay?" I rushed out.

"Fine. How bad are your injuries?" he blurted before I could disconnect.

"No injuries." Except for the scar on my stomach from being stabbed.

"Then tomorrow it is." He disconnected and I turned to find Mephisto relaxed back in his chair, brow hitched, and an amused smile curving his lips.

"That was interesting," he said.

I shrugged. "Ms. Harp, my neighbor, has me on her radar for some reason. It's strange, not interesting." I waved it off as inconsequential.

"Ah, yes, this is clearly about Ms. Harp and has nothing to do with the Alpha's obvious interest in you."

My life was getting complicated enough, and I wasn't ready to unbox that, so it had to wait. I needed to find out more about Malific, the Huntsmen, and the Veil's hell.

"Malific was sentenced," I said in redirection.

"Yes, your mother—"

"Malific."

"Malific was sentenced to the Abyssus. The decision was made while we were on recovery missions to find the prisoners she'd released. Instead of waiting, I assume in another bout of sibling sentimentality, Oedeus decided to apprehend her. Alone. Underestimating her mercilessness and viciousness was a mistake. She killed him."

Releasing the breath I hadn't realized I was holding, I remembered Ian telling me of a god that Malific had killed. He didn't tell me it was her brother or the Lord of the Abyssus.

"She killed her brother?" I eked out in a low, incredulous croak.

"She killed the Lord of the Abyssus. The person who'd taken her army away twice and stood between her and what she wanted. Incapable of the same sentimentality, she responded the way she would to anyone else. That's where

7

they differed. Malific was able to separate the two: Lord of the Abyssus and brother. He was incapable of it." Anger hardened Mephisto's words and with noticeable effort he relaxed, allowing his frown to ease and his jaw to unclench.

"Despite killing the Lord, her sentence stood. We were tasked to retrieve her and that was what we'd planned to do. She'd been sentenced to half a century, but it should have been life."

The violence and anger in his words led me to believe that he didn't want her imprisoned, he wanted her dead.

"She was never apprehended by you all but placed in an Omni Ward?" I said.

"Yes. We never had the chance to apprehend her because she discovered our true-god's name and used a Laes to cast us out of the Veil, preventing us from returning. It works similarly to the Caste curse. Unlike fae, our name doesn't give others power to compel us, just to bespell us."

He stood and started to pace the floor. "I've collected so many magical objects, performed thousands of spells, and nothing has worked. If I can get the Laes and destroy it, then it will lift the spell, allowing us to return home."

It's not like he was suffering outside of the Veil. He lived in a mini mansion, wore exquisitely tailored suits, obviously wasn't hurting for money, and had access to the most coveted magical objects known.

"You're anxious to get back to hell?" All the jokes I made about him being Satan were apropos. The Huntsman for Hell.

"Back to my duty. This side of the Veil has its pleasures and enjoyments"—his lips curled as his eyes lifted to meet mine—"but this is not where I belong."

My eyes breezed over his lavish gourmet kitchen. "You seemed to have made it your home."

"I adapt."

"Did your adaptability include how you respond to

magic? Because you didn't respond to the Immortalis magic but you did to a witch's during the poker game," I asked, recalling the spell that had left all attendees frozen in time while the witch and her dragon-shifter partner looted the place. My eyes narrowed on him, pinning him midstep. "Why do I suspect that it didn't?"

A sly smile drifted over his lips, reaching all the way to his eyes and making me remember the first time I borrowed magic from him. He had responded like everyone else, but when I returned from the Veil, he was on his feet, intrigue in his eyes as he watched me.

"The best hand a person can have in any game is the one he never shows. It leaves those in it speculating the cards being held." His smile widened. "You were to do a job, and I was there to get to know more about Erin. I suspected there was more to you than just a mundane death mage, a typical raven cursed. I just needed to find out what."

The glare I bored into him was blistering cold and unwaveringly virulent. A pang of feeling like a specimen under his microscope, having been manipulated, him infiltrating my life for the sole purpose of using me to get back into the Veil wouldn't allow me to release the glower.

"Their magic doesn't affect you, but your magic works against them, doesn't it?" I guessed.

Again, his head barely nodded into his acknowledgment.

I scowled. "When we battled with the Immortalis, you could have done something."

"We did do something. We helped and retrieved Victoria," he pointed out. "No one died, we made sure of that."

"I've been a toy you've been playing with for the past few years," I said.

His placid smile disappeared and his eyes became dark and austere as they held mine with the same intensity. "You may not agree with my tactics of obtaining information or the role that I've assumed in this world, but I have my reasons." He moved closer to me, in that undeniable other-ness of swiftness and grace that made the eyes seem as if they'd lost moments. He exuded carnal self-assurance and flirtatious amusement. "You, Erin Katherine Jensen, are no toy, but I think we'd both enjoy playing together." He was back in the chair across from me by the time I'd pulled the glass of wine toward me.

"You're able to loan me magic because you're a god."

He nodded. "But doing so weakens me. It's the reason your mother will want you dead. As long as you are alive, she's not strong enough to make more Immortalis. She's significantly limited in her ability. As someone who reveled in her strength and her power over others, she will hate not having that advantage. Before, it would have taken the four of us to bring her in, to be strong enough to contain her. But if I were to meet her now, I suspect it would be a level playing field. The Obitus blade can kill both Immortalis and gods. She may have created you as a way to help her escape the ward. You were never to live long enough to be a weak-ness to her."

His look was grim. He gave me another appraising look. "For now, you are not at risk. It's not until she discovers you are alive that she will come for you."

The glass wasn't enough. I was past pristine sipping and pretending to be unaffected by the knowledge that a ruthless god would soon be hunting me. I finished the glass and pulled the remaining bottle to me, opened it, filled the glass just short of the brim, and chugged it. Mephisto looked remarkably calm for someone who was watching me chug down his expensive wine that was meant to be savored, not gulped. Having had my fill of life-altering information, I needed a reprieve.

"I'm heading to the room. When I wake up, I'd like to go home." Going home alone was more appealing than hearing more about the Veil, Mephisto, Hell's Huntsmen, and how

Mommy Dearest would want me dead. No, I was done with finding out more atrocious information about my life and longed for the liminal period: pre finding out I was The Raven.

But my feet were like lead, rooting me into position because of one pressing question I needed answered. "How did you all save my life?"

He approached me with a mirthless curve of his lips. Settling just inches from me, he took my hand, the one without the bottle, and allowed his fingers to trace an imperceptible marking on my arm. After a few seconds, I realized he was tracing the mark of the raven that had appeared on my arm when we went through the Mirra.

"It was a magical death. The knife wound didn't kill you; it was the Tactu Mortem used during that spell that did. We performed a necro-summoner spell. There's always a penalty for performing one. The sacrifice for your life was years of ours," he admitted softly.

The guilt train was right back on track. "How many?"

"Five hundred."

Years.

"Thank you," I whispered, my voice ragged as it broke.

The grim curve of his lips hadn't faltered. "It was between the four of us. A hundred and twenty-five years. Just a drop of time."

For him. Or maybe me. "I'm immortal, too, right?"

"Depends on your father. Witches and mages aren't immortal and their lifespans are similar to humans. Fae and shifters live longer than humans but aren't immortal. Gods and vampires are by definition. We don't age out of life."

"You still gave me back my life. I appreciate it." Taking the hand that was still tracing the image of the raven on me, I gave it an appreciative squeeze.

The wine, the new knowledge of what he was, my role in the world, or my brush with death—or rather, my short

11

period of being dead—still hadn't diminished my desire for magic. With Mephisto no longer suppressing his, I was more aware that I required magic. It was no longer a yearning; it was a need. I had to find a way to get my magic.

His finger gently stroked my hair, then traced the planes of my face. "I'd love to say my motives were selfless, but they weren't. We need her weaker, and keeping you alive is the answer. She is capable of making hundreds of Immortalis and access to unimaginable magic."

Dude, take the win. Sometimes you have to smile, nod your head, and keep the truth to yourself.

As if he read my expression, he said, "I don't want your feelings of appreciation to be conflated or misinterpreted by your desire for me." Unabashed arrogance colored his words.

Moving away from him, I secured the bottle in my hand. "Am I as strong as she is?" I asked.

"We don't know who your father is. If he's another god, yes. Even a demigod's magic would allow you to contend with her power. You come from the strongest bloodline."

Great, now I needed to find the man who decided to father a child with a psychopath whose sole purpose for doing so was to use the infant to release her from prison.

"I'm taking a nap," I announced, knowing that I'd never fall asleep. I needed a reprieve from all the information and time to figure things out.

"Alone?" His dark eyes were wells of salacious and devilish intent. A distraction was exactly what I wanted, and the way he was looking at me ensured that the Huntsman of Hell would offer me a torrid and hedonistic distraction I wouldn't be likely to forget. Mephisto closed the distance between us and the minutes ticked by as he stood just inches from me.

I wanted so desperately to blame my faltering willpower on my status as formerly dead, or the bottles of wine I'd consumed, or my desperate need for a distraction, but there was more. Something nagged at me, as if there were still so many things unrevealed about him that I needed to know.

Clutching the bottle to my chest like it was a floatation device keeping me from drowning in decadent thoughts, I turned and fled up the stairs before I changed my mind.

CHAPTER 2

*A*s I'd suspected, sleep was impossible, so an hour later, with the overnight bag Cory had packed for me hoisted over my shoulder, I searched through the house for Mephisto, who hadn't been in the kitchen, conversation room, or his office. After searching for nearly ten minutes, I walked past the room where Benton was stationed, his head down, reading a book.

Seriously, what is your job and may I submit a resume?

During my pass by the door, he decided to *work*. "Go to the end of the hall, to the left, and follow that hallway downstairs to the gym. He's there with Kai," he provided before returning to his book.

"Thank you, Benton, you're always so helpful," I said in an overly cloying voice.

"Of course, Ms. Jensen, helping you is never a bother." His tone matched mine for artificial sweetness.

"Enjoy your books and...tea?"

"Coffee. And I shall until the next interruption." His voice, saccharine to match his smile, simply told me he couldn't be shamed or out-pettied, but instead of conceding defeat, I accepted it as a challenge.

14

"Carry on. I'll just navigate my way through the house and hope I find it."

"Or you can just follow the directions," he responded, still keeping his ebullient disposition as he made a show of taking a long drink from his cup, keeping his gleeful eyes on me the entire time, before returning it to the table next to him and dragging his attention back to his book.

He was King Petty of the Land of No Shame. Part of me admired it.

The large space was a direct contrast to the rest of Mephisto's home. Muted dark-gray walls and an assortment of blades took up half of one wall, and the other half contained a display of swords from a katana to a broadsword. Mephisto had a sai in hand, and Kai a double-edged karambit, like my weapon of choice. The smell of cedar spiced the air.

All the new information plaguing my thoughts disappeared as I watched them spar. Magic pulsed through the air, and Kai directed the frenetic energy that typically permeated off him like a charge into his movements. The blades were just blurs of silver striking through the air. The sound of steel clinking at a quick steady beat filled the air. Kai soared at Mephisto as if he'd extended his wings and taken flight. Mephisto's movement was a haze, eerily similar to vampire speed. Strike, parry, strike. A quick thrust of Mephisto's weapon grazed Kai's side. Blood spilled from the injury, wetting his shirt. Expecting them to stop, I took a step forward, scanning the room for a first aid kit.

But the fighting didn't stop.

Kai moved as if uninjured, and the duo continued as if this wasn't just sparring but a death match. I swallowed a gasp when Kai thrust a sphere-shaped bundle of magic into Mephisto's chest, flooring him with a loud thud. Before he could stand up again, Kai advanced, the karambit moving in a whirl of figure eights, causing Mephisto to roll away, several of the slashes kissing his skin and leaving cuts.

I watched in a strange combination of horror and intrigue, drawn to the magic that inundated the air, the prowess of every strike and parry, the skill with weaponry. I was fascinated by the fluidity of movement and their adroitness in their use of various fighting techniques, and I was mortified by the unrestrained vehemence. This was half of the Huntsmen, the warriors tasked with retrieving the worst of the worst in the Veil.

Mephisto had guided me to the best part of the Veil. Not where the most power hungry, strong, and cruel dwelled. I'd only seen the innocuous part of it, and I wondered what the other parts were like. Was it war-torn and hostile? Did people who weren't the strongest live in constant fear?

Drawing my attention back to the men, I remained conflicted. I'd sparred many times and it was never like this. The dichotomy of it was confusing as hell. It wasn't hostile but violent. It was aggressive but had undertones of camaraderie.

Standing, Mephisto advanced, thrusting the sai at Kai, who blocked it twice with his weapon, but not the third, lower, that pierced his skin. He made a light hissing sound, his shirt blooming red again.

"Stop," I blurted.

They continued as if I hadn't spoken. Kai's lips lifted into a smile and he advanced in a combination of kicks, thrust, and strikes, putting Mephisto on the defensive and fighting to get enough distance between them.

Mephisto Wynded away, reappearing behind Kai, who flipped back in time to miss the bolt of magic from Mephisto. His wings flicked from his back in many hues of blue, cerulean the most dominant as he distanced himself from Mephisto. Airborne, he slowly descended to the ground, looking more peaceful and relaxed than I'd ever seen him. Kai needed to fly, which I speculated was the reason he was usually a coil of unspent energy.

"We should stop. We're upsetting The Raven," Kai said, his voice low and concerned.

"Erin," I corrected. "I'm sorry, did I overreact or should I have let you two kill each other? I just need to know the rules of engagement."

"Kill each other? Neither of us was in any danger of death." Kai extended his weapon to me with a twirl of his finger. It was clean, all evidence of him trying to slice and dice Mephisto into bite-size pieces gone. "It's just steel," he said.

The Immortalis could only be killed using an Obitus blade, I suspect the same was true of gods.

I examined the craftsmanship of his weapon; the blade was much sharper than mine. I turned to Mephisto to look for the wounds I was sure would be there. Lifting his shirt, he showed unmarked skin, a reminder of the time in his kitchen when I'd ripped off his shirt and seen velvet skin stretched over the delineated muscles of his stomach and definition in his chest and back. I dragged my eyes from him and focused on Kai's deep-tawny skin and his seraphic features, fitting of a person with wings.

He snapped his wings back, then they disappeared. I assumed I was gawking. "Nice wings," I said.

He looked away, a smirk curling his lips. His eyes closed momentarily, causing his long lashes to brush against his cheeks. His skin was slightly flushed along his high cheekbones.

How much had they held back during our encounter with the Immortalis to hide their identity? Seeing their movement, command of magic, the otherness that enveloped them was a clear giveaway.

Kai lifted his shirt, where Mephisto had speared him like a steak, showing healed, unscarred skin.

I don't need any more show and tell, so everyone can stop flashing me. I get it, you're immortal and damn hard to kill. Or even scar.

Getting increasingly frustrated with so-called being a god without any of the benefits, I said, "I get injuries all the time."

Mephisto deliberated on the comment. "Magic heals us. We need to figure out how to remove your restrictions."

Kai wasn't able to hide his doubt as well as Mephisto could.

"It doesn't seem like an easy task?" I asked.

"I wish we knew who your father is. It would make things simpler. If we knew the source, mage, witch, god, or hybrid..." Mephisto mused, cleaning off his weapon with magic and returning it to its position on the wall.

"If it's hybrid magic, it will be harder to remove the restriction," Kai said.

"Why would anyone restrict my magic?" It seemed like such a cruel thing to do. Leaving me in a world of magic, craving it and needing it.

He shrugged. "I don't know."

"Maybe they thought I'd be like Malific and too dangerous to have it."

"What if it wasn't an act of malice but one of kindness? To keep you from being found," Kai offered. "Like magic can find like magic. You're Malific's child, a magical link. She'd be able to track you each time you used it. The beauty and the curse of our magic."

My eyes quickly snapped in Mephisto's direction, fixing him with a hard stare. "When I borrowed magic from you, I could be tracked whenever I used it?"

"Yes." His face was indecipherable as we held each other's gaze, and I flushed at the memories of the many times I'd considered running with his magic, thinking that I wouldn't be found. This was one of the innumerable things I didn't know about Mephisto.

18

His finger trailed along the area on my arm where the raven had been imprinted.

"I would like to try some spells in an effort to remove it. Can we?"

I nodded. As if I'd object.

———

Clayton and Simeon were already in the room where Mephisto kept his collection of magical objects. Clayton was slumped in the corner, thumbing through a book. I tilted my head to get a look at the cover. At my approach, he looked up.

"That's *Mystic Souls*," I said. Had Asher stolen it from them? Or had they "borrowed" or taken it from the same person Asher had? Or was this the second one?

"How do you know of this book?"

"Because I tried to use it to prevent me from killing when I borrowed magic."

He pushed away from the wall, his face brightened, eyes alight. "You have the second one?"

"Not anymore. It didn't work."

His brow furrowed and he slumped back into the corner of the wall, eyes unblinking. "You got rid of it because it didn't work. There are only two in the world."

"It wasn't mine. I returned it."

"Who has it?" Mephisto asked. The Huntsmen had surrounded me. I doubted they realized how bad an idea that was. Neither death nor the knowledge that I had my own magic had subdued my longing.

Their magic unmuted, the full intensity of it over-whelmed the room—and me.

Step back, please.

I closed my eyes and took several breaths, and when I

19

opened them, they had moved away. Apprehension and intrigue were on their faces.

"Who has it?" Mephisto repeated.

"I can't disclose that."

His lips pressed into a tight line.

"Do you plan to use the *Mystic Souls* to try to remove the restriction?" I asked, hoping to redirect them to the task at hand. No matter how I tried to tamp down my hope in the face of innumerable failures, I was working with gods now and it seemed like anything was possible.

While they prepared for the spell, pulling magical objects out of drawers and Clayton flipping through the pages of the *Mystic Souls*, hope became a blazing inferno in my chest. The reassuring smile Clayton gave me only made things worse. I was blissful when he opened the book and placed a scribed rectangular granite-looking object next to me, despite my apprehension of using anything from the *Mystic Souls*. Despite a sudden memory of Madison's tears.

"Ready?" he asked.

I nodded a little too enthusiastically.

Glancing down at the spell, I had no idea what he was about to do and should have been more concerned that he was doing a spell that Madison said looked like Akkadian but wasn't certain.

"What language is that?"

"Akkadian."

Madison would be happy to know that she was right, but it wouldn't have helped because we didn't speak it, nor did we know how to translate it.

"You can translate it?" I asked, my optimism unfazed by him using a spell written in a dead language.

His confident mien, reassuring smirk, and comforting warm chestnut-colored eyes would reassure anyone.

"You need to hold this." He gave me the granite object, then he retrieved a peculiar-looking blade with markings on it and handed it to Simeon. This wasn't a spell they'd just come up with on a whim.

"Pearl is fine. I checked on her yesterday," he informed me.

Cue performance. This was the time that I had to pretend to be overly concerned for murder kitty—the apex predator with fangs and claws that could tear through flesh. *Okay.*

"Thank you. How's Victoria?" My performance must have been believable because he flashed me a smile.

"Victoria's fine, but we think that Pearl is getting a cold."

How am I supposed to respond to this information? Kitty got a cold. And?

"Oh, poor kitty," I cooed.

"Yeah, Victoria is going to take her to the vet today."

My imagination went wild. I envisioned Victoria requesting an airlift to the vet for her poor sick, spoiled kitten while stroking her murder paws.

Before Simeon could give me any more updates about Pearl, Clayton cued him to use the knife. He moved so quick, it wasn't until I saw the blood welling on my finger that I knew he'd cut me. A droplet fell onto the granite slab.

Clayton's deep melodious voice made the spell like a rhythmic stanza, making the lost language sound poetic. Enthralling to the point my skin felt like it was being singed, making me gasp in pain. The raven flashed on my arm, then disappeared, only to reappear, sending more shocking aches throughout my arm. Clayton continued with the spell and I gulped more air, tears welling in my eyes. The concerned look on Mephisto's face made me wonder if my tears were similar to the sanguineous ones that Madison shed. Then clear droplets fell onto my arms.

Mephisto's jaw clenched before he looked away from me. The slab in my hand disintegrated into ash and the raven made one more appearance, pain pulsing around it like needle pricks until it formed a red circle and disappeared.

"What the hell?"

Kai's bellowing drew our attention to Clayton, who was gaping at an empty page.

Mephisto rushed to the book and both he and Clayton let out a string of curses, flipping through the book and letting out sighs of relief when they found that only that page had disappeared.

After giving each other knowing glances, their attention turned to me. They didn't say it, but I could see the apprehension on their faces.

I needed to find my father.

CHAPTER 3

$\mathcal{T}$he motorcade of Clayton and Kai on the motorcycles and Simeon bringing up the rear wasn't as dramatic as the elaborate light show performance they were putting on in my apartment. Wisps of dark smoke and striking light interwove throughout the room. It became dense with magic, powerful, omnipotent, and arcane. I remained awestruck, watching them move in unison, magic twirling, merging, twining, and twisting as it formed a magical grid to create obstacles and complicated wards, barriers to prevent anyone using my home as an exit from the Veil and also to prevent Wynding. It also meant I couldn't go through the Veil from here, either. It was a necessary trade-off to prevent Malific from just popping into my home.

Focusing on the magic being performed, I used it as an excuse to not look at Mephisto. To ignore the furtive glances he kept casting in my direction. When it was done, the magic-drenched room was hard to tolerate. Room stuffiness or an odor could be improved by opening a window, but not the remnants of strong magic. I'd have to wait until it settled. Knowing what these Others were, the type of magic they possessed and the sheer power of it, should have been a deterrent.

After using every distraction possible to keep from looking at them, I lifted my eyes, taking in what and who they were. Immortals tasked with apprehending and punishing gods and the worst of the worst in the supernatural world. The Huntsmen of Hell.

My lips twisted but soon faltered at the absurdity of me calling Mephisto "Satan." It wasn't a misnomer. In a way, that's what they were. Warriors by duty. Bounty hunters by necessity. But in the end, they were the guardians of hell.

Kai looked bored but not in need of burning off stored energy. He didn't seem frenzied but subdued, as much as someone like him could be.

"We're done," he said, not above pointing out the obvious. He looked at the other three.

Clayton kept a considerate but seemingly cautious eye on me. I suspected he was wondering about the other *Mystic Souls* or recalling what had happened earlier.

Mephisto's eyes moved in the direction of the bottle of vodka and the glass I put on the counter. I brought out more glasses; we could all drink.

Instead of coming to the kitchen, Simeon, Kai, and Clayton offered me faint smiles laden with apprehension and intrigue. They tossed another look in Mephisto's direction then at the glasses on the counter before leaving.

Don't judge me.

Mephisto lingered. Slipping the drink from my hand, he brushed strands of hair from my face, his finger brushing delicately across my skin. "Are you sure you want to do this?"

"Do I want to get so drunk I forget I died four days ago, released my mother from a prison that she rightfully deserved to be in, and discovered that the magic I don't really have use of has been magically restricted? A restriction that you and the other super-gods can't remove, which means it was put in place by someone stronger than you all combined." I took the drink from him. "Yes, I want to do this. I want to finish this bottle and then possibly work on another and figure out what I'm going to do tomorrow. I'll find a way to fix this." I lifted the glass to him. "But today, I drink."

Mephisto didn't deserve my anger or my frustration, but with each moment, it was harder to contain my emotions. Taking the bottle from me, he poured a little into one of the glasses and tossed back the contents. It was cheap vodka, a brand he'd never drink.

He didn't comment on it. Instead, he removed the distance that remained between us. His vodka-laced breath brushed lightly against my cheek. Not quite a kiss. Just a gentle brush against my skin. Then he pressed his lips to mine, the vodka lingering on his lips and tongue. His mouth was exploring mine, deep and passionate, and for a moment, all the drama of the past few days escaped as his fingers splayed against my back, pulling me closer to him. When we broke apart, we stayed close, shallow pants escaping us both, heat radiating. I didn't want to move to break the connection.

"We'll figure this out. I'll remove your magical restriction," he vowed. He backed away, his dark eyes fixed on mine, until he made it to the door. Then he left me to my day drinking. Or more. I took a mental inventory of my stash: weed, Oxy, powder in my drawer. All had been tried or sampled as a way to manage the magic cravings. I took a sip from my drug of choice. I wanted to forget, just for today. Tomorrow, I'd handle things.

———

I didn't drink the bottle. Not even a glass. I had been nursing the same glass for the past hour. Being drunk or so high my thoughts were clouded wasn't going to help my disaster of a problem. I needed magic. If Mommy Dearest was in fact coming after me, I needed magic—a lot of it. Strong magic. An Obitus blade or whatever else killed gods. Bile crept up my throat. I might have to kill my mother. What the hell type of torrid Greek tragedy had my life become?

My inappropriate boom of laughter filled the room.

"Can I get in on the joke?" said Asher's voice from the other side of the door.

I groaned.

"I can hear that, too."

Still seated on the sofa, I held my breath and turned my ear toward the door to hear if he was still there.

"Erin, do you think when you hold your breath, I think you disappeared?" he asked, humor in his voice.

Glass still in hand, I answered the door. His deep-gray eyes dropped to the glass and then roved leisurely over every inch of me, from my fluffy socked feet to my leggings to my fitted V-neck t-shirt. "Are you hurt?" he asked.

No, just died and had to be brought back to life. How was your day?

"No, I'm fine."

His attention fixed on something behind me. I looked over my shoulder. The network of magical webs, lines, and wards that remained visible for a few minutes after the Huntsmen had left was now gone. Could he still see the fragments?

Drawing his attention back to me, he asked, "May I come in?"

I nodded and stepped aside. He kept looking around the room, brow furrowed, eyes scanning over everything, then moved to the sofa and sat. "Is Mephisto still here?"

"What did I tell you about smelling people and things?"

"It's not intentional. I can't help that I'm hyperaware of

26

things. Like the erratic beat of your heart and your ragged breathing."

He made a face. "The heart doesn't change much when you hold your breath. Stop doing that, it's weird hearing your breath just cut off."

"Most people don't hear any of that!" I plopped down next to him. "Want a drink?"

Before I could object, he took my glass from me and sipped. Then he handed it back to me.

"I meant from your own glass."

Flashing me a devilish smile, he relaxed back. "I don't mind sharing." He stopped smiling. "Your drink." He took another look around the room and frowned. "What's going on, Erin? You leave with Mephisto, go missing for days, and come back smelling"—he leaned in and inhaled—"different."

"Stop smelling me."

"Your eyes look different, too. I can't figure out what it is."

"Stop looking at me."

"Really? Stop looking at you? What should I look at?" he asked, humor in his voice.

"Don't listen to me. I'm being terrible. Sorry."

"Your words, not mine." He slipped the glass from me and took another sip.

"So…we're just drinking from the same glass now."

Taking another draw from it, he flashed me a wicked look. "Seems that way." Then he placed the glass on the table in front of us. "You were gone for three days. Ms. Harp was convinced Mephisto had abducted you. Her story changed, becoming more elaborate with each retelling. And things are different with you. What's happening with you, Erin?" The concern in his voice matched his eyes and was hard to bear. Was the weight bogging me down that apparent? Did my eyes look vacant? Was I some type of revenant?

Throat tightening at the thought of answering, I sank

back into the sofa with a sigh. When I laid my head on his shoulder, he reached for my hand and stroked it.

"I can't talk about it right now." *Or maybe ever.* How much of this was mine to tell? I culled through all the information for something I could tell him, hoping it would offer some relief.

"I'm adopted," I said.

He remained quiet, then, "There's more, isn't there?" His voice was so soft I could barely hear him. He must have forgotten I wasn't a shifter.

Feeling the weight of his chin resting on my head, I sighed. *You don't know the half of it.*

The need to distract myself became more urgent. Surprising both of us, I suddenly moved, sitting bestride him, resting my head on his chest. He stilled. Part of him stilled. One very prominent part of him was awake. *Very* awake.

I cleared my throat and looked down, and he shifted a little and looked away. A light flush of color swept over his cheeks. "You surprised me," he explained.

"Hmm." I rested my head in the crook of his neck. I'd shocked myself. At that moment, I understood the complexity of an Alpha's existence. When his arms encircled me, I realized why the people in his pack found such comfort in the Alpha's touch. His excessive heat was like being wrapped in an electric blanket. His fingers caressing my back was as soothing as hot chocolate on a snowy day. The feel of the mug's warmth against cold fingers. I closed my eyes and melted into him with a sigh.

Asher ran a comforting hand over my back. Was it just Asher who made me feel like this, or did every Alpha possess the innate ability to soothe and invoke such calm? I found myself pondering how I could test this with Sherrie, the Lion Pack's Alpha.

How would I test my theory? Did I just walk up to her, jump into her arms, and bury my face in her neck, forcing her to cuddle me? The image brought a smile to my face even though I knew that situation would end up with me on the ground, her teeth bared and her claws at my throat.

"You have a devious look on your face. What are you thinking about?" Asher asked.

I contemplated whether to tell him. It helped with my effort to distract myself from the events of the last few days.

"I'm just wondering if Sherrie's as cuddly as you are because she's an Alpha, or is that just an Asher thing?"

"I'm cuddly, despite the claws, teeth, predator tendencies, and the thrill of the hunt?"

"Yeah," I admitted, sighing against him. "That's just the useless part I ignore."

A chuckle reverberated in his chest, causing my body to vibrate.

"Being with me, like this, makes you think of Sherrie?" He laughed again. "Erin, you are such a peculiar woman."

"What do you think she'd do in that situation?"

"You're not part of her pack and I doubt she cares whether or not you are uneasy or in need of comfort," he finally admitted after several minutes of deliberation. Despite the time, shifters tended to be direct to a fault.

"She doesn't like me," I said. It didn't bother me, but I liked to know my enemies or potential enemies.

"She believes you're a wildcard and questions your loyalty to my pack."

"Sherrie thinks I should be loyal to *your* pack? I'm not a shifter."

"You're not, but she assumes there's something going on between the two of us and because of it, your loyalty should be to me and my pack."

"What do you think?"

His hand ran idly over my skin, gentle and attentive. "I think," he said softly, "that you have your own pack and it

29

consists of Madison and Cory. That's where your loyalty lies. The two of us will always have split allegiances."

I'd returned to my position pressed against him, my face cradled in the crook of his neck, inhaling his scent, considering what he said. A pack wasn't what I'd call us. Cory was my friend and Madison was the closest thing I had to a sister. I'd protect them as vehemently as I knew they'd protect me.

After several minutes, he eased me away, his arms resting on my waist. "Tell me the part you can tell me," he urged. "There's something bigger going on and it has something to do with Mephisto." He stopped abruptly and made a face and I suspected that somehow I had confirmed it. My heart rate? "I realize you have to keep a great number of confidences if he's involved. Tell me what you can and let me help."

I frowned.

"Please." He pulled me to him, his voice warm and entreating, his touch liquid and soothing.

"I'm adopted. Or, rather, I was just left on a doorstep. I can't believe that happened. That should only happen in the movies," I said. His arms tightened around me. "And I found out that my mother is a psychopathic god in the Veil, who was imprisoned for killing another god. Apparently she wants to kill me, too."

I recounted the stories I'd read and had been told about her. Her violence against shifters, attacking them mid-change, while they were answering the call of the moon. Killing the witches who'd aligned themselves with the shifters. Her goal to take over the Veil, forcing all the other supernaturals to live under the gods rule. Abruptly I stopped, astonished that I'd revealed that much. My mind raced over everything I knew of shifters.

"Shifters can't compel, can they?"

His finger brushed against my cheek. "No, Erin, I'm just that alluring." His lips curved into the overly assured Asher smile.

30

"Well that just broke the spell," I countered, rolling my eyes.

I don't think they did. Tentatively, he pressed his lips against mine, coaxing a response from me. And I responded. Kissing him, my fingers tangled in his hair, pulling me closer to him. Tasting him and the alcohol, the warmth of his tongue sensually caressing mine. Firm fingers kneading into my skin. I wanted a distraction and Asher delivered.

He kissed me more fervently. Nails grazing my back sent a shiver through me. Desperately wanting more, my hand slid down over the defined muscles of his arm, the corded muscles of his chest, the definition of his abs. Before I could unbutton his shirt, he pulled away. Panting, he pressed one finger against my lips and looked at the door. His thumbs continued to glide gently and rhythmically over my stomach —and my new scar.

Someone knocked.

"Erin," said Ms. Harp's wan voice. We remained silent. Motionless on the sofa, I tried to ignore the finger on one hand lazily stroking my scar and the other spanned across my back, toward the clasp of my bra.

"Asher." Her voice was rough and distressed. Within seconds, Asher was on his feet, his hands cupped under my butt. He lowered me to the sofa and quickly headed for the door. Not even taking the time to fix his disheveled hair or his clothing, he opened it.

"What's wrong?" he asked in a concern-drenched voice.

I never thought I'd have to share a man with a septuagenarian woman, but there I was. My life was never simple. She kept moving her head, ducking and weaving, trying to get a better view behind him. I could just see her gray bun bobbing in and out and slight glimpses of her face.

"Is she okay? Did *he* do anything? She goes out with him one night and is missing for three days. She travels clear across the country with you and returns that same day

31

unharmed. He's dangerous to her," she said in a stage whisper.

Unharmed? Trees kicked my ass, I thought, recalling our visit to Dante's Forest.

"She's fine. He didn't take her. She chose to stay with him."

"Did she tell you that? Then why are you here? Who says something like that? I told you things aren't right with her."

I'm still here.

She was talking loud enough for me to hear; I might as well join the conversation. Inching in closer to Asher, I ducked under the arm blocking the door.

"I was sick," I told her, hoping she wasn't as good as detecting a lie as Asher.

"For three days?"

"Yes."

Her lips twisted to the side. She fixed me with her skeptical topaz eyes. "And the three other men who left your house with him this morning, were they doctors to address your ailment?"

Now who's the Chatty Cathy, you gossip?

She pulled a look of innocence when my eyes narrowed on her. Patiently, she waited for an answer.

"No, they weren't."

Her inquiring brow hitched. "Who are they? I'm sure Asher's curious, too. He was quite worried." Then she looked at Asher and beckoned him to lean down. She brushed his mussed waves. "And your hair, what on earth happened to it? You look like you've been in a fight."

I'd be damned if I was going to let her interrogate me. Placing a big smile on my face, I said, "Well, you wanted to discuss something with Asher, so let me leave you to it."

Taking my cue, he asked, "What do you need, Evelyn?"

I turned around to see her pull a phone out of her pocket and extend it to him, nearly shoving it into his chest.

"I hate this thing. Give me my old phone back."

"This one is better, and if anything happens, I can find you."

"It keeps blocking my calls and most of the time I can't unlock the stupid thing. And no, I don't want it to recognize my face. I want to just pick it up and use it. How hard is that?"

With a heavy sigh, he looked over his shoulder. "I'll be back."

"I'll be here." I gave him a glib half smile. I didn't miss the narrowed-eye sneer she gave me when she turned around. I wondered if the whole phone thing was a ploy to get him out of the grips of the siren.

Pressing my finger to my lips, they still felt warm. I slid the glass away and propped my feet on the table and tried not to review the past five days of my life. It was hard not to.

What am I going to do?

I was still wondering about my next course of action when Asher knocked and then opened the door.

"Your date's over already?" I asked the frazzled Alpha, who was sporting a rigid scowl.

"Her old phone belonged in a museum. It was a flip phone without an ability to track it. I've seen better burners."

"Why do you need to track her?"

"I don't *need* to track her. I can usually find anyone in the city if I need to, but scents vanish. It's hard telling her the gravity of what she is without scaring her. She's a person born of a cat-shifter who lived as a loner. She never changed and has enhanced senses. Especially her eyesight and hearing."

"I knew she didn't need that hearing aid!"

Asher laughed. "No, she doesn't need that hearing aid, or the cane for that matter. She slipped on ice a few years

33

ago and got it." He stopped and chewed the bottom of his lip.

"I know. She's a friend of the pack and I can't reveal anything you tell me."

"That's not it. She fell on the concrete and didn't sustain an injury. She's resilient like shifters—it takes a lot to break our bones."

"Except when you change," I pointed out. Although shifters with experience do it with exceptional speed, bones break and realign, tendons stretch, and muscles tear and reform to accommodate their animal form. Considering that it all happens in a matter of moments, it doesn't seem so absurd that humans didn't immediately accept them. And they didn't seem to exert the same energy to change as I had when I used a transformation spell to turn into a cat.

"If her shifter parent is a cat, why isn't Sherrie handling her?"

He shot me a devilish smile. "I can't turn it off. Women, no matter the age, are drawn to me. It's a curse and a blessing," he drawled. Stepping closer to me, his lips quirked into a half smile.

"It's getting easier," I shot back. He leaned down and kissed the tip of my nose. I inhaled his earthy musk. When we pulled away, his face was serious. "I have a rapport with her. It would complicate things to abandon her and heighten her anxiety. No need to put her through that, if she can't change. She's a friend of the pack, that's all that matters. Sherrie will treat her as such, if I'm not able to help." A frown emerged and quickly disappeared, but hints of it remained in his narrowed eyes.

"And?"

His brows inched together in question.

"And, what's concerning you besides her being a cantankerous anomaly who's fallen for your *alleged* charisma?"

Flashing me a wolfish grin, he said, "There's nothing alleged about it, and you know it."

I rolled my eyes. *Ugh, this guy.*

His smile quickly fell and his mood grew heavy. "I'm torn," he admitted.

Typically taciturn when not dealing with his pack, Asher sharing with me took a great effort, I knew that. Asher washed his hands over his face and sighed. "I'm curious about her, too. I've debated bringing people in to study her." By people, I knew damn well it wouldn't be anyone outside his pack, or at the very least another shifter.

"What concerns you?" I asked, keeping my voice soft and as unobtrusive as possible, surprised I'd gotten this much from him.

"Studying her opens up doors to knowing of her existence. And if by some chance it gets out, I can't control what others would do with that information. Shifters who don't have to answer to the call of the moon but possess all the heightened senses and abilities? People can be cruel when they think the results are worth it."

I wondered if he was including himself. Blinded by good intent, everyone can blur the line between good and bad, ethical and unethical, moral and immoral.

Before I could question him further, he started moving to the kitchen. "Finish what you were telling me earlier," he urged. With my refilled glass in hand, I followed him and sat at the breakfast nook while he made himself comfortable. After taking a moment to look in my refrigerator, he glowered. Then he searched the small pantry next to it, and then my cabinets.

"You don't have any food," he announced. I didn't miss the judgment in his voice.

I need none of that.

"I have plenty. There's a large multipack box of popcorn

and two bags of chips. Look farther back in the freezer, you'll find a bag of pizza rolls."

"Pizza rolls?" His eyes widened and his lips twisted.

"Yes, Your Highness, *pizza rolls*." I hadn't had a chance to shop. *I was busy fighting a rogue fae and dying.*

"What have you had to eat today?"

"A bag of popcorn, cheese sticks, and this." I raised my glass.

Taking out his phone, he scrolled through it. "Chinese?"

I shrugged. "Fine, I'm not picky." He glanced at my fridge and I could see the comment *obviously* glint in the recesses of his slate-gray eyes, the devilish smirk that pursed his lips. My eyes narrowed on him, daring him to say it out loud.

He met my gaze and his lips twitched, fighting the urge to meet the challenge. Jaw clenched, after several lulling moments and considerable effort, he did.

Once Asher ordered the food, I returned to the sofa, plonked down on it, and refilled my glass. Asher joined me in silence, but I could feel his intense gaze on me. When I turned to face him, I took another long sip from the glass and handed it to him. It was a communal drink now.

"Your mother's a god, but what about your dad?"

I took the drink from him and nearly emptied it. "I don't know who or what he is. I'm not a death mage, never have been, so I doubt he's one. My parents had been hiding that from me for years. Not raven cursed. I can't use magic because somebody decided to restrict it."

"Why?"

I shrugged a response and filled my glass again. There was so little ice in the glass that I might as well have been drinking the vodka straight. I took a sip, my eyes remaining on Asher's disapproving gaze. Taking the glass from me, he tossed back the remaining contents. Then he grabbed the bottle and drained it.

"If you didn't want me to drink, you could have just said so."

He leaned in, his finger brushing rhythmically along my cheek, and whispered, "I want to have this conversation with you sober."

"We should have had this conversation five hours ago," I teased.

He went to the kitchen and returned with a bottle of water and handed it to me. "Why was your magic restricted?" he asked.

I shrugged. "Either because my mother is a psychopath and they didn't want her daughter out there doing the same, or they were trying to protect me and prevent me from being found each time I used my magic."

He considered my answer for a long time. "Hmm. I think it was your father who restricted your magic."

"Why?"

"You were adopted as a baby, right?"

I barely nodded my confirmation.

"Who else would want to protect you other than your father?"

"My father—" I stopped abruptly. Why was I calling these people mother and father as if they were anything more than people who helped give me life? Egg-lady and Sperm-dude didn't seem right either. Donor number one and donor number two? Perfect. "My *father* had sex with a certifiable evil goddess with a thirst for violence, murder, and domination. I'm not sure he's the nurturing, protecting type."

"I wouldn't rule it out. Sometimes people fall in love with people they never expected to. Perhaps she seduced him, for the sole purpose of making you."

No, she desired a death that would trick the spell that bound her into thinking she was dead and releasing her. But I kept that part to myself.

"The question still remains, why would she want to kill you?" he asked.

Was that information I could give him? Again, I found myself trawling through all the information Mephisto had given me, trying to determine which information wasn't privileged.

How do shifters keep this straight?

The arrival of our food gave me more time to sort through the information and edit what was necessary. The Huntsmen's secrets meticulously intertwined with mine. By the time I made it to the kitchen to help him with the food, I'd sorted things out the best that I could.

Shifters had helped with taking down the Immortalis, and I wasn't under any illusions that Asher didn't know about them. The shifters might work for the STF, but everyone knew where their true loyalty lay.

"My mother created an army, the Immortalis. A lot of them have been killed, and because of me, she can't make another army. Her magic is shared with me."

"And you're sure she's able to get you?" he asked between bites.

I nodded. Unsure of anything, I relied on Mephisto's information.

His eyes assessed me with uncertainty. "Are you sure?"

I shook my head. Something would give me away. The human lie detector was making it difficult to navigate and dance around the information.

"How did she escape?" he asked, ignoring his food.

That was something I couldn't tell him. Shoving several more bites of food into my mouth, I shrugged.

"Does it have anything to do with that new scar near your stomach?"

"No."

His lips kinked into a disapproving scowl.

"I'd rather you tell me it's confidential than lie to me. There are no lies between us."

Nearly choking on my food, I hurried to chew it and chugged the remainder of my water. "There aren't?" I asked. "Asher, I think there are plenty of lies between us, the only difference is you're usually the one telling them."

He gave me a smug, indulgent look as if he was standing by his statement.

"How did you get the *Mystic Souls* book?"

"You wanted it. I acquired it."

"Did you steal it?" Cory was convinced Asher had stolen the arcane book that I tried to use to allow me to borrow magic without killing the donor.

"You wanted it. I acquired it," he repeated, the look on his face intensifying. If he didn't want to give me the truth, he wouldn't. People who are good at detecting lies tend to be great at telling them. Even if I hooked him to a lie detector, I was confident he'd pass.

"The Salem Stone. How did you get to it before I did?"

"I'm a really good hunter."

I glared at him.

"No lies, just secrets between us," I said.

"Semantics."

We finished our food, allowing the conversation to devolve into nonsensical and superficial topics, which I appreciated. I had a lot to think about, including me wanting to use Asher as a distraction. I wasn't totally convinced that's all it was. When we decided to watch a movie, my leaning against him with his arm wrapped around me was the bottom of the list of bad choices.

Asher offered to stay but I needed to be alone.

It wasn't just solitude I wanted. I needed time to sort things out. My dad could have been the one who took me and restricted my magic. Who and what was he to possess magic like that?

CHAPTER 4

*A*sher finishing off the vodka was probably for the best because instead of waking up with a throbbing headache, I awoke motivated to discuss the past few days with Madison. Asher probably woke up without any problems—the benefits of a shifter's metabolism.

Madison's decision to give me time to process things was appreciated, but unfortunately Cory didn't share the same belief or possess the discipline. Since informing him of my leaving Mephisto's, I'd received at least ten text messages and one call while Asher and I were watching the movie.

"Movie! Your life is in shambles, probably in peril, and you're cuddling with Asher!"

I wanted to snap back, *I died! Can't I at least enjoy a movie before battling my mother?* But with Asher so close, I just snarked back something and told him to meet me at Madison's, so I wouldn't have to repeat the information.

The conversation with them would be easier than it was with Asher because I could give them the truth, straight no chasers. And maybe the tightness that had settled in the muscles of my neck and chest would ease.

Weaving my way through traffic that was heavier than

usual for a Saturday, I got off the highway, two exits from Madison's, and watched the black R8 that had been following me since I'd left my apartment exit as well. And the matte-black SUV with a modified grill that made the vehicle look more hostile than any vehicle should. It was easy to assume mere coincidence when I first noticed them, but when they remained close after my coffee stop, I knew I was being followed.

Not wanting them to follow me to Madison's, I pulled into the shopping plaza and parked close to a convenience store. There was enough activity that if I wanted to draw attention to myself, I could. When they parked on either side of me, making it brazenly apparent they were tailing me, I realized I hadn't been at all cunning in spotting them.

With my double-karambit in hand and a knife sheathed at my ankle, I stepped out of the car and quickly made my way to the driver's window of the R8, rapped on the window, and jerked my head at him to get out.

"Shifter," I groaned under my breath as the tall, olive-skinned man who had me by nearly seven or eight inches stepped out. If it weren't for the glint of predatory awareness in his chocolate eyes, I would have been met with boredom. Thin and wiry, his short-sleeve shirt exposed sinewy muscled arms and a tapestry of ink snaking up them when he crossed them over his chest.

"Yes?" he inquired, brow hitched up. The purse of his lips hinted at the same boredom I saw in his eyes.

The shorter woman who stepped out of the SUV had a predaceous mien that made me grip my karambit tighter. Although stout in build, she moved with the fluid grace and self-assurance of shifters. She looked like she was on a secu-rity detail job, dressed in a black shirt and pants. I noted the bulges in her clothes that I suspected were concealed weapons.

"What's wrong?" the female shifter asked.

Mr. Bored shrugged. "I don't know."

"You've been made." *I have to stop watching police dramas and thrillers with Cory.*

Mr. Bored smirked. "Made? We weren't hiding. We were following you in plain sight. Asher wanted our presence to be known."

"Asher? He put you up to it?"

"No, we had nothing better to do than go with you on a Starbucks run," the female shifter quipped.

Fixing the comedy duo with a hard look, I said, "I don't want to be followed."

They responded with disinterested and dismissive looks.

"That's not really up to you. Maybe you should take it up with Asher," the female shifter finally said, ending the awkward silence.

Standing up taller, my hard glare shifted to her first. Her diminutive size made me think she'd cower easier. She didn't, returning my glare with one of her own: icy, steely, and indomitable. And a little bitchy. Served me right for judging a book by its cover. Mr. Tall and Bored's gaze mirrored hers with just a skosh of jackassery to drive home the point.

My badass stare-down has been honed from years of practice. It got results and I gave them the full intensity of it. "Stop. Following. Me. I command you." My voice was dagger sharp and arctic cold. For effect, I shifted my weapon, allowing the sun to gleam off it, making it look more menacing.

Their roars of laughter and looks of amused incredulity were, frankly, insulting and ignited my anger.

Shifters are the worst.

I was the reason they were immune to magic. Shouldn't I be their queen or something? Or at the very least Alpha by proxy.

Their narrowed gazes followed me as I stalked back to

my car. Yanking open the door, I snatched my phone off the seat. Then I gave myself several minutes to get hold of my emotions before scrolling through my contacts and calling Asher.

"Erin," he answered in a raspy purr. A smile was in his voice and I could envision the half grin and its unyielding self-assurance.

"Call them off."

"Ah, you're out and about, I see."

"Yes, I'm out and about and being followed by *your* shifters. Send them away."

"No," he responded without consideration. Hearing the amused satisfaction in his voice just made me more determined.

"Asher, this isn't a debate."

"Exactly. Yesterday you told me someone wanted you dead. I'm not about to let that happen. You're right, there's not going to be a debate. The answer is no. If we're done here, I'd like to get back to work. No matter how effortless I make it look, running a business is a challenge."

I didn't immediately respond and let him hear me seething. He had to know this wasn't going to end that easily for him.

"Goodbye, Erin." With that, the phone disconnected. I couldn't bear to look out my window and see the smug looks on my sentries' faces.

When I started the car and pulled out without warning, I knew it wouldn't take long for them to catch up. Out of the rearview mirror, I got a glimpse of the female shifter's grin when I got back on the exit in the opposite direction and sped to my destination. The towering building at the beginning of the street dwarfed all the others except for its twin at the end, the Lion Pack's building. Both were a dark brown, with lush manicured bushes flanking the entryway. A lighted fountain decorated the front lawn along with newly installed statues of howling wolves, facing in opposite directions.

That's not terrifying. Way to assimilate, packs.

Slate-gray textured walls were complemented by black-framed pictures of woodlands. Sleek and expensive-looking modern furniture was situated throughout the space. Over-sized windows gave a picturesque view of the lush trees, clear blue sky, and the surrounding buildings that looked diminutive and plain next to this one. Which I imagined was their point: a subtle display of dominance.

I expected my detail to follow as I made my way through the building, but they were apparently content to wait parked next to my car in the lot. Despite the erratic drive to the Northwest Pack's building, it had calmed me, allowing time for introspection. I no longer had the desire to make a dramatic scene by storming into Asher's office and spewing some choice and indelicate words.

I appreciated Asher's concern. But it felt overbearing and uncompromising, two things I hated. A man who commanded hundreds without any resistance or challenges wasn't used to pushback, and I wasn't used to his way of handling situations. He took on the responsibility of caring for his pack and in return, they followed him without a lot of questions. If they ever questioned his ability to be astute and strategic in his decision making for the best interest of the pack, he'd be challenged.

I wasn't a shifter or part of his pack. Following uncondi-tionally wasn't for me, and besides, sometimes I challenged things for the hell of it. *Eh, sometimes I'm a jackass, too. I'm owning it. It's not as bad when you're aware of it, right?*

But Asher was a self-proclaimed jackass, too. He owned it like a badge of honor, had told Cory there was a benefit to being one: that it allowed him to get down to business without the impediment of being overly pleasant or amiable.

I had that in mind when the elevator opened to the top floor, which consisted of Asher's office. A whole floor for Mr. Alpha, CEO himself. At my entrance, his assistant smiled. Warm, lucid, hazel eyes, the most welcoming I'd seen. I had forgotten his name and had to look at his name plate. Xander. But his honey-colored complexion that brightened when he smiled, displaying the solitary dimple in his left cheek, and an easy countenance made it hard to imagine that he shifted into a massive jackal. Falling under the corporate umbrella of the Northwest Wolf Pack, it was common to find a jackal, dingo, coyote, or fox working at the company. The largest group were wolves.

Xander sat behind a sleek glass table with metal legs, wearing a suit that seemed too tailored and expensive for most assistants. I looked at the desk plate again: *executive assistant*. Still, his suit looked like it would pay my rent for several months.

"Ms. Jensen," he said, "Mr. Sullivan is expecting you."

Of course he is.

It was good I'd abandoned my plan of surprising him. I reached for the door before Xander could release the lock on it.

Really? Oh, Mr. Sullivan's too important to let just any riffraff in. People have to be allowed entrance.

Mr. Sullivan was waiting for me, insouciance itself as he settled back in the large chair, a cup of coffee in hand, watching me as I entered. Extending his hand to the chair in front of him, in a professionally neutral gesture, he offered me a seat.

Dropping into the seat, I declined his offer of coffee. "They didn't tell you that I already had coffee," I said.

"No, they didn't. They're not spies; but extra protection if you need them."

I sighed. "I get that, but I still need you to send them—"

"No." It was the same uncompromising tone as earlier. I

stood and moved to the window that took up the back wall of his office.

"I appreciate your concern, I do," I said. "But I'm not your pack, and besides having a life I'm trying to live, I still have to work. Having shifters following me isn't going to help anything."

He stood and moved to just inches from me, his finger gliding across my shirt where the scar remained from me being stabbed. Biting my bottom lip, I held his sharp, penetrating gaze while he rolled up the edge of my shirt. We both looked down at the scar that was healed more than it should have been at five days.

"Each scar just shows I survived whatever was trying to kill me," I said proudly. But I hadn't survived.

"Mmmhm," he said, devouring the few inches that were still between us. Leaning in, he inhaled, and I wondered what he was taking in. What did I smell like now? Asher had said it was different, but how? Did it have a dark, ominous feel to it? A smell of desecrated earth or freshly turned soil? Petrichor or morning dew? Flowers or fruit? Was it pleasant or noxious?

A vampire once told me I smelled like strawberries and Riesling. I took in Asher's response as he leaned in and inhaled again. Clearly my smell wasn't noxious or unpleasant, just different. Letting my shirt fall, he stepped back just enough to examine my eyes again.

"Something has changed about you, Erin. You survived, but at what cost? You stayed at Mephisto's for days and he's"—he sucked in a ragged breath—"*unique.*"

We directed our attention out the window as if looking at each other would reveal too much.

"We're immune to magic now," he said. "I can sense things differently. I can tell when a witch, mage, or fae is near, not by their scent but by the smell of the magic."

"Me too. It's similar but they all have nuances to them, don't they?"

He nodded. "With that in mind, believe me when I say there's something different about you."

I returned to the chair. This line of questioning would probably lead to him figuring things out, and I couldn't have that happen.

"I appreciate your help and concern. I'm not too proud to ask for help when I need it."

"You aren't, but you seem to seek it only from Mephisto."

"Asher, I won't do anything dangerous without asking for assistance. I'm not in a hurry to go to a family reunion without backup."

"Give me your word?"

I'm very particular about giving my word, because I stand by it. "What am I giving you my word on?"

"If you need help, I'm the first person you call. Not Mephisto."

I leaned into the desk and shot him a defiant glare. "That doesn't sound like you only want to help me, but rather that you don't want it to be Mephisto."

His lips quirked up and he met my accusing eyes. "Fine. If you need help, *only* call me."

"No." That shouldn't have felt as good as it did. But after being treated to his defiance, it was a glorious feeling. And watching him try to let it roll off him made it feel even more delightful.

Easing back into his chair, he clasped his fingers behind his head and a roguish look flitted over his face. "If two shifters following you bothered you, I bet six is going to drive you nuts. You're going to have some hard days."

"Asher," I pushed out through gritted teeth.

"Erin." His tone was light and laden with amusement. His brow rose as he waited for me to respond.

"If I'm in need of help, I will call whoever can do it the best. That's the best I can offer you."

He didn't respond.

"And I'll keep you in the know."

After several moments of consideration, he nodded. "You have a deal. My shifters won't follow you."

I turned the words over in my head, replaying them.

Oh Asher, you're always playing your wolfie games, aren't you?

"*No one* will follow me. Not one person who falls under the Northwest Wolf Pack."

His tongue slid lazily over his bottom lip before he gripped his lip with his teeth. Asher didn't possess the humility to be embarrassed; this was as close as I would get. A vulpine smirk. A snared trickster.

"Of course." He stood in one graceful move. "I'll keep my promise as long as you do."

I stood and headed for the door. I needed to get to Madison's. She and Cory were waiting for me. When Asher called me, I turned and found him right next to me. His lips pressed lightly against mine. The raw intensity from such a light kiss surprised me.

"Be careful, Erin." There goes that insipid tautology again.

Careful. Of course I'm going to be careful.

"Erin, don't try to command my wolves again, okay?" In a falsetto and dramatic imitation of my voice, he said, "Stop. Following. Me. I command you."

His robust laughter followed me out of the room. At least Xander had the good manners to suppress his response into the tight smile he gave me.

CHAPTER 5

The door swung open the moment I made it to Madison's doorstep and I was face to face with a very anxious-looking Madison. Narrowed eyes skewered me with disapproval as if by some chance I'd managed to miss the reprimanding scowl.

"Running late. Have a problem I need to deal with," Madison ground out, reciting the text I had sent her.

I wasn't going to get any help from Cory, who was seething. His left eye was twitching.

"Sorry. I had an Asher situation I had to deal with. It took longer than expected," I explained, brushing it off with a wave of my hand. I should have known it wouldn't work.

"As if anything with Asher can be handled quickly," Cory said.

I'd expect that to come from Madison. Years of dealing with Asher, his pack, and their overly aggressive team of lawyers always elicited an eye roll from anyone working for the Supernatural Task Force.

"What issues?" Madison asked.

"Apparently he's under the impression I need a body-guard," I said with an indolent shrug.

"He's not wrong. You didn't send the shifter away, did you?" Cory said.

"Not one shifter, two. And I couldn't because apparently in the world of Asher, his wants override my rights."

"Yes, you have the right to be murdered. Cool." Now he was just being bitchy for sport.

I glared at him. "Well, yes. And speaking of death, you were right, I did die."

Madison paled and dropped onto the sofa, her hand covering her mouth. It made me instantly regret being so flippant with that information. Even having had days to deal with it, the thought of it was still troubling. I took a seat next to her, placing my hand on her leg.

"I shouldn't have told you that way. Forgive me." I sighed. "I'm trying to deal with a lot of new information and issues that have irreparably changed my life, and I'm trying to hold on to some semblance of it," I explained. "It's not easy."

Cory nodded, giving me an apologetic half smile, pressing his hand to his chest, his way of asking for forgiveness. I nodded back, but us making up didn't return the color to Madison's face. Her expression was indecipherable, blank faced and hollow eyed. I wondered if she was in shock. Taking several deep breaths, she closed her eyes and relaxed back on the sofa and folded a forearm over her eyes.

"Tell me everything that happened, starting with what preceded you dying. Give me very specific details as to how you died yet are here now," she instructed in a low, modulated voice.

Because I didn't have to edit the way I had with Asher, retelling everything went smoother, with the exception of their interruptions: "What do you mean hell?" "It's less draconian than it sounds," "They're all gods?" "That's what I said," "No, only Kai has wings. Clay has oceanic and elemental abilities, Simeon can communicate with animals, and Mephisto can Wynd and has the strongest defensive magic," "Malific exiled them," "A spell similar to the curse that the Caste used on the Immortalis. It was payback."

Madison was leaning forward, looking at me, studying me, concern in her eyes. I knew it was because I didn't seem scared and delivered the information like a report: emotionless and measured. It was an act. A façade I was struggling to maintain. It was enough that I was worried; I needed to do whatever it took to mitigate theirs.

"You seem to be handling this well," she observed.

Not at all, my life is a crapshow. The circus of the damned.

"Yeah, too well, Erin," Cory added softly, his tone laden with suspicion.

"I'm sober and haven't taken anything," I assured him. "If I stress, you two stress," I finally admitted under their scrutiny. "She killed her own brother and we're pretty sure she only had me to use as a tool to release herself from imprisonment. And now I'm the only thing standing between her ability to restore her full power and create more Immortalis." Malific was an evil I wasn't sure I was prepared to deal with.

We lulled into a stiff silence, and I watched Cory fidget. If we were at my house, he would have busied himself with straightening the room, folding blankets on my sofa, aligning things on my tables and consoles. But being at a fellow type-A's home, there wasn't anything to straighten or any unrequested suggestion to offer for improving the home's efficiency.

"Do you think Mephisto can find a way to remove your restriction?" Cory finally asked, his gaze bouncing around the space as he intermittently wrung his hands. I considered dumping the contents of my purse on the floor just to give him something to tidy.

"He thinks so." I wasn't as confident. Magic was mercurial. In all the time Mephisto had been here, he hadn't been able to find a way back into the Veil. I explained what happened when they attempted to remove the restriction.

Neither Madison nor Cory seemed surprised that the Others had the second copy of *Mystic Souls* or that they could speak a dead language. I suspected they'd become desensitized. After all, they were sitting next to someone who had been brought back to life by a spell. Not too many things were going to be more shocking than that.

"Your magical restriction is similar to a curse by the Caste. Only they can remove their curses. If there were enough Caste, they could remove the curse on the death mages. Only the person who invoked the spell can remove it." Madison looked dejected. It wasn't what I wanted to hear because it was something I had considered after the removal attempt.

"Probably, and everyone seems to think my father invoked it, and we have no idea who or what he is." Resting my face in my hand, I sighed. "I need to find my father."

Then, feeling just as fidgety as Cory, I stood, shifting my weight from ball to heel, ball to heel, unable to present the brave, calm, and collected front that I'd tried to project earlier.

"I don't think it's going to be that easy," I acknowledged.

Cory started pacing, his long legs eating up feet of the walkway with each step. "Blood can be used to track people of the same bloodline," he cited halfheartedly.

"Cory, you know the success rate is less than one percent," Madison said. We all knew that.

"Less than one percent is better than nothing," I said, sounding more optimistic than I felt.

Madison shrugged. "It can't hurt."

It was a time waste and we all knew it, but the need to do something was too great. I didn't want to feel like I was just sitting around waiting to be attacked by my mother or for some clue to be miraculously revealed. I needed to be proactive.

Cory didn't possess the spark of anticipation that he

usually did when he performed a locating spell. Going into anything with a success rate of less than one percent was enough to dampen anyone's enthusiasm. His finger danced over the glow of the golden map that presented itself to him, but not even a trace of red coloring showed to indicate someone. Even when the sample was weak, it at least showed some dim coloring that displayed for just a second, sometimes just long enough to get the general area as opposed to specifics.

At least we weren't dejected by the result because it was expected. We spent an hour putting on the greatest performance of pretending that it wasn't doom and gloom. I made a sketch of the raven that showed up on my arm and the markings I saw on the Huntsmen when we went through the fire Mirra at Elizabeth's. They wanted to use the information for research, but it was just busywork. We needed to do something until there was nothing to do.

———

Confession was good for the soul, or at least it was good for sleep, because after returning home, I fell asleep fast and didn't wake until my phone buzzed at three in the morning. Looking at the number, I groaned. They weren't creatures of the night although they seemed to prefer it, which was why Landon, the acting vampire Master of the city, was calling me.

"Erin," said Landon, his silky voice twining around me.

"Bring it down several notches. I have no intention of ever being your midnight snack or sleeping with you," I informed him, my voice rough from sleep.

"You say that every time."

"And yet you do the whole seductive voice thing. Every. Time." Compelling was against the law. Because vampires were only able to compel humans, the law was strictly

53

enforced. But there was something so intrinsically alluring and seductive about vampires that they didn't really need compulsion. Humans convinced themselves that, like the vampires' immortality, their allure was another facet of their magic. When humans were ensnared by the vampires' seduction, they attributed it to being similar to the vampires' compulsion magic. They just couldn't help themselves.

Whatever. You want some hot and freaky with a vampire —own it. People will judge you for a lot of things but desiring the vampire experience wasn't one of them.

I'd had my share of salacious nights with vampires. The bite was as seductive as their voices and as enchanting as any spell. The raw, unfettered hedonism always made me forget my magic cravings. At that moment, they offered a false fulfillment.

"Do I ask you to stop being a feisty, snarky spitfire?" Landon asked, laughter in his voice.

"I'm only two of the three," I countered, sitting up and rubbing my eyes. I didn't want to wake up too much; I planned to immediately go back to sleep, but I needed to be alert enough to talk to Landon.

"What can I do for you?"

"I'll be at your apartment in an hour. I have a job for you."

Nope. So many nopes. I had an office for that. Too many people knew where I lived, making renting my little rundown office nearly unnecessary. But I had eight more months on the lease and I was going to use it.

"I'll meet you at the office tomorrow at ten."

"Ten." He scoffed. I knew he was giving the phone the look of disdain meant for me. Landon was dramatic, born from the same thing that drove Victoria: self-indulgence, privilege, and an overly heightened sense of self-importance. I considered it a societal obligation to squash it every chance I had. No, the world doesn't revolve around you. If I thought it was important, I'd have met him.

"I'm going out tonight. I'll hardly be up in time to meet you."

"Then you have to make a hard choice. Stay in and meet me at ten or go out and miss our appointment. If you do, you're still responsible for my consultation fee."

"I'll triple the fee if you meet me tonight." It was so tempting, but sometimes I had to set expectations. Principles came at a price or, rather, a loss of revenue.

"Is twelve better?"

Sighing heavily, he sounded petulant. "Better but still not what I want."

I'm sure that hurt your feelings. You couldn't buy the results you wanted.

"I'd like to get this started tonight," he pushed.

"Is someone going to die?"

"Eventually."

His voice was hard with repressed anger directed at whomever the call was about. Vampires preferred to dole out their own form of punishment, which was often violent, macabre, and with medieval elements. The STF watched them closely for that reason. The vampires enjoyed not having to live in the shadows. Most supernaturals did, so there was an unspoken and tenuous truce between us all. Humans had the numbers and access to weaponry and a military, but they also had human vulnerabilities. Supernaturals had magical abilities and resilience but were lacking in numbers.

If there were a war between the two, it would be a Pyrrhic victory. We all enjoyed and benefitted from the truce and, in theory, we policed our own, or rather the STF did, and it was that careful eye and threat of repercussions that ensured the vampires played nice. Or at least made sure no one ever found out if they didn't. Before, they liked to use people as a cautionary tale of what happens when you cross them. The stories lived on in journals and history books but not in current events. At least, not in a way that could be traced back to them.

"Tomorrow at twelve and I'm not cleaning up a vampire situation, Landon," I said firmly. "Are we clear?"

"Meet me tonight, and I can assure you that you won't have to."

At times like this, I felt like my business world was like one of those spinning plate performances and I was darting about attempting to keep them all rotating. If Landon was in fact considering handling the situation, then depending on what it was, the Supernatural Task Force might have a situation that would indirectly and possibly directly affect Madison. If I didn't set boundaries with the vampires, Landon would spend most of the time during this job ignoring the drawn lines as if they weren't there.

"Twelve. If someone dies, I won't be working for you but for the STF to bring your ass in. Are we clear?"

"Of course, Erin." Hints of dark delight tinted his words. "Good night, I'll see you tomorrow."

No, you'll see me tonight, I thought, getting out of bed. At least it was on my terms, and anyway, there was nothing wrong with a little unpredictability. Especially when dealing with vampires.

Quickly showering and dressing, I pulled my hair back into a sleek ponytail, taking more care than usual. It made my sharp features look more severe, which, when dealing with vampires, wasn't a bad thing. Nor was putting on my least favorite color and outfit. Black leather pants, eggplant tank, and leather jacket. I hoped that at the end of the day, I would regret wearing my leather. It would mean no one tried to drag me. Except for my recent stab wound, dragging injuries are the worst. It only happened once and I still vividly remember the ground ripping against my skin. Sharp needle pricks the entire time.

Despite hating wearing my leather jacket and pants, I got

the chance to wear my favorite boots. Soft supple leather, with two slits where push daggers could fit. The reinforced toes ensured that if I kicked someone, they would definitely feel it.

Getting dressed to meet clients was a bigger hassle than actually meeting them. Vampires in particular. They were a finicky group and a little too judgmental for individuals who drank blood to survive.

I had a healthy glow to my olive-colored skin, so a few strokes of mascara and light blush and I didn't look like I'd just rolled out of bed. Nor did I look nearly as embittered as I felt about Landon's call. I would be fine meeting them in worn leggings, an oversized stretched t-shirt, slip-on shoes, a messy bun, no makeup, and a crabby disposition, but they wouldn't take me nearly as seriously, even if I were carrying a flamethrower. I tried it once, but instead of a flamethrower, I had a broadsword. And they couldn't pull their attention from my attire to care about my slice-and-dice weapon.

A person holding a weapon that could take their head off was less offensive than my unkempt clothing.

I headed to my car with a goodie bag of weapons and gadgets, hoping I wasn't going to have to use them against Landon to prevent whatever massacre he was planning. The hushed darkness was unsettling, making me recall Ian swooping in and snatching me up. Getting stabbed. The feeling of helplessness. Giving the area another quick sweep, I pulled my weapons bag closer to me and clutched the karambit tighter.

Once in my car, I breathed a sigh of relief. I didn't have to worry about Ian anymore. It was my mother I'd eventually encounter. No one said she had wings. But could she Wynd in? Part of me regretted sending Asher's sentries away. Grabbing my phone and taking a calming breath, I called Landon.

"I'll be at your house in twenty."

"Twenty? Oh my, time has passed faster than I thought, if it's twelve already," he teased.

"I'm protecting you from yourself."

"I can't think of better protection," he said. Pressing my ear closer to the phone, I heard a low mewling sound, hissing, and a deep moan. I had no idea what he was doing but I wanted to get off the phone.

"Is that okay?"

"Of course. I'm in the middle of dinner, but I should be finished by the time you get here."

You better be finished by the time I get there. Because it didn't sound like he was just feeding from someone. And why did he have his phone with him?

CHAPTER 6

$\mathcal{T}$he sharp lines and defined geometric shapes of Landon's stark white home personified the ostentatiousness and eccentricities of a vampire who used priceless and rare magical objects, artifacts, and artwork as knickknacks and ornamentation. Landon's home defied preconceived notions people might have about a century-old vampire who was a mélange of dangerous seductiveness, brazen selectiveness, and disturbing otherworldly anachronisms, all of which made him an unpredictable and difficult client.

I was used to seeing him in crisp tailored shirts and his preferred Italian suits with bold patterned ties and his hair meticulously neat and coiffed to perfection. Now, his shirt jacket was missing and his shirt was opened by three buttons, giving me a peek at his chest. Disheveled hair and red-tinted lips made him nearly unrecognizable.

"Erin," he whispered in an airy voice, baring more of his red-tinted fangs. It was oddly comforting. He'd fed, which meant he wouldn't be coveting my neck the entire visit.

"Are you finished with dinner?" I looked past him at his guest, who'd decided it was a good idea to carry her dress rather than putting it on to traipse through his home in the direction of the kitchen.

Moving aside, he directed me past him into the den. He didn't follow but instead disappeared into another room, returning with his hair neat and his shirt buttoned. Landon's lips were still ruby-colored and his eyes heavy-lidded and euphoric. I wasn't sure if it was from feeding or sex. Vampires tended to prefer to indulge in both simultaneously, so it was probably a Pavlov dog situation where either act invoked the same reaction.

Languid and relaxed, he eased into one of his highbacked chairs that resembled a throne. It was new.

Erin, don't roll your eyes.

I rolled them so hard I thought I was going to give myself a headache.

Well, at least don't comment.

"Nice chair."

Dammit.

Running his hands along the ornate patterns in the wood and settling back into the plush-looking leather, he said, "It is, isn't it? I thought it would be ostentatious but it has a certain panache that is quite fitting."

"Definitely, it's very fitting." It looked like a self-indulgent vamp should be sitting in it.

His eyes narrowed and roved over me, taking in my attire, lingering on my neck, then slowly moving past my lips until his gaze met mine.

"Why don't we hang out more?" he inquired earnestly.

"Because you host poker games where you bet priceless objects and ancient artifacts. You drink brandy that costs my consultation fee plus some jobs," I pointed out. "I drink cheap tequila, vodka, and wine."

"That's by choice, not by necessity." He flashed me a smug grin. Head tilted, he studied me for a few moments. "Yet you had no problem with Grayson. We run in the same circles and share similar interests and have common predilections. How are we different?"

Adrenaline-ridden job, liquor—lots of it—attempting to stave off magic cravings, relentless flirting, and lust. That's how I ended up with Grayson. But our shared history didn't stop me from apprehending him and turning him over to the Supernatural Task Force when he stole a dangerous magical object and put Madison's job and reputation at risk. But instead of saying any of that, I simply redirected him.

"What's the job, Landon?"

"I think I'm going to kill the Lunar Marked coven," he said, far too casually for someone admitting to premeditated mass murder. Landon regarded me with slightly pursed lips and narrowed eyes, I assumed trying to gauge my stance on it. My reputation had definitely put me on the gray side of things, perceived as morally ambiguous with capricious behavior. Clients liked to determine where my ill-defined lines lay. How far they could push the envelope before I either declined the job or established my boundaries.

"Hmm," I mused. "And you want me here to call STF and have them arrest you once you do?"

"No, I want you to help me do it and get away with it. I don't want any of my vampires to suffer because of a fleeting moment of anger."

Landon's calm, measured tone was the reason I found vampires so dangerous. I was sure he was quite angry, killing angry. And a person wouldn't know until the second before their neck was broken or their throat ripped out. Sometimes it was like dealing with a temperamental toddler. The fact they were calmer, or pretended to be, showed that the behavior could be controlled, but they were unwilling to do so unless there were consequences.

"No, I'm not going to do that."

With a dramatic flick of his wrist, he tossed the idea aside.

"Very well. I'm being blackmailed by them and I'd like you to make it go away."

"How do you want me to do that?" I inquired, needing clarification and an explanation for him outsourcing something that seemed quite simple.

"I have to pay them, of course. But I'd like to negotiate it down and they are reluctant to meet with me or another vampire. I need an intermediary."

"Did you tell them of your gallant plans to slaughter them? I bet you did. People don't like to meet you after you've told them you plan to murder them. You know, that whole self-preservation thing kicks in. Damn that stupid fight or flight system." I flashed him a mild smile in response to his glare. "Ingratiating goes a long way. So does flattery. You should try that sometime."

I was making an attempt to ease the thick tension in the room. The smartest thing the Lunar Marked coven did was require an intermediary. The coven was new; I didn't know a lot about them. Covens, because of their size, were numerous, and it wasn't uncommon for a witch to leave one to start their own. It was rarely contentious, but severing their relationship meant they were starting from scratch with few resources.

Apparently this was how the new coven decided to fund theirs: blackmailing the vampires. It was a bold plan albeit not the safest. Strangely, I was enthusiastic about meeting this ballsy new coven.

A shadowy cast moved over Landon's face and darkened his eyes, along with a very subtle look of murderous intent. Jutting his chin out, he said, "I made my displeasure with the circumstances known and the lengths I'm willing to go to rectify the situation."

In plainspeak: You did. Jackass.

"They have Amber Crocus and would like me to pay to have it."

"How did they get it?"

"That's something I'd like you to find out as well. It's my understanding that not even places like Dante's Forest have it. Growing it is difficult and they've managed to nurture a whole garden of it. You can imagine how concerning it is for me to know there's a garden of plants that can kill me."

Landon always did have a flair for the dramatic. It wasn't like a vampire could brush the plant on their skin and it would kill them. It had to be ingested or injected. But if it was, they'd respond as if they'd been staked in the heart, except that if the stake is removed and they are fed, they can survive. My research revealed it's not the same with Amber Crocus.

"This is what they are asking," he said, handing me a piece of paper.

Damn, that's a lot of zeros.

I understood his frustration, even his anger. It wasn't enough to send me into a murderous rage, but I think I might have slapped them with a glove for the ludicrous offense, and questioned their audacity.

Seeing that he looked more irritated at the gall and not the lack of funds made me question how much money the vampires had. People said the reason for their wealth was their long lives. That never made sense to me. Some came from money, invested well, and the vampires, like the shifters, had multiple businesses but rarely worked among humans. I suspected a great deal of their fortune came from a time when they were able to compel people legally. How many times had they compelled a person into inside trading, to give them permits, sell them thriving businesses, leave their inheritance to them?

"Are you willing to pay this?" I asked.

"No, I don't want to pay any of it. What I want is to make them rethink it." He gave me a "tell me how to get rid of them without it being traced back to me" look.

"I'm sure this is just starting negotiations. Offer them half," I suggested. The Lunar Marked coven wasn't very large and if they divided the money equally, they could still live off it for a very long time.

"You're more generous than I am. I'm willing to give them twenty-five percent of what they are requesting, along with all coven members taking a death oath that they will never grow Amber Crocus again, nor show anyone else how to grow it, and that they will inform me of anyone having the Amber Crocus or attempting to grow it. I don't want this to open the door to others."

"That's understandable."

Cory wouldn't like it, but he'd perform the oath. No one liked doing them. Magical oaths required a great deal of magic, not technically dark magic but so close to it that calling it white or natural was incorrect. Opaque? Wording the spell is what took the longest because once it was cast, it was binding, and unbinding it was quite difficult. When there is a penalty of death, wording is everything.

"I doubt they'll agree. They're witches, they understand the magnitude of it."

A death oath was one of the few spells that endured past the life of the casting witch. It was a good thing, too, because the casting witch's life would be at risk from anyone who wished to break the oath.

"That's the only thing that I'm willing to agree to," Landon said firmly.

The creases of agitation had smoothed out and he'd returned to the image of refined beauty, indulgence, and ostentatious wealth. Effortless aloofness and ease that accompanied having all the time in the world to do something. Unhurried by limited time or resources.

"Tell me your parameters," I said.

"I've told you," he said breezily. "Perhaps you should start the negotiations by asking them to put a value on their lives."

"I'm not going to threaten them."

"It's not intended to be a threat. This matter will be handled, hopefully with no blood on my hands. That's clearly a statement of fact, not a threat."

It was odd, but I would have preferred it if he showed more emotion and was vocal with his anger. Bluster, a torrent of fury, melodramatic spewing of threats, and vivid descriptions of the pain and havoc that he planned to cause were rooted in emotions, and once the person calmed down, they rethought things and chose a rational path.

When people were as calm and matter of fact as Landon, I grew concerned. His thinking wasn't coming from a place of anger but from calculated planning.

Taking another look at the number on the paper, I forced my face to stay neutral and kept my frown and groan to myself.

Did the coven have any businesses?

Their ploy reeked of desperation and wish fulfillment. But maybe it wasn't; maybe it was a well thought out endeavor. If you were going to blackmail anyone and didn't mind living dangerously, vampires were the best people to blackmail.

"You have to give me room for negotiation."

Anger flashed over his face and in his eyes. "They didn't even have the integrity and decency to come to me. I was made aware of it and sought them out."

This was getting worse. "How did you find out?"

I knew he heard me but he didn't respond, so I repeated my question.

"He's coming," he informed me, and I knew whoever it was, was in the house and Landon had heard him. Supernaturals without preternatural hearing made my life simpler. He might have been on the estate for all I knew or outside parking his car.

Or stepping into the room, as he was now doing.

Flawless, warm, deep-umber skin; striking angled features; full supple lips, and lashes that made me envious. I could achieve that look with maybe ten coats of mascara and definitely some lash extensions.

"Dallas," I greeted and his faint smile widened.

"You remember me?" His asphalt-black eyes sparked. Was he kidding me? No one met him and forgot. One, his name wasn't something one would soon forget, and two, his appearance was memorable.

Dallas moved farther into the room, reminding me of the request I made the night I met him, which was to turn off the vampire charm. For some, it was as fluid and natural as water. With others, you could tell it was honed from years of practice, and then there were vampires like Dallas who I suspected were charming, charismatic, and alluring before becoming a vampire and only enhanced by it. A sincere sweet smile lingered and brightened his midnight eyes.

"You know each other?" Landon asked, a cold undercurrent to his tone. Landon didn't care about me; he probably didn't even find me attractive. I'd seen the people who kept his company and captured his interest, and I didn't compare. Now I'd become a conquest and that was the worst. First Grayson and now he assumed I'd been with Dallas. I needed to nip it in the bud.

"I met him at a club." I flashed Dallas a grin. "He found someone far more interesting than me." I gave Dallas a wink.

A roguish smile curled his lips. He'd captured the attention of a Grup who initially had her eyes set on me. Those were the worst. Drawn to me by the prospect of a dangerous night, it was Dallas who was able to deliver it for her. Grups were drawn to vampires more than anyone else, I guess for the same reason I had been. They were exciting and exhilarating. A vampire feeding from you could take you to the brink of death and snatch you right back. Sex with them was just as intoxicating and reckless as letting them feed from you, and if you didn't give them any boundaries, they weren't going to offer any. And if that was what you were looking for, they didn't disappoint.

"If I'm not mistaken, you were more interested in my friend Kieran than me."

That wasn't true. I was interested in his friend's magic and the third person in the trio, whose chaotic, rhythmless dancing had amused me. Thinking about it still brought a smile to my lips.

Landon's brow still rose, his attention moving from Dallas to me. Everything always looked appealing when it wasn't in his possession. The grass was always greener for him.

He was quickly becoming my least favorite person.

"Dallas, how did you find out about the Lunar Marked having possession of Amber Crocus?" I asked.

"It was discovered by a friend of mine, a loner witch. She showed me a piece." He reached into his pocket and retrieved a small plastic baggie with pieces of plant in it.

Landon's face tensed. Mine did, too. They didn't just have the dangerous vampire-killing plant but were being very careless with it. How many other people had pieces?

"She just found it?"

He shook his head. "They found her. Hired her as a consultant. She's a horticulturist, with expertise in herbs and mystical plants." He shrugged. "Their plants were starting to die and they needed help."

"They are very careless with such a dangerous plant." Landon's voice was tight.

"They searched her prior to her leaving."

I wondered why she was a loner witch. There weren't many. Most were witches who participated in dark magic and got kicked out of their coven. The few who were loners by choice were a conundrum. Witches and mages were apolitical and didn't have a lot of rules. The rules they did

67

have seemed to be: Don't play with demons, stay away from the dark arts, share with the coven or consortium, and don't be an ass. I wasn't sure what would discourage a person from being part of a coven or consortium.

"I had no idea what it was, but she overheard them mentioning vampires and thought it prudent to bring it to my attention." He examined it again. "I didn't know what it was."

The lack of knowledge embarrassed him. His eyes dropped from mine to the floor, lifting periodically to make furtive glances in Landon's direction.

"You're still young, and it hasn't been around for years. My wish for you was that you and the others your age would never know what it's like to be controlled by a necromancer and to see someone die from Amber Crocus," Landon said. He sounded so earnest in his desire and his commitment to preventing it that he earned a removal from my dislike list.

"We are vampires. Where there aren't gods, we offer a pleasing alternative. Someone holding power over us in any form can't be accepted or tolerated."

Well, there you go. Right back on the list where you belong.

Dallas didn't seem to share Landon's belief or his unabashed hubris.

Landon's face became rigid, and he directed his attention to me. "Our acquiescence into society wasn't out of necessity but out of benevolence." His dark gaze sharpened on me.

His hubris had elevated to such dizzying heights that the journey with him was making me a little lightheaded.

He controlled the city because the original Master of the city lived in seclusion, no longer desirous of being part of civilization. I had no idea where he was or what led to his decision. Vampires grew tired; one of the disadvantages of immortality was that it took more and more to make the tedium of life worth it. But I wondered if it was just the banality of life that the former Master grew tired of, or if it was the over-the-top, unyielding, egregious arrogance of their personalities. Carrying such an ego had to be like Atlas holding up the world.

Instead of correcting him about the pitfalls of us going to war with humans, I traveled back from Landon-ville, the city of self-aggrandization and hubris, and asked, "Who do I need to speak with?"

I needed to make sure the coven wasn't sharing their acquisition of the plant with others. I also needed to take them to task over the fact that they were expecting the vampires to be the coven's retirement plan—preferably before Landon decided to take this situation into his merciless hands.

CHAPTER 7

"*F*uuuuuck," I mumbled under my breath at River, who was parked right next to my car. Dr. Sumner would think I was intentionally late to decrease our session time. Maybe today would be the day he discharged me. It was that hope that made not being able to go back to bed after my visit with Landon tolerable.

The witches had been contacted and I was just waiting to hear from them. Not only did I have to deal with black-mailing witches who were perilously close to being wiped out by the acting Master of vampires, I was debating whether or not to tell Madison.

"Ms. Jensen," he croaked out, my name always said like a curse. He forced a smile on his face, but it looked like a grimace. "Can we chat?"

Since he'd gotten out of his car and was now blocking my way to my car door, I didn't have a lot of options other than listening to him or figuring out a way to navigate around him. Something he wouldn't have made easy to do.

"About what?" I breathed out in exasperation. At what point did I start to consider this police harassment? He wasn't going to rest until he'd seen me sentenced at the Enclave.

Shoving one hand into his pocket and running the other through his salt-and-pepper hair, he was attempting to seem casual, but malicious intent dwelled in his eyes and the cruel hitch of his lips. River had a dazzling endearing smile, but he was unable to summon it for me.

"It seemed that we had a weird incident a while ago. The shifters were attacking people for no reason—first you, then they were behaving in an erratic and unusual way at the park around the same time people reported sightings of a winged man."

"Hmmm, and you think I'm involved?" I returned the same contrived aloofness he gave me.

"Seems a little odd that things start happening just when you seem to have acquired magic. That's the reason you were at the magic fight, right?"

"People go there to watch."

"Did you go there to watch?" He pushed up from the car just inches from me, his gaze homed in hard on me, as if trying to convince me he'd know if I lied.

"Have you had any more reports of shifters behaving erratically?" I asked, ignoring his question.

"No. There haven't been any reports of the winged man, either. I guess that's coincidence."

I shrugged. "Possibly. Maybe you should go and investigate it further," I suggested coolly. *Or just go away.*

"The winged man disappears and you acquire enough magic to participate in magic fights." His lips dipped down into a painful-looking scowl. "I don't think that's a coincidence. Why don't you tell me again how your magic works?"

I was done playing his games. "Perhaps you should research it, or you could leave supernatural problems to the STF."

"They're compromised, and at the root of it is Ms. Calloway and you. Most of the time, you're linked to the problems, and Ms. Calloway finds a way to make them go away and tie things up in a neat little bow." The edge of threat in his voice ripped away the few tendrils of patience I had maintained.

"If you don't have a warrant for my arrest and you just want me for questioning, I'm going to decline." I hip checked him away from the door and got in.

With a slow, deliberate swagger, he walked back to his car. He tossed a look over his shoulder in my direction. "It would be terrible if Ms. Calloway was no longer in her position. There'd be no one to clean up your messes. Things would get really complicated for you," he eased out airily.

My face was a placid mask, although I was seething inside. "Possibly, but perhaps my energies have been misdirected. Sometimes I can be a real bitch, especially when I direct it solely at one person. It would be a real shame if you were that person." The airiness of my tone matched his and held the same level of undisguised threat.

He stopped abruptly, the color draining from his face as his eyes narrowed on me.

Sometimes my reputation worked to my advantage.

————

It took a lot of effort to push thoughts of River out of my head. He was just an obnoxious memory by the time I walked into Dr. Sumner's office twenty minutes late.

Really, I thought when I got a look at Dr. Sumner. His moderately obtrusive squarish round frames in various tones of brown, gold, and tan had been replaced by oversized midnight-blue rectangular ones that would make even a hipster shoot him a derisive sneer. There was a dark shadow of hair that was undoubtedly going to be a full beard.

His tweed jacket was complemented by a white, pastel-pinstriped shirt. At least Dr. Cliché refrained from the patches on the elbows this time.

Plopping into the seat, I rummaged through my bag and pulled out my flask and two shot glasses.

His brow raised at them.

I filled both glasses, downed my tequila, and filled it again. He watched, amusement glinting in his eyes.

Head cocked, I asked with a half grin, "Who hurt you?"

"I'm not sure what you are asking."

"The glasses, the beard, and this"—I waved my hand at his outfit—"*ensemble.* Clearly it's to repel. Why? What's wrong with being a hot doc?"

I grinned as his cheeks grew rosy. My smile faltered, though, when he took the notepad off the table, placed it on his lap, and started to scribble something.

"Did you put 'hot doc' or 'hot doctor'?" I teased.

"Okay." His voice remained neutral as he looked at the shot glasses again and frowned slightly. "What do we discuss today?"

"Everything I say is protected, right?"

"Depends."

"I want it to be."

He nodded absently. "If you don't plan on injuring yourself or anyone else, then my goal is to help you."

When I hesitated, he sighed, leaning forward until I held his gaze.

"I don't plan on hurting myself," I offered in concession as I debated what to tell him.

"Someone else?" he speculated, keeping me under his watchful eyes.

I responded with a deep sigh of exasperation. My tension and his speculation consumed the room.

His face became earnest, his eyes warm, inviting, and sympathetic. "Erin, obviously you want to talk about it.

Based on our past experiences, you have no problem canceling or rescheduling, but you didn't. You want to talk. I'm here to listen and help you."

I opened my mouth to speak but before I could, he added, "The full story…not the abridged version." Responding to my frown, he said, "Nothing you say will leave this office. Okay? I give my word."

Nodding in assent, I grabbed the shot glass and threw back the contents.

"Erin, perhaps you should put the flask and the glasses away."

"You're going to want it once I start talking."

Curiosity widened his eyes before he pulled himself up taller, his interest palpable. He leaned back in the chair.

I lay back on the sofa.

"I might have to kill my mom," I tossed out, far too nonchalantly to be discussing murder.

He sucked in a sharp, ragged breath.

"No worries, not the one who raised me. The psycho one who probably wants to do the same to me."

"Hmmm." He scribbled away on his pad. "Why do you think that?" Tinges of fear and intrigue tightened his voice.

"I have reason to believe that she's no longer imprisoned. Remember the man who attacked me during therapy?"

He nodded and glanced at the changes in his office that were a result of that. The fire extinguisher that I'd used to disarm the Immortalis had a twin placed closer to Dr. Sumner's chair, and his briefcase remained partially open, more than likely holding a concealed weapon and the fire-starting obsidian stone—which would serve as a distraction if needed—that he'd purchased after the attack.

"Those are her minions and she'll want them back and I suspect she'll want to make more and she can't do that because I cheated death and me being alive makes her weaker."

He blinked once and I told him everything as if I were talking to Cory and Madison, but it was different. There was a detachment; he wouldn't lose sleep over this and it was relieving. Emotions broke like a dam and I showed fear, got upset, felt frustration, sat up too often because lying down made the weight intolerable. Several times I took a shot, and when I felt the burden ease, I stretched back on the sofa. By the time I finished unloading I was sitting up.

Picking up the glass I'd poured for him, he sipped some, made a face, and replaced it on the table.

"But they're restricted from the Veil, right?" he asked.

I shrugged. "Based on everything I know, they are. But maybe she'll find a way to get them there, or leave them here and create another army in the Veil. Or she might come here and decide to stay and wreak havoc and destroy, like she did in the Veil. I have no idea."

His prescription-less oversized glasses came off and he massaged the bridge of his nose. Silent for a long time, he eventually asked in a soft voice, "Do you want to meet her?" The sincerity in his voice made me pause to really consider his question. I wanted to give him an honest response.

Closing my eyes, I thought about it. "Yes," I whispered. "There's a part of me that's curious. I don't know who I am and it sucks," I admitted. "For years I struggled with my magic, thought so many things were wrong with me, lived in this state of perpetual guilt and shame, only to find out that some of it wasn't my fault. But..." The heaviness in my chest had returned and my muscles were so tense, I felt rigid. There was a long stretch of silence that I was unable to end.

"Go on," he coaxed gently.

"How can I not be like this? I'm the daughter of a goddess who murdered her own brother. A person, perhaps my father, restricted my magic and I don't know why. Was it because I was considered a menace before I had a chance to prove myself? Why would someone do that to me?" Tears welled in my eyes and I fought hard not to let them fall. "The only reason I exist is because I'm a tool to be sacrificed so that she can be released. Perhaps it's wistful and naïve, but I'd like to meet her so she can tell me that it's all false. That there's an alternative story and it's less grim than the one I know."

A tissue brushed against my hand and I took it from Dr. Sumner and quickly wiped away the tears that had spilled. Face flushed with embarrassment, I looked at the wall for the clock, needing to use it as a way to escape. Clearly, our time was up. The clock was gone and I slid an accusing look in Dr. Sumner's direction.

His lips tipped into a wayward smile. "It was distracting for people," he explained.

"People, or me?"

"You're people, aren't you?"

I welcomed the silence that followed. Sitting there, I watched Sumner sip from the tequila shot. He tolerated it better than I expected.

There was nothing normal about my life and definitely nothing normal about my therapy sessions.

I suspected my life had cured him of his fascination with the supernatural world. I could see it in his eyes. There was still intrigue or unsated curiosity but also fear and apprehension. Once again I had introduced him to another facet of the world, and I wasn't sure he appreciated it. With a blink of his eyes, the expression was gone.

He attempted a congenial smile, but it was mirthless and grim, obligatory.

"I didn't see it, but a spell was done to release her."

Although the awkward silence continued, I didn't have the desire to leave or end the session. This time it felt different. Safe. I didn't have to feign indifference or be braver than I felt for fear of making others worry. Nor did I have to pretend that things weren't as dire as they were.

"Why didn't you tell Madison you lost time during the incident?"

Looking at my shot glass, I opted for the water sitting next to it and took a long drink. "Because she would have made sure I stayed in the Stygian."

He blinked hard once but his face remained impassive.

"Madison cares a great deal for me," I said, "but her sense of duty would not have allowed her to let me out knowing that I was losing time." I shrugged. "I wasn't a hundred percent sure it happened. I wanted his magic and he was just a guy I'd met for coffee and drinks a few times. And when he offered, I didn't think twice. There were spells I wanted to practice, defensive magical skills I wanted to hone, and..." I drifted into silence.

"And you wanted to feel magic?"

Nodding, I reached for my tote and took out my phone. "We've been at this an hour and a half. Time's up." Feeling raw and exposed, I was ready to leave. Because I was so close to admitting that when I found that guy dead, if I hadn't been seen leaving with him, I would have taken off. I called Madison first to ask her to do what I knew she would: clean it up. Shame intermingled with my guilt and the large room became a closet.

"Next week. Same day, same time," I threw out, coming to my feet and heading for the door.

When he called my name, I was reluctant to turn around. I could hear the sympathy in his voice. The gentleness with which he said my name, making everything I knew about the situation worse.

"Next week, okay? I don't have more to share."

"I think you do," he said. "You'll feel better if you let it all out. You can't fight the demons if you pretend they aren't there."

There he is, Dr. Cliché. I've missed you, buddy.

"I'm not pretending they aren't there. I'm just choosing not to confront them. Not today."

I didn't give him another opportunity to offer his sage wisdom or hit me with any more of his tautologies.

———

Outside the office, I looked to see if I had any messages or voicemails from the Lunar Marked coven's representative. Debating the consequences of contacting them again, I considered that it would make Landon look desperate and hinder negotiation. But if they didn't get back to me soon, he'd get restless, believing his initial plan of seeking and destroying was unavoidable. Or at least that would be the excuse he'd use.

A few feet from my car, I was surprised that Dr. Sumner hadn't followed me out. I was more astounded by the vacant streets. Not one person came out of the restaurant three buildings down, or the café across the street, or the dance studio on the opposite corner of Sumner's practice, or any of the numerous office buildings on the street.

Familiar arcane magic swept through the air, rosemary with hints of tannin. The signature hum of energy from compulsion magic was confirmed when a woman with a coffee in hand headed in my direction and then stopped abruptly. Brows furrowed, her lips curved down into a grimace and she quickly turned and scurried off in the opposite direction.

Dropping my tote bag to the ground with a thud and grabbing a dagger in one hand, the karambit in the other, I scanned the magic-drenched street, looking for them. Heart racing, I hoped there was only one Immortalis, maybe two. I could handle them.

Compulsion magic required a lot of energy and concen-

78

tration, which should have worked to my advantage. They would have been weakened by doing it. That's the way it should work, but they were a creation of an Arch-deity from the Veil, immune to magic and immortal. Fear of death at my hand wasn't something they had to worry about. Just pain I had every intention of delivering.

At the overpowering noxious change in the air pressure near me, I whipped around to see an Immortalis approach. The strain of the compulsion magic furrowed his brow and tensed his face. He was tall, nearly seven feet, and approached me with purpose. It wasn't just his height that was intimidating, it was his resolute presence, his broad build. His muscles contracted and bulged with each step. He looked like he'd be part of an indomitable army.

The sword sheathed at his back remained there, but I still didn't know if this was an assassination attempt or an abduction. Did mom want to meet me before she killed me?

His approach was met with me charging at him. His attention focused on my karambit moving in swift figure eights, putting him on the defense. He might heal fast, but blades against the skin hurt. He was tasked with healing and dodging and having to make the decision to risk further hurt and go for his sword.

He moved faster than I'd expect of his imposing frame, but the karambit blade still sliced into his right arm. His face flared red and he hissed. His eyes promised painful retaliation.

The pulse of magic behind me changed. The compulsion magic was gone. We'd soon have an audience, which I was sure he didn't want. He backed away, trying to put distance between us that I refused to give. The karambit worked as a distraction as he watched the glinting blade, dodging from left to right, keeping him from being able to perform his rote magical movements or go for his sword.

He sacrificed the pierce of my karambit blade to go for it. I thrust my dagger into his hand, and he howled in pain. If this had started out as an abduction mission, it had just changed.

"I will be the one to kill you," he promised.

"It won't be today." The dagger thrust to his chest and he moved back, fast but not before I sent a front kick into his crotch. I don't fight to look pretty; I fight to survive. Kicking someone in the crotch is an often-used tactic.

He didn't go down but drew in a breath. Then he lunged at me, his arms bloodstained and red without any signs of the slashes they had endured. Taking the pain of my blades, he slammed a punch into my side. The crack of my ribs pushed the breath out of me. I stumbled back, dropping my karambit so I could grip my side. Huffing out ragged breaths, I reconciled with the pain, keeping the dagger extended, ready to protect.

He offered a malicious smile, and I got a peek at the terror an army of people like him would instill. Responding to the thrum of arcane magic behind me, plus the noxious smell, I whipped around. Compulsion magic restored to the surroundings, magic from the new arrival hit me in my chest, sending me flying onto my back. Nothing else broke, but the pain made me cough out a breath. My next inhalation brought tears to my eyes, blurring my vision. Through the distorted vision I could see two figures advancing.

Get up, Erin.

My mind raced. What should I do? I saw a blurry image of the karambit several feet away. The knife was still in my hand, and each time I took a breath my broken ribs screamed.

Get up, Erin. Now!

I tried pulling my legs under me, sucking in the pain and trying to use it as fodder to ignite my will. Dagger in hand, I forced myself to stand.

A sweeping earthy aura consumed the area. It was refreshing, all-consuming, and overwhelming, like a meadow with hints of evergreen. The magic around me changed. Its suffocating force could not be ignored.

Blinking my eyes to clear the tears of pain, I looked around for the source but saw nothing other than the Immortalis shuffling back, their tension apparent. Faint indistinguishable words carried on the light breeze of the wind, enveloping me like a soothing blanket. Dropping the dagger, I covered my ears, refusing to give in to the lure of its power.

I reacted too late.

———

I awoke to a crowd of people surrounding me asking if I was okay. Another person announced they were about to call an ambulance.

"I'm fine," I choked out, trying to come to my feet, only to have lethargy force me right back down. I had a feeling a significant amount of time had passed but I didn't know how much. Losing time was becoming all too familiar. I sucked in a deep breath and held it, trying to keep from spiraling out of control. What was I waking up to? Another body? Another death? Stolen magic?

Dammit.

I looked around, ignoring the woman with a round face and a determined expression kneeling next to me, taking my pulse.

"I'm okay." My voice sounded stronger than I expected. "I haven't eaten. I'll be fine."

She didn't look convinced, but when I stood up, she backed away.

Putting on a face braver than I felt, I gathered my tote and all the things that had spilled from it. Discreetly, I looked for my missing karambit and dagger, aware of the audience of six around me.

After I promised the concerned bystanders that I'd get something to eat first and if I didn't feel better, I'd go to the doctor, two people left. But the determined woman stayed. Rigid scowl in place, she seemed reluctant to let me out of her sight.

"Let me help you." Moving closer, she questioned me on whether this had happened before, if I was hypoglycemic, and extensive medical questions that I tried to answer without getting irritated.

"Dr. Cambridge." Sumner's voice held an easy confidence. "I'm familiar with her, do you mind?" His presence eased the remaining onlookers enough that they dispersed, and after he gave her a nod of assurance, Dr. Cambridge left as well. Or maybe his wacky glasses just scared them all off.

Him standing close and cradling my face felt weird. He held it firmly as I attempted to tug away. "What happened?" he asked quietly.

"I don't know." My voice broke and I despised how vulnerable I felt. "Magic. I don't know what kind." When I jerked away, he let me and gave me some space. I washed my hands over my face and evaluated the area. The easiness of my movement made me recall my ribs were broken. It should have hurt to breathe, to move. But it didn't. I lifted my shirt to find unbruised skin.

"They were broken," I whispered.

"What was broken, Erin?"

I shook my head. "Nothing." How could I tell him I lost time again? How could this happen again? "Nothing," I repeated.

"Erin?"

I shook my head. "Nothing. Just go back to your office. I just need to eat."

"Erin," he pleaded.

82

"Just go. I'm fine. I promise."

He accepted my assertion with the same lack of enthusiasm with which it was given. He didn't believe me because I didn't sound believable.

"Erin, I'm here for you if you need me."

"I know." I looked around the area again, feeling the pang of desperation that I couldn't get rid of.

"It happened again, didn't it?" he asked in the same quiet voice as before.

"Yeah," I breathed out. "The magic was different."

Sighing, I relaxed against the car, washing my hands over my face again before telling him what happened. When I finished, the stoicism that he'd often displayed wasn't there. Concern, frustration, and even fear moved along the planes of his face.

"Was it your mother?" he asked.

"If it was Malific, I don't think I'd be alive." Or maybe I would. I hated not knowing the play. She didn't want me dead immediately. The wistful, naïve part of me thought maybe she didn't want me dead at all. But the Immortalis threat doused that hope.

Dr. Sumner stared at me in silence. "You're not okay, are you?"

"No, but I'll have to be." I moved away from him, dropped to the ground, and was flooded with relief when I found my weapons under my car, neatly hidden behind the tire. Moving as if I wasn't under Sumner's scrutinizing gaze, I removed them and placed them in a protective bag. The Immortalis had found me, and now I could use the blood on my dagger to find them—or at least one of them.

Unable to hide his concern at the clinical detachment with which I was handling things, Sumner frowned.

"I'll see you next week."

Based on the look on his face, I figured he said it to release me. My life had morphed into something unrecognizable from what he thought it was. Magic and monsters. It had to be a lot for a human to handle.

"You didn't do it. The first time. It wasn't you." His lips pulled into a wan smile. He opened his mouth to speak again but decided against it. At my silence, he simply gave me a sympathetic nod and disappeared into his building.

CHAPTER 8

y plan was to talk to Mephisto about the attack and figure out a way to get an Obitus blade because my weapons were useless against Immortalis. The next time I encountered them, I didn't want to be in a state where they could attack me again.

I had been mulling over whether to tell Madison and Cory about the attack, debating whether it would just cause them to worry unnecessarily, when a representative from the Lunar Marked coven finally responded to my request to meet, giving me only half an hour to get home and change.

Them texting me proved they weren't criminal masterminds. Most people I dealt with preferred to make arrangements by phone, not text. Messages left evidence. But maybe they weren't dense after all; their texts may have left evidence of the blackmail, but if anything happened to them, it would implicate the vampires.

If the witches' goal was to create a tableau that suggested shady dealing, they had succeeded. The small, dilapidated yellow ranch home with its unkempt lawn and ragged bushes flanking the house didn't look like the location of a seven-figure deal but an underhanded deal that would probably erupt in gunfire or a standoff. I followed the privacy fence surrounding the house and slammed into a ward. Unable to get to the plants, I backtracked to the front door.

It swung open before I could knock, revealing a bare room. The hardwood floor was scarred and had a black circle burned into it. It looked as if someone had attempted to scrub it out. A dated sofa stretched along one side of the room, and two oversized armchairs flanked it. The coffee table was discolored, and the scent of tannin, verbena, ginger, and oak stained the air along with other unrecognizable scents.

"Is this where you all practice?" I asked whoever had magically answered the door. It was a dramatic, unnecessary, and flagrant display of power to which I'd grown accustomed.

Big whoop, you can open a door with magic.

"Yes, we practice here."

I groaned. I'd heard that voice just a week ago. Wendy. The so-called Maestro of Magic. The wizard robe-wearing peddler of magic. When she came into view, she wasn't wearing her costume, which was good. Despite knowing what she was capable of, it was hard to take her seriously when she was wearing it.

Now if she'd just get rid of the petite woman standing next to her, who *was* wearing a robe, we could get through this without me trying to hold back my laughter.

The petite woman returned my derisive look with her dark-brown almond-shaped eyes. Her long, straight, coal-black hair was pulled back into a tight, high ponytail with bangs that were a little too long and overwhelmed her round face. Her lips were twisted into a scowl, and her khaki-colored skin flushed with indecipherable emotions. Whatever she was feeling, there was a lot of it and it was all directed at me.

"We know what you are, and please let Landon know that

sending you here is the highest of insults," Wendy said. And with that they stepped back, far from the circle. Wendy's mouth moved, and orange and gold sigils appeared along the perimeter of the circle, forcing me to stay locked where I was.

"What was his plan, for you to take my magic and leave us for dead? Or force the others to turn it over in order to return my magic?" Wendy ground out through clenched teeth.

"Neither. I'm here to make you an offer. I don't want you dead, nor do I have any plans to use violent methods to make you comply."

Their magic was strong. When I first met Wendy, I had my own; the urges had been satiated. Now, I had no magic, and as theirs wafted around me, I inhaled, trying to find the fortitude to not give in to my desire for theirs. Being magically bound in the circle helped.

After several cleansing breaths, I had wrangled in my control and focused on the fact that I wasn't the one they needed to worry about.

Eyes narrowed, Wendy studied me.

"Fine," she eventually conceded. Stepping back, with an invocation and a wave of her finger, a small paper manifested and floated in front of me.

Wendy was a magical badass and spell-wielding extraordinaire with ridiculous taste in clothing. "That's where he can send the money," she said.

"He's only agreeing to half."

"If we wanted half, we would have asked for it. This isn't up for negotiation. Either he pays what we ask or we start selling it. I'm quite sure we would make that amount rather quickly."

People would buy Amber Crocus for the same reason people kept silver, and if they could afford it, iridium cuffs. The sense of security. They could kill a vampire. For people who lacked vampiric strength and speed, it had to be empowering to know they could disable one.

"He'll pay half and you'll have to agree to a death oath on your silence and to refrain from ever growing it again or instructing others on how to do so."

"No." Her tone was decisive with hints of offense.

"If he paid the full amount, would you agree to the oath?"

"No. There isn't anything he could offer that would convince us to agree to that."

"Perhaps you need to bring the offer to your coven for discussion," I suggested.

"I have the voice of my coven."

Either she was in a coven full of superfans who followed her blindly, or she was the one who figured out how to grow Amber Crocus. Covens worked as units and had a communal relationship, usually making decision as a group by vote. Mages and witches had the most democratic leadership of all the other denizens. It was unusual for one person to have the voice of the group.

"He's not going to agree to it unless you do. If I were you—"

"You're not me. In fact, you would say anything to make sure this goes in his favor. After all, you are working for him."

I shrugged. "True, he's paying me to handle this, but I have nothing to lose in this situation. No horse in this race. You can continue to be stubborn, refuse to compromise, and have Landon handle the issue in the manner he finds most fitting." My voice held a warning measure. "I'll still get my fee whether this is settled by you getting his money and giving him his oath or your coven no longer existing."

"Are you threatening me on his behalf? It's quite arrogant on his part and bold on yours to do that." Her fingers began to move, a precursor to what looked like pretty wicked magic.

Dropping my eyes to the sigils in the circle, I tried to make sense of them. Without magic, there wasn't much I could do about whatever Wendy was planning. And without the ability to move outside the circle, I couldn't get to them. Yanking the gun from my holster and the small knife from the sheath at my waist, I dragged my eyes from Wendy to the other witch and back.

"Contrary to what you believe, it is in my best interests to handle this amicably. I need the vampires to feel they've been treated fairly and for you to feel it was a just agreement and discourage you from trying this again."

She frowned, but I was still met with defiance. I wanted to urge her to review her vampire history. To recognize that most of the stories aren't about the vampires' forebearers but about the vamps we see daily. Living for centuries didn't allow them the privilege of saying they can't be judged by the actions of their ancestors. I wanted to warn her not to underestimate Landon. With his baroque mannerisms, stylish dress, and appealing benign looks, people often forgot or overlooked his history. He was as equally dramatic in his violence as he was in his disposition.

"I have a gun and I'm pretty damn good with it. You'll try to physically or magically dodge the bullets while I'm unloading. You're good with magic. I'm better with a gun. No matter how gifted you are, it's really hard trying to perform a spell with a bullet in you."

I directed my attention to the robe-wearing witch with the resting witch face.

"I get it. You want a payoff. But what you don't want is for the vampires to feel slighted. Hurting me and refusing their offer won't work in your favor. They'll use it as justification to retaliate. Landon's just looking for a reason. All the malicious things you've read about vampires aren't accounts of their ancestors, it's them. The same ones living among us."

I stopped to let that sink in.

Wendy attempted to remain stern, unmoved, and indifferent. The other witch's scowl had given way to a look of concern.

"I'm not here to bully anyone. I have no desire to see any of you hurt. While you're only looking at it from your perspective, I see the whole picture and I'm able to be objective." I wanted to add that I was the only person standing between them and carnage.

"Stacey." Wendy jerked her head toward the other side of the room. They backed away, but instead of going to another room, they went outside.

After several minutes, Wendy came back in and said, "We won't do a death oath, but we'll agree to an *evanesco* spell. It's as binding as the oath, and in the event we break it, we face the consequence of losing our magic, not dying."

Loss of magic. A magic restriction. Every spell can be reversed. Some are harder to reverse than others, but they can always be reversed. Oaths are the exception, which is why they aren't entered into lightly.

"I'll ask, but I'm not confident that he'll agree to it."

"And the original cost. We will not haggle."

I nodded, considered the figure again, and inwardly winced.

With a quick flick of her finger, made with the ease of an afterthought, the sigils disappeared.

"He'll want an outside witch to perform it, so I'll need the spell."

"Once the money is in the account, I'll give it to him. Just say it's included in the fee."

I needed to figure out how to befriend the robe-wearing witches. If I could manage to control my eye rolling at their robes, they could become valuable resources.

Before I left, I asked to see the AC as confirmation. They led me through the house to the kitchen that looked into the backyard. Whoever didn't want anyone to learn about AC did a splendid job, removing any images of it. This was my first time actually seeing the plant and not just reading a description. Opening the door, Wendy revealed a garden containing healthy, vibrant, verdant, fern-like plants with a distinctive white-and-goldish tip growing out of dark, rich, moist-looking soil. They clearly received better care and attention than the home.

———

The dark-haired woman who answered Landon's door looked up from her phone long enough to greet me with a bored smile.

"Erin?"

I nodded. She was too casual and disinterested to be his assistant.

"Come in. Uncle Landon's waiting."

Uncle? The only familial resemblance were the dark eyes, hers a lighter brown to his onyx. With a vibrant apricot complexion, this woman was definitely human. Sired vampires never used family titles, like mother, father, uncle, and aunt. She was completely team human; the expensive-looking ombre-dyed hair of black and white, heavily lined eyes, and thickly coated lashes gave her a creature of the night mystique, but she was human nevertheless.

"Uncle Landy, your assistant is here."

I should have corrected her, but she was so preoccupied by her phone, it was doubtful she'd care. I got the distinct feeling that to her, people fell into two categories: vampire elite and the help. She'd denoted me as the help.

"Thank you, Robyn, love," he said. Avuncular adoration bloomed on his face. Something that must have been rooted in her familiar bond because she wasn't that adorable.

Her fingers speeding over the keys of her phone, she didn't look up as she turned lengthwise in the oversized chair in the corner of his office, making herself at home. Sensing the change in the atmosphere, her gaze finally moved from her phone to look at us. The dark eyes were definitely where the family resemblance ended. A rounded face, wide expressive eyes, full lips, and a pert nose gave her a doll-like appearance that was a stark contrast to Landon's imposing sharp features, narrow face, dark and intense guileful eyes, and supple lips that pulled back too often to display fangs.

"What?" she asked.

"We need a minute," he informed her, giving her a plaintive smile that I was sure would vanish the moment she was gone.

"Of course." She bounded to her feet with liquid grace. As she moved from the room, she gave me the impression she was a dancer. That may be what spawned his expression. Landon remained tethered to the human world, unlike the original Master of the city, because of his investment in it. He was discerning, I'd go so far as to say snobbish, about the company he kept, preferring to only interact with the city's elite, but he loved the arts, often investing in dance and theater companies, donating to the arts in the schools, and financing art showings.

"Uncle?" I asked.

He took a sip from the wine glass he held. I wondered if it was red wine or the blood/wine mix they enjoyed. "Yes," he said. "I have three nephews and another niece. Of course, there are many 'greats' before that title. My other nieces and nephews are far less impressive than Robyn," he admitted.

Something told me he would definitely tell them that. They could be a well-renowned scientist, a CEO of a Fortune 500 company, an elected official, but as far as Landon was concerned, if they didn't make art with their body, enhance the landscape of the world with their painting, make awe-inspiring sculptures, or write prose that made a person sit in contemplation, they didn't count. Violence and beauty—the dichotomy of his existence didn't escape me. I snapped my eyes from him when I realized I was staring.

"She's the principal of her company. You should join me sometime, to watch her. She's fascinating."

And whatever the others were doing would never be as impressive as her performing on a stage. In one nimble sweep of movement he was behind his desk, glass still in hand, taking another draw from it. "Would you like a glass?"

Unconvinced that it wasn't their special wine, I declined.

"What was the result with the witches?" he asked after taking another indulgent sip. The wistful look he gave the glass confirmed that declining his offer was the right decision.

"They won't reduce their price, nor will they agree to a death oath. They will agree to *evanesco*. If they violate that, they lose their magic. You can have the spell customized to extend to them and any future members of the coven, only to expire upon your death."

He considered it. "I reject their counter. Spells can be broken. If they go back on their word, I want them to die."

Before I could offer a suggestion, he added, "They are blackmailing me for two million dollars. I will not negotiate the terms. There need to be dire consequences. I will not go through this again in a few years." He jutted out his chin.

I knew what wasn't being said. Landon was handling this as amicably as he was willing. There would be no more concessions. Pushing him any further would make his brutal option look even more desirable.

Stepping out of the office and house until I was far enough away, I called the robe-wearing, greedy blackmailer.

For fifteen minutes, she continued to attempt to negotiate.

"Do you understand how much money you're getting?" I said. "This is his less violent offer. Keep pushing and you and your coven will walk away with nothing and possibly a bounty on your heads, or lifelong enemies of the vampires. Remember, they're immortal. Not only will you have them to contend with but also anyone they can compel. Your sweet little neighbor who waves at you and loves your little kitty might be the very person who plunges a knife into your back." I wished I was being dramatic and hyperbolic, but anyone who'd ever read any of the tales of vampires would know that I wasn't.

"Compelling humans is illegal," Wendy reminded me in a huff.

"Are you kidding me? You're asking for two million dollars! If Landon feels he's being taken advantage of or affronted in any way, do you think he's going to care about a law? He's working within the confines of it now. How long do you think it will last? I don't think it's unreasonable to agree to this. But you can decline and take your chances on the black market."

"I already have a buyer. Mephisto. We won't be just selling it to random people on the streets. Since you've worked for both of them, I do believe you're the one in a compromising position. So it is in *your* best interest that you work something out. Landon's going to assume you were playing both sides. Mephisto is offering less but without any oaths."

Wendy's greed and obstinacy were rapidly diminishing my desire to protect them.

Afraid that Landon might read the fury on me or I might say something I'd regret, I called him to tell him I needed to handle it in person. Buying some time, I headed to Mephisto's.

CHAPTER 9

The gate swung open before I made it to the entrance. I managed to keep the anger out of my voice when I called to ask to speak with him. The drive hadn't calmed me down and I was still seething by the time I walked to the front door. How did he find out about the AC? Did the witches approach him or did he contact them? Did he know I was involved and not care?

Benton had abandoned all door duties and had adopted the role of beverage drinker and book reader. When I entered the unlocked house, I passed him in his favorite room, doing exactly that.

"He's in his office," he offered, glancing up from his book.

Great job. You, sir, are in need of a raise.

"Don't get up, I know the way," I sniped. I was feeling good about my comment and thinking I'd scored a point in the pettiness tournament we were somehow embroiled in.

Until he responded with, "No problem, Ms. Jensen. I wasn't planning on it." Then he punctuated it by taking an exaggerated slurp from his cup. I'd wanted to take my win with pride, but he snatched it from me with one simple act. Who was I kidding? Benton was the Master of Quips and

Snark and the Grand Pooh-bah of Pettiness. I was a mere novice and out of my league.

I stopped in my tracks and turned to get a glimpse of the twisted look of satisfaction on his face.

He was lucky I had a god to yell at and therefore didn't have time to try to out-petty him, but he was definitely going on my to-do list: Yell at a god, stop Landon from killing Lunar Marked coven, convince said coven to stop being stubborn jackasses, figure out what to do with my mother and the Immortalis, figure out who kept bespelling me to sleep, and win my tournament of pettiness with Benton.

Mephisto met me in the hallway, coming from the direction of the room where he kept his magical objects. Probably looking for a space for the Amber Crocus.

His head tilted and he studied me. "You're upset," he surmised. "What happened?"

Was he messing with me?

"Are you kidding?" I asked, louder than intended. It was me yelling that brought Simeon out of Mephisto's office to look at me. I turned at the sound of him walking into the hall. His attention moved from me and then to Mephisto, where it stayed. Without any words exchanged, Simeon ducked back into the office and returned with a small bag in his hand and headed for the front door.

Mephisto was quiet, his face unreadable as he led me into his office, closing the door behind him and immediately moving to the window. He lifted his face as if allowing the setting sun to warm it.

"Am I kidding about what?" he finally asked.

"The Lunar Marked coven has Amber Crocus and I was just informed that you've made an offer."

"Yes, there isn't anything untrue about that." He moved from the window to the front of his desk, crossing one leg over the other. Folding his arms over his chest, he asked, "What part of that seemed to be in jest, or kidding you?"

"I'm working for the vampires trying to purchase the Amber Crocus from the witches."

"Hmm, I wasn't aware of that. This must be an incredibly awkward and complicated situation for you," he eased out airily.

"You know what the vampires can be like. I'm trying to prevent the situation from becoming one of those stories you cringe at when you read it. Right now, that's exactly where they are."

Mephisto heaved a sigh, a look of censure and annoyance flashing over his features and quickly disappearing. "For all Landon's love of the humanities, appreciation of life, and his indulgences in its banalities, he still seems to revel in gruesome violence. Ever willing to demonstrate his talents."

"Yes, and if you purchase the Amber Crocus, you will give him license to turn those skills on that coven. And possibly on you."

A cold dark look passed over his face, a look that people must see when the Huntsmen swoop down on them to deliver justice.

"I have no fear of Landon or his retribution," he said aloofly, but an edge of malice lingered on his face. You don't apprehend the worst in the Veil, go against other gods, and not be adept in violence, maybe even have a penchant for it. I was sure that the call to be a Huntsman wasn't for the faint of heart or pacifists.

"What about the witches?" I ground out in frustration.

"They approached me. I'm assuming they feel confident enough to protect themselves."

"Sometimes stupidity is the misguided cousin of confidence. They are being blinded by greed. Wendy is skilled and might be able to protect herself, but I think she's overconfident and it will lead to the death of that coven."

"Is it Cory's coven?"

I shook my head.

"Then why do you care?"

I had to snap my mouth closed at his question. "Because it's the right thing to do."

His movement toward me was so swift, it made me miss the times when he'd moved like he was human. When he'd muted his magic enough that it was less distracting. Now, I was swathed in it and wondering how deadly his strike was.

Studying me, he traced a finger languidly along the curve of my jaw. Knowing that he gave part of his life to bring me back from death didn't remove my desire for his magic. Nor did finding out that he was closer to the devil than I'd jokingly thought take away the attraction I'd been denying.

"Tell me," he urged, his face just inches from mine. His cologne inundating my senses, his warm breath against my lips were distractions that were getting harder to ignore. "How much must I surrender to you?" The accusation in his gaze was a punch to the chest. It was an unfair question.

I closed my eyes for a moment, attempted to pull in a cleansing breath. That failed. Stepping away from him and his touch, I gathered my thoughts. "I'm trying to do my job and prevent a group of foolish witches from getting killed and a mess that ultimately will involve the STF and Madison. Whether you understand or care to, it will have a ripple effect. I just don't need that in my life right now. Please. Withdraw your offer."

He frowned. "I have a job, too. I'm a collector, something you are aware of. In fact, my collection is what saved your life. You must have some appreciation for that. Walk away from this and let them handle it in the manner that fits. That will allow you to be blameless in the matter."

"I won't be blameless. Neither will you. It's cruel to let this happen if we can stop it."

Mephisto regarded me for a long time, his face an indecipherable mask. "Pragmatism and cruelty aren't the same thing," he offered softly, his eyes whetted with insight.

"But far too often they run in the same circles," I said.

Moving until I rested against the wall, I remained under the weight of his dark inquiring gaze as magic swept through the room with a turbulent force.

"Stop it," I demanded in a low, rough voice. For someone who claimed I was his weakness, he had Herculean strength when he wanted, but I couldn't help feeling as if I was exploiting it. Was it wrong to do that?

It was a selfish request but it was to save lives. "Will you do it for me?" I entreated softly. "Please."

He moistened his lips, his gaze tracking my every movement as the seconds quickly became minutes of stilted silence, and once again, I felt that anything that took that much deliberation should go in my favor.

"No," he asserted in a low, raspy, and uncompromising tone.

Landon would have to make an offer that was just as appealing, but I had no idea what it could be that would match a sale without any restrictions.

Dragging his gaze away from me, Mephisto eventually meandered back to the window. I was convinced he must live most of his life underground, because outdoors just wasn't that damn interesting.

"Are you finished?" Although he asked, the finality of his tone indicated we were.

"Besides the Obitus blade, what else can be used against Immortalis?"

"I just know of the blade," Mephisto said.

Now I had his full attention and he, along with washes of magic, was right in front of me.

Move normal. Not your normal. The other normal. Pre-confession normal.

It had to be freeing to be able to be himself. To move in a godly manner and indulge in his magic and be who he was behind the Veil, but sometimes it was off-putting. Besides the other Huntsmen, I was probably the only person who he could be like this with. Then it dawned on me that Benton wasn't just the answerer of doors, the drinker of beverages, and the laziest employee ever, but also the keeper of the Huntsmen's secret.

"You were attacked again?" he asked before I could inquire about Benton.

I nodded and told him everything that happened. His hands went to my ribs when I told him about them breaking. "They're fine now." He didn't move his hands.

"Why wasn't this the first thing you told me? Landon and his problems are the least of your worries."

"I wasn't expecting to be attacked. You can't expect me to just wait around for Malific to kill me, so I accepted a job."

"No, but more should be done." He was examining my arm as if it would prompt his memory of a spell. Frowning, he said, "She's here."

"How do you know?"

"They wouldn't have attacked without a reason. You said they seemed like they were trying to take you."

"Initially they appeared to be content to break rank. He threatened to kill me after I kneed him. I get more threats that way."

Mephisto fought the smile that flickered at his lips before shooting me a disapproving look. "You are trained and quite skilled," he said.

"And? There are no rules when trying to save your life. I fight to win. Training is fine, but I've never brought a man down faster than kneeing him in the groin. All my fancy hand work, throws, tosses, strikes, and parries don't compare to a punch to the man berries."

He chuckled, still looking at the area on my arm that bore the mark of the raven. "Do you have your weapons?"

I nodded and headed out of the office to my car with him behind. *Oh great, now I have a god as a bodyguard.*

I retrieved the weapons and we returned to his office where he examined them. He kept questioning me about the magic.

"Were the Immortalis gone, or were they disposed of?" he inquired, his scent teasing my nose and the turbulence of his uneasiness a reminder of the Immortalis attack.

"I don't know," I admitted. "But if they are immune to magic and only an Obitus blade can kill them, perhaps they left."

Mephisto didn't seem convinced. My eyes attempted to track him as he moved back and forth. It made me appreciate not having gods living among us, even if I was one, or a demigod, anyway. I was a magical dud until my restrictions were removed.

"You have to be more careful with your life, Erin."

Irritation bloomed in me. I was at my therapist's office. I had my weapons on me and I fought back. "Go to hell." Wrong choice of words. "Don't blame me for being attacked. I didn't ask for any of this," I shouted. "A month ago, my life wasn't nearly as crappy as it is now. The only thing I had to worry about was staying away from magic and trying not to kill someone. Now my life is in jeopardy, someone's using magic against me, and I can't stop it. I'm magicless and in a situation where I really need it. And my mother wants me dead. You think I'm not being careful? How can I not be?"

He didn't deserve my anger. I was an emotional bomb and he'd unintentionally detonated me with his words. His lips pressed together and he kept the distance between us, his expression impassive, his silence disconcerting. I needed Mephisto as an ally and I was doing a terrible job at it.

Exhaling a heavy breath once the silence became too much, I backed myself to the door. "I'm trying to be careful." The uncomfortable silence remained and he didn't stop me from leaving. That bothered me the most as I sifted through what had happened between us. A part of whatever we had had wilted, maybe even died.

It tugged at me enough that I didn't go back for my dagger that Mephisto had been assessing. I could use it as an excuse to come back. What I would be returning to, I wasn't sure.

CHAPTER 10

I couldn't be more careful then being behind the secure walls of the Supernatural Task Force, which consisted of well-trained shifters, talented witches, skilled mages, and adept fae. And one sat across from me picking at the chicken roti I'd bought her for lunch. It took a lot to distract her from her favorite meal, and I felt bad telling her the unedited version of what happened with the Immortalis. She took it in stride, even the attack, nodding as she picked at her meal.

"Is Sumner going to discharge you?" she asked, holding a forkful of food. If it bothered her that I kept that from her, she was doing an excellent job hiding it.

"I think so. I'm seeing him for something that never happened."

She frowned but didn't comment. "The blacking out—"

"I didn't black out. Someone used magic on me, a sleep spell without the need for ingredients." If I hadn't been bespelled, that person wouldn't have died. I would have felt the tug that notified me to return the magic.

"Another god?" she asked. I had a feeling she felt like I did about them, that our world was better without their existence. She shoved her fingers through her hair, which was starting to show the ringlets she'd cut off and the hints of her natural deep-sienna color. Mussed up, she looked out the window in her office at the small park where she liked to have lunch.

"Erin, I have no idea what to do." Her tone was despondent and defeated. "It's like we're waiting for someone to kill you."

In a way, we were. We were sitting around, waiting to play defense when the time came. It was frustrating. Proactive measures had failed.

"We tried to find her. We don't have a lot of options. But she can't make any more Immortalis," I emphasized, with a level of confidence and optimism that I hoped would ease the strained look on her face.

Giving me a weak half smile, she said, "Yeah."

We tried to let the conversation fall into something more lighthearted, but her questioning kept coming back to me describing the magic. "And it wasn't like Mephisto's and the other...Huntsmen's magic?" She paused over the title, a strain in her voice. Did she imagine them as ruthless overpowered mercenaries as I sometimes did? Images of them fighting the Immortalis resurfaced and a reminder that there's always three sides to every story: his side, their side, and the truth, which often lay somewhere in the middle. I couldn't help but remember the way the Veil shifters regarded Mephisto. There was more to them.

I shook my head. "It was different. More similar to witches' magic, maybe." I wasn't confident about that. The magic felt too different and it overwhelmed me. I was lulled into the spell in a manner that I hadn't been with any other magic. It overtook me so quickly, I felt helpless.

Giving up on finishing her food, Madison packed it away. "Do you think they can be trusted?" she finally asked, pensive.

Mephisto wanted to avenge Oedeus's death. For that reason, I knew he could be trusted when it came to me and dealing with Malific, but I was still left agitated by his bid for the Amber Crocus and his indifference about the complication his acquisition of it might cause. But I didn't disclose that to Madison.

"Yes," I simply said. Something in my response made her eyes narrow and her lips pucker.

"Then our goal is to remove your magical restriction. At least if Malific comes for you, you can make her see how bad a decision it was."

I smiled at her overly ambitious and enthusiastic confidence in me. Yeah, the only thing standing between me and defeating an Arch-deity was magic I wasn't totally sure how to use.

But it did embolden me. Now I just had to fix the situation with Landon and the coven and have one less thing to deal with.

———

When I looked at the incoming call, I figured the fates were having a time screwing me over or betting on who could make my life the most hellish.

"Landon."

"Ms. Jensen," he purred. "It seems as if you've decided to play on both sides of the fence. Your perfidy will not be tolerated." His voice was so calm it sent more chills through me than if a bellowing voice had reverberated throughout the room.

"I'm not sure what you are talking about," I said.

"Oh, but you are. Apparently Mephisto has made an offer. I'm not blind to your history with him. He's made it quite clear that what he wants he expects to get, and you've been instrumental in making sure it happens."

I was a retrieval specialist, I helped him find things. A glorified bounty hunter. But it was just jobs.

"The same can be said for my relationship with you. I've worked for you and acquired things for you on more than one occasion."

"True. The question is, who are you working for now, me or Mephisto?"

My mind raced through every possible scenario and the most likely outcomes. If I told Landon that the witches approached Mephisto, would he feel the urge to take matters into his own hands out of offense?

"Landon, you hired me to handle this, and I will. You'll have the Amber Crocus, okay?"

"That's what I wanted to hear." The menace had left his voice and he quickly ended the call.

My job for Landon wouldn't take priority. Magic had stolen time from me, my magical restriction was leaving me vulnerable, and there was an impending face-off with my mother. That had to take priority. Because if the stories were true, me running into my mother without magic or the ability to defend myself would have the same result: The Landon situation wouldn't be resolved because I'd be dead. Staying alive had to be my first objective.

I needed to talk to Cory.

CHAPTER 11

Trying to ignore Cory's scowl and his scathing sidelong looks was becoming increasingly difficult as I navigated the unpaved road and wound farther into a stand of trees. If I managed to miss those signs of irritation, occasionally he'd let out a huff of annoyance.

"What's with the mood?" I asked with a sigh.

"It's not a mood. I seem to recall receiving a lecture about dealing with witches who dealt in dark magic. Hmmm, let me see if I can remember who gave me that lecture. The name escapes me at this moment." There was a long and very unnecessary pause. "Oh, I remember now, it was you. And I agree."

I had chastised Cory for going to Harrison for help when we were trying to stop Ian.

"I just have a few questions," I said. "The magic I felt was so different, what if…"

"You think it was a demon?"

"I don't know, but since neither one of us is really versed in anything more than what we've read in books, and Harrison dabbles in dark magic, I'm not convinced he hasn't summoned a demon."

"You know what he is, how he operates, and if you're asking about dark magic, he'll be more than happy to oblige."

I grew silent. Desperate times called for desperate measures.

"You're going to let him summon a demon on your behalf, aren't you?" Cory accused.

I pressed my lips together for fear that the words would spill out. Cory and I didn't keep too many secrets from each other, and glancing in his direction, I could see the look of betrayal, sense the frustration and the glint in his eyes as he pondered how to take control of the car.

"I'll be careful," I promised.

"Careful wandered out the door and gave us the finger the moment we decided to deal with Harrison."

"You dealt with him," I reminded him.

"Just to question him," he said softly. "Erin, I have a feeling you're willing to do more than just ask him questions." His finger curled around a lock of my hair. It was a reminder of the many times we'd lain next to each other. I thought just being close to magic would ease the urges and prevent me from giving in to the cravings. It didn't. But Cory would stay there for as long as I thought I needed him.

"I'm desperate," I admitted. "You have no idea what it feels like knowing someone wants you dead."

"I might know. Do you know how many women I dated before I realized I didn't like them?"

My breath hitched. He was finally saying it. Out loud. He was dating Alex, which was the first time I'd seen him openly date another man. But this was the first time he'd admitted he didn't like women.

"Look at me, I'm a total smokeshow. I'm charming. My body looks like it was sculpted out of marble. My wit is amazing. And I effortlessly straddle the line between hot boy next door and sexy guy in the gym you want to bonk—"

"Don't you dare forget modest. Modesty is where you

truly shine. It is your wheelhouse. Hands down you might be the most modest. The modest-est. Your humility makes me want to be a better person."

"Good, that's my goal. I want people to see me and want to do better," he countered, flashing me a teasing smile. "I've left a string of broken hearts. They might not want me dead, but I'm sure they hate me."

"Wait. You think that's equivalent to a sociopathic god wanting me dead?" I asked, my mouth agape at the absurdity of the comparison.

Giving my chin a light nudge, he said, "Let's close that, sweetie. Okay, it's not *exactly* the same." Then the humor melted from him and his face became aggrieved. "I just don't want you to become so single-mindedly focused on this that you make decisions with your emotions. We both know choices made solely on that aren't always the wisest."

Sighing, I wished I had more options. It wasn't my first choice to deal with a person who peddled in dark and demon magic.

"I won't let my emotions drive my decisions," I promised. That was a promise I could keep.

When I pulled up to the motorhome, the man with curly chin-length strawberry-blond hair, docile amber eyes, razor-thin lips, and a pudgy nose didn't strike me as a demon magic dealer.

But he walked toward us with a confidence that made me wary. Cory must've sensed the eeriness, too, because he tensed. Our eyes narrowed on the dark witch.

"What can I do for you?"

His quick approach didn't leave a lot of room for me to assess the area. I did a cursory scan. The grass was healthy and verdant, a wealth of large trees surrounded the area, a barbeque pit was just a few feet away, and off in the distance was a large circle where the grass was stained brown. I assumed it was from the use of tannin, salt, and whatever other ingredients were needed to summon a demon or perform dark magic. Near the perimeter of the circle were half-buried stones marked with sigils.

Harrison noted what I was looking at. "It's good to have a backup to prevent them getting out," he said. "They're corporeal by choice, it keeps them strong. But if they see an out, like a weak boundary, they take it. Those stones are a magic-keyed defensive perimeter that can be quickly invoked."

I wasn't well versed on what was needed to summon a demon. If I were ever in need of one, I'd have to go to my shadier sources to get it. The information was guarded—or rather very well hidden. If you decided to summon a demon, you had to work for the information on how to do it. Most people didn't want to risk being ostracized by admitting they were peddling in demon-summoning magic.

"So, you do summon demons?" I asked. There was a hint of accusation and judgment in my voice that I didn't like. I hoped he missed it. I was the last person with any right to cast aspersions on another.

His genial smile faded into a rueful smirk. "Don't be coy. Me peddling in dark magic and summoning demons is the very reason you are here. On that note, what can I do for you?"

Powerful caustic magic bathed the air, reminding me of the time I pulled magic from the Immortalis. Magic that felt acrid and toxic, making me turn from him and inhale a breath of clean woodsy air.

Good question. What could he do for me?

"A magical restriction has been placed on me, marked by a raven, and I want to know if you have a means of removing it."

"Where is it?"

I extended my right arm.

"There's no raven."

"It's there. It seems like magical fire and certain spells make it appear. A fire Mirra made it appear the first time."

"And the spells?"

"I don't remember."

He gave me a look as if he knew I was lying, but I didn't care. I wasn't about to tell him I had access to both *Mystic Souls* books.

"We've tried to remove it several times, but nothing worked."

"And you think it's demon magic."

"No, no one thinks that. But since you have a vast knowledge of magic, we thought you might be able to tell," Cory offered.

"Vast, meaning dark." Harrison's brow rose as he shot Cory a derisive sneer. Cory sounded a little judgmental, too, but when it came from me, it seemed to roll off him. My reputation probably made him see us as kindred.

He went on. "Jung said, 'Unfortunately there can be no doubt that man is, on the whole, less good than he imagines himself or wants to be. Everyone carries a shadow, and the less it is embodied in the individual's conscious life, the blacker and denser it is. At all counts, it forms an unconscious snag, thwarting our most well-meant intentions.'" He directed a castigating look in Cory's direction. "The fact that you are here means that you aren't opposed to dark magic, just opposed to doing it because you feel that it will make you bad. Does having someone do it on your behalf make you good and your magic light?"

Cory's chin jutted out, but his eyes glinted with uncertainty and introspection. Several beats of silence passed before Cory conceded. "No," he admitted, "but for me, it's a last resort. Is it for you?"

Harrison didn't even wait a beat. "Light magic is weak because it's limited by so many rules and the nebulous perception of good and evil. No, light magic is never an option. I deal with whatever magic will give me the results I need." He responded in the neutral timbre of a sociopath admitting to a heinous crime without any remorse.

I scored high on the personality disorder test and I suspected that I would continue to do so until I had magic. It was embarrassing and shameful to admit that I wasn't sure I wouldn't be a wraith sucking magic from people and leaving them for dead if there weren't any consequences. That knowledge didn't make me feel good. When it came to magic, ethics got a little blurred. I didn't want to kill, but the need seemed too hard to deny. But I did it. Often.

There were some similarities between me and Harrison. He'd do anything for the results he needed, and I struggled with not doing anything and everything to get magic. But was it that struggle, my desire to not kill, that separated us?

"What do you want from me?" Harrison asked, dragging his searing gaze from Cory to me.

"Can you make it appear again?"

He frowned. "A Mirra is very strong magic. I can't do one, but I can do something very similar. Who did the first one?"

"The Woman in Black."

"Hmm. I'm sure I can make it reappear, but after that, then what?"

"Once you see it, you might be able to identify the magic."

"If I can't, would you be willing to show it to someone else?"

"Someone else or a demon?" Cory asked.

"A demon is someone," Harrison pointed out. His docile amber eyes grew hard. "If you want my help, that can't be excluded as a possibility."

"What will this help cost?"

"An oath that you will give me a favor in return."

I didn't like bartering with favors. I'd rather reach into my bank account and pull out everything in it than trade in favors. Most people like to keep them open ended. Anyone who agrees to that is just asking for trouble.

"What's the favor?" Although I had no intention of paying in favors, I was curious if he would be one of the few people who was specific enough to make me change my mind.

He shrugged nonchalantly. "Just a favor. I'll let you know when I call it in."

Yeah, right. There's no way I'm agreeing to that.

"I don't deal in favors. Payment only. How much do you want?"

He nodded. "Very well." He went back into his motorhome, where he stayed for several minutes.

"What's he doing in there, discussing it with his accountant?" Cory sniped.

Unless you were in one of the innumerable witch shops around town, as I was, witches didn't really have a fee schedule. They just came up with a number that wouldn't make you walk away. I did it as well. I had a baseline consulting fee, but I'd add a surcharge just because the client was being annoying or an ass; I called it a hazard fee.

I suspected Harrison used a similar system. He handed me a piece of paper and I grimaced at it. What was he trying to do, upgrade his motorhome?

"Half up front, and if you're successful in giving me an answer, you'll get the rest when we leave."

"And if I can remove it?" His voice held a level of confidence that piqued my interest.

"What do you want?"

"Since you aren't offering favors, double." The fact that a favor was worth the egregious amount he was asking made me glad I didn't peddle in favors. "Fine. If I walk away from this with my magic permanently restored, you can have double."

There goes the down payment on my house, I thought

sadly. How much more was this endeavor going to take from me?

Whenever fire, reptiles, tannin, knives, and a bunny are used in a spell, believe me, things are about to get real. Real gross. Real messy. Real dark. Real bloody. And real painful. I prepared myself for the worst.

It made things even more unsettling when, once we were settled in a circle formation around the campfire, the bunny hopped into my lap.

Harrison had already taken blood from the serpent. It was done with such clinical proficiency, I knew he'd done it many times before.

"I need the rabbit," Harrison told me.

"No," I blurted without thinking, holding the bunny to my chest.

"I need the blood of a mammal."

I extended my arm.

"I need a great deal. Enough to fill this." He showed me a shot-sized container. When I kept my arm extended, he rolled his eyes and without any warning slashed my hand. I squeezed my balled fist. Each time the blood flow slowed, I received another slash until the clear glass was totally full. After I cleaned the cut with the damp paper towel Harrison handed me, I tossed it into the fire. I wasn't leaving anything that could be used for a spell against me.

Bunny had the good sense to hop out of my lap and run.

That's right, bunny, get as far away as possible from this bunny blood-draining jackass.

Despite knowing that the magic Harrison was doing was dark, I couldn't help but be mesmerized by the beauty of the tenebrous tendrils of black, gray, and crimson twining over the fire. The crackling sound of it created a tranquil melody, and a strange sedative feeling overtook the area. Pepper and tannin wafted from Harrison, removing the initial aversion I had for his magic. Even the forbidding aspect that marked his presence seemed diminutive now.

"Ready?" he asked.

"For what?"

"To reveal your mark?"

Dammit. If it wasn't a Mirra, it was an excellent fabrication. Like the one at Elizabeth's, which had not only looked like fire but felt like it, too. After having my hand sliced several times, I wasn't keen to go through fire. But I simply nodded.

With a simple swipe of his finger through the air, fire rose from the campfire and drifted to him, settling in his palms.

If it burned or caused any discomfort, he was doing an excellent job of hiding it.

I stuck my arm through the fire and winced at the pain that lanced through me, biting back the scream in my throat. My eyes blurred with tears.

When I pulled it out of the fire, the only thing that marred my arm was the raven.

Cory hadn't seen it before.

Both he and Harrison studied the bird, perched on a gilded branch with several archaic-looking symbols around it. I hadn't noticed the small insignia next to it, or perhaps I just hadn't paid it any attention. Cory and Harrison got their phones out to capture a shot of it, but one snap and the raven disappeared.

Harrison had me go through the Mirra-replica again. This time he scribbled away, sketching the markings and the bird. When he turned the sketch to me, it bore a striking resemblance. He was talented.

The raven remained for several minutes, giving the witches time to examine it.

"I don't know what these symbols are, but I'm assuming it's a protection spell."

Duh, no kidding.

Harrison's mouth twisted to the side in concentration. "This is the witches' old language," he said, pointing to symbols at the top of the raven. He made a face, his fingers traced along the other markings. "I have a rudimentary knowledge of fae and this is theirs."

Cory frowned. I don't think it was just Harrison's connection to dark magic that was bothering him; something in Cory's posture led me to believe he didn't trust Harrison.

"If you're willing to do anything to find out what this is, there's another source who I'm sure could decipher the sigils, maybe even break the curse."

"A demon," Cory said tersely, negating Harrison's need to tap dance around the topic.

"Demons are old, have been around for years, and have experienced far more magic than we'll ever know. I think a demon could help us."

I agreed without hesitation or even looking at Cory.

"There's always a bargain with a demon and they won't accept cash. They don't need it. Hosting them—" Harrison said.

"I'm not hosting a demon," I told him firmly. People survived hosting a demon, but I'd heard of more failures than successes. The horrors of the host's mind never being the same or feeling as though they'd lost full volition of their body once they were no longer a host, for example.

"Sometimes they just want things: blood of a mammal, hair of a witch, an item of yours. A book or something just as benign or inconsequential. Once, one only wanted the sound of a fae's laughter." Harrison scrunched his nose in dismay.

"Why?" I asked. On the hierarchy of stupid and innocuous things, that ranked pretty high.

He shrugged.

"You didn't want to know?"

"Not really. It was simple enough. I don't like to give them

116

spell books or magical objects, but it's a better trade than letting them host."

"How many times have you hosted a demon?" I asked.

"Once," he said nonchalantly as if it wasn't a great feat that he was still around to tell about it. "It's not as bad as you're led to believe. It's like anything else: People like to sensationalize it. 'Never make deals with a demon or you'll die,' 'So and so made a bargain with the demon and he hasn't been right since.' Usually it's the favor requested that leaves them messed up. If you've dealt with the Woman in Black, then you're used to tricksters. The fun in it all is getting one over on them. I've done it several times."

He beamed. Tricking a trickster had to bring some level of satisfaction.

I'm not sure if it improved your magical street cred to tell someone you'd tricked a demon. It only made me warier and consider him more duplicitous than I had originally.

"Mostly, you don't hear about the successful ones because people who summon demons and make deals with them get stigmatized, and no one wants to be looked at the way"—his accusing gaze snapped in Cory's direction—"he looks at me."

Cory flushed and dropped his gaze to the ground.

The air was still thick with smoke and magic, distracting enough that I hadn't paid attention to the circle of salt, tannin, and a maroon blend he'd made into a circle inside the engraved stones.

"You stand here," he instructed me. Cory was next to me, examining the circle.

"This line isn't as thick as the others. In fact it's barely a line. Perhaps you should go over it again," Cory suggested.

Harrison's face flashed with irritation. "I have a ward. He won't get out."

"Perhaps, but this will just add a second level to your existing security."

Harrison rolled his eyes, reached into his pocket to pull out the ingredients, and secured the circle.

"Satisfied?" Harrison's voice had a hard frost that sent shivers through me.

Cory nodded.

"You'll need to be over there. Otherwise he'll assume you're part of the deal, too."

Cory's lips pulled into a taut line as he scrutinized Harrison. "Remember, Erin has to agree to the deal," Cory reminded him.

"Of course."

Cory looked uneasy as he stepped back about two feet, splitting his attention between the circle and Harrison. There wasn't any trust.

"Keep going until I tell you to stop." The satisfaction from getting Cory away showed on Harrison's face. Cory was being uncharacteristically overbearing.

It wasn't until Cory was close to twenty feet away that Harrison told him he could stop.

Summoning a demon was a lot simpler than I expected. A few words spoken in Latin, words scribed on the ground, and an invocation. I was positive I could do it. There were enough steps to ensure no one accidentally summoned a demon, but it was easy enough that it wouldn't deter someone if they wanted to do it.

The apparition of a man appeared. He was of average height, with olive skin and features so sharp they gave him a severe, stark look. His snake-slit eyes were hard, unwelcoming, and fixed intently on Harrison.

"You summon me again…" he hissed.

"*She* needs help," Harrison rushed out.

His attention turned to me. The demon gave me a smile and brushed the nutmeg-colored hair away from his face. His weird eyes studied me with interest.

What the hell is this? I want my demons gross looking with messed-up teeth, a snout, horns, disfiguring scars, and goat eyes. Not enchanting snake eyes.

Just in case he could entrance with his eyes, I didn't look directly at them.

"What do you need?" he asked in an Australian accent.

And they shouldn't have cool accents, either. I want them to bleat or at least make a mangled garble.

The markings of my raven were gone, so Harrison stepped next to me and held out the drawing. "She has this mark on her arm."

Dragging his eyes from me, the demon still regarded Harrison with disdain. Slowly his gaze moved back to me, roving over me, and if it got anywhere near my arm, it was clearly by accident.

My sneer and dagger glare got his attention and he straightened.

"Dareus," Harrison said, pulling the demon's leer from me. And that was a good thing because he was about to hear all the curse words, insults, and hostile language I'd accumulated over my lifetime.

"May I see it again?" he asked politely. If not less than a minute ago he was ogling me like a perv, I would have been fooled by it.

Dareus studied Harrison for a few seconds and it was obvious they shared a long history, a long, tumultuous history. Harrison showed him the sketch again. Dareus's slitted eyes moved to it. A slow smile curled his lips.

"Then they do live," he said brightly. His gaze snapped to me. "You are being protected by elven magic." He looked to Harrison and smiled appreciatively. "She will do. I'll take her."

Harrison blurted a word in Latin.

A blast of magic sent me across the clearing, landing on my butt, shocked and bewildered. When I came to my feet, Cory was near the circle, moving some of the ingredients of the circle to fill in the part that Harrison had kicked away. Fury was in Cory's eyes. Harrison took a defensive stance, magic curling around his fingers but not executing it fast enough before Cory blasted him with enough magic to smash him into a tree. He crumpled against it, and when he tried to come to his feet, Cory hit him again. Then again. And once more, leaving Harrison shuddering in pain.

Rage marked every step of Cory's advance. Behind the bright smile, the charismatic and amiable personality, and quick wit, I often forgot he was a strong, military-trained magic wielder. I forgot he'd killed before and was capable of doing it again. It had slipped my mind that among the witches, he was one of the most skilled. Watching him go at a beleaguered Harrison like a single-target missile was a reminder. White-hot magic that looked like sparks of bound electricity ready to be released made me recall that he'd had access to the *Mystic Souls* and had taken several spells away from it. I suspected this was one of them.

Unfettered anger shone in his eyes, and I was neither reckless enough nor did I care enough about saving Harrison to jump in front of him. But I did care how Cory would feel knowing he'd killed someone in a fit of rage.

"Cory!" I yelled.

His gaze flicked to me. Some of the anger leached from his eyes and awareness took over. He threw the magic. It soared to the left and slammed into a large oak tree, blasting it to pieces and scattering bark and chunks of wood throughout the area. Some of the pieces landed just a few feet from Harrison.

With effort, Harrison pulled himself to his feet. His eyes went to the demolished tree and his face paled. Mixed with the fear, I could see hints of frustration and irritation. He whispered an invocation, made several swipes with his hand, and the demon started to disappear. I realized he was sending Dareus away before I could finish asking my questions.

Dareus screeched, "You still owe me!"

Harrison's eyes screwed shut for several moments. When he opened them, he gave a passing look at Cory and then at me.

"The remainder of the money is forgiven. Do not come here again."

Talk about gall. Harrison tried to give me to a demon and he was telling *us* not to return. He had no idea how much I didn't want to see his smarmy ass again. I looked over at the closed circle and was hit hard with what had nearly happened. I needed to get away. Cory looked as if he felt the same way.

I drove to Cory's place, keeping a comforting hand on his leg, but it wasn't helping.

"Thank you for stopping me," he said softly once I'd pulled into the parking space in front of his apartment. His expression was as hollow and dejected as his voice. It made me ache.

"He was trying to give me to a demon. Your reaction was warranted."

"Even after I'd fixed the situation and beaten him up?" he inquired in a low voice. "What happened to that tree would have happened to him."

We all knew that.

"He was going to give me to a demon," I repeated. That had to offer him some consolation, but it did nothing to ease the grimace on his face.

There was no way I was going to let him stay at home wallowing in his misery. When I grabbed my keys and started to get out of the car, he stopped me.

"No, I really want to be alone."

"Are you sure?"

He nodded. I wasn't sure he wanted to be alone, but he didn't want me there—a reminder of the reason he reacted that way.

I nodded, repositioned myself in my seat, and watched as he got out of the car. He quickly made his way to his apartment.

I drove for several blocks feeling the weight of my guilt and concern. Eventually they got the best of me and I pulled over and scrolled through my contacts until I came to the name I needed. Hesitating for an excruciatingly long time, I looked at the name on the screen. Alex.

Was I crossing a line? Meddling too much? Making a mistake that would change my relationship with Cory? But as Cory's look of disappointment and despair flashed in my mind, I pressed the call button.

"Erin?" Alex's voice piqued with curiosity.

"Yeah. Um…Cory—"

"What about him? Is he okay?" he rushed out. The level of concern in his voice eased my apprehension. I was doing the right thing.

"He's fine…sort of…well, yes and no. He hasn't been physically hurt but…when is the last time you talked to him?"

"This morning," he offered in a strained voice.

"Oh," I sighed softly. Silence lingered as I debated how much to tell him.

"But I was thinking about calling him later. I'd like to see him."

"I think that's a good idea," I said, thanking the fates for all the things I disliked about shifters and their preternatural perception finally working to my advantage. "I think that's a really good idea."

"Okay, then I'll do that."

I relaxed back in the seat. I had made the right decision. I hoped.

CHAPTER 12

*R*esting my head back against the seat in my car before going into my home, I tried to corral all the thoughts running through my head. What had happened at Harrison's sent shivers through me. I was drowning in so much new information. At what point did it get to be too much?

That was what I was thinking when I got out of my car. I was finding it difficult to ease the tension building in me. People could Wynd near me, use magic against me, and attack. Cautious as I moved up the walkway to my apartment, I scanned the area again before I neared it. At the sound of light footsteps behind me, I whipped around with my karambit, ready to strike. A hand grabbed my wrist and instantly I was against the side of the building just inches from my door, the arm with the karambit pressed overhead, my other with the exposed push blade pinned at my side.

Mephisto. When I relaxed, his hold on my arms eased, too.

"Next time announce yourself. You almost got hurt."

"Ah, *I* almost got hurt." His brow rose. He lifted his head slightly to look at my pinned arm, then at the other secured at my waist. "Yes," he said in a low husky voice, "I feel in harm's way. I should be quivering in fear, shouldn't I?" His lips lifted into a sensual smirk with traces of amusement.

"Because I let you get the upper hand," I countered.

Chuckling, he leaned in. "Of course, because you always give in to me so easily," he teased.

"Look where my knee is." I moved it just a smidge to let him know how vulnerable a position he was in.

"You did warn me that you fight dirty."

"No, I fight to win," I corrected.

"I do, too. And I have no problem getting down and dirty. Perhaps someday we should test how dirty we can get."

"Why do I get the impression you're not talking about sparring?"

"It's whatever you want it to be, Erin," he said, but my smile and the way he said my name in a deep growl made it apparent he *definitely* wasn't talking about sparring.

Before I could respond, Ms. Harp peeked her head out her door. She took one look at Mephisto with his dark pants, heather-gray shirt, and slightly mussed dark hair. Then she looked back to his shirt and frowned. Following her gaze, I noticed a small splatter of blood on the edge of his shirt but wasn't sure if she could see it from her position.

"There's blood on your shirt," I whispered.

"No worries, it's not mine," he said as Ms. Harp continued to glower at him. She dipped back into her apartment and returned with her cane in hand. Literally. It was nestled under her arm, held horizontally. She started in our direction, flashing a smile so dulcet it was impossible not to return it. But her eyes glinted with devious intent as they narrowed in our direction. Her paper-thin lips stretched wider into a forced smile.

"Pardon me, I need to get to my car," she announced from a few feet away. Instead of taking advantage of the nearly ten feet of unobstructed path behind me and Mephisto, she stood near us, her brow raised, nonverbally requesting him to move away from me, so she could pass through.

Returning her inauthentic smile with one that was mirthless but polite, he moved back a few feet.

"Oh my, I forgot my keys." When she turned, her cane whacked Mephisto in the side of the hip. He grunted from what I suspected was surprise rather than pain.

"I'm so sorry," she gasped.

Sure you are. Her subsequent performance was worthy of some form of acknowledgment. Tony? Oscar? Golden Globe? I considered applauding and throwing roses at her feet. She touched her hand to the injured area, but after seeing him barely respond to being sliced by Kai, I suspected he was delivering his own performance as well. Everyone's a thespian.

Hand pressed to her chest, she continued her act of being terribly sorry for hitting him as she backed away toward her apartment. "Please forgive me, that happens sometimes."

"It's difficult to get the gait pattern correct with the cane. I see it used incorrectly all the time." I could sound cloying and sweet, too. I pinned her with a glare, but she continued with her look of wide-eyed innocence.

You are an artist. We are not worthy of this performance.

Borrowing her cane, I said, "I've seen people use it like this." I demonstrated, planting the cane tip on the ground then walking up to it. "Or you can do it like this." Holding the cane in my right hand, I moved my left leg and the right hand together. After hearing Cory complain about people using the cane in the wrong pattern, I had him show me the patterns, useless information I'd never need. I was glad I'd paid attention. Or rather, that Cory made me pay attention.

"I'll keep that in mind," she said, taking the cane from me and grasping it in her hand as if she was about to use it.

"I can wait for you to get your keys and walk with you to

your car. Just to make sure you're okay," I suggested in a hollow gesture.

"No worries, I'll get it later." She turned and seemed pleased by the distance remaining between Mephisto and me. She trekked to her apartment, barely touching the cane to the ground as she "used" it.

The corners of Mephisto's lips moved into a small deliberate curl as Ms. Harp kept the door slightly ajar for a few moments once she was in her apartment, peeking back out before closing it.

In silence, we both slipped into my apartment.

"Whose blood is on your shirt?" I asked, closing the door and placing my weapons on the table.

In response, he handed me the blade I'd left with him. Cleaned and sharpened to a razor's edge.

"We've ensured that your mother doesn't have an army any longer. Or if any are left, there aren't enough to be of any use to her," he informed me. Something dark, ominous, and dangerous lingered behind his midnight eyes, discouraging me from asking further questions.

What did I need to ask? How'd they do it? They were the Huntsmen from Hell. I'm sure it was violent, efficient, and probably bloody. I didn't need specifics. It was one less thing I needed to worry about and for that, I was grateful.

I licked my lips. They'd become increasingly dry, along with my throat. My hand ached. I went to the kitchen and ran water over the open area, giving it a better cleaning than the quick swipe of a damp paper towel I'd given it at Harrison's. Without any of the red stains from the poorly cleaned dried blood, it didn't look as bad as I'd thought. Especially since it hadn't been magically healed.

After tending to the cuts, I grabbed a bottle of water and drank most of it.

"She doesn't have an army or a way of making one, so she'll definitely come for me now," I pointed out in a remote voice, keeping my face emotionless. I could feel the color slowly draining from my face.

Moving in that unnerving way, Mephisto swallowed the feet of distance between us and took my hand into his to examine the cuts.

"She wasn't with them," he said, "so I suspect she has been in contact, instructing them to bring you to her. She's never worked from the shadows before. This is a new approach. I suspect it's because she's weaker. And we're here. God to god. She doesn't have the same advantage she once had and that probably bothers her. Whether we took her army or not, she'd want you dead because you make her weak."

He frowned at my hand. His long fingers traced along the outside of the cuts as his eyes held mine during the languid movement.

"She must not know I'm a magical dud." I gave him a half-hearted smile. It was wearing on me. It wasn't just a craving or a desire, it was a genuine need. I *needed* magic or undoubtedly I was going to die from the lack of it. Based on everything I knew of Malific, I couldn't imagine surviving an encounter with her without magic. Even without an army, it would be me, virtually human, trying to ward off a god.

"I can't continue to be without magic," I said.

He sucked in a sharp breath, aware of what I was asking. But his emotions were unreadable. Was he considering it? Evaluating the cost/benefit? Or formulating a kind way of rejecting me?

"I know," he whispered, gliding his finger over the cuts. The familiar cooling breeze of his healing magic wisped over my palm, numbing the throbbing that lingered and healing the wound. I snatched my hand away. "Don't remove the scar."

His expression became a mask of curiosity. No doubt he thought it was a weird thing to ask. I doubted it would leave a scar but I wanted it to heal on its own. I had the memories

127

and couldn't explain why I wanted to hold on to the proof, but I did.

I shrugged, displaying more bravado and nonchalance than was actually in me. "Kind of a little reminder of my first encounter with a demon."

His expression faltered, his mouth parted, and dark intense eyes bore into me like spikes. "What?" he asked sharply. "You summoned a demon?"

"I can't summon anything. I don't have magic, remember?" *So, give me some of yours.*

"Cory?" Shock and disappointment replaced his usual calm, professional demeanor. In that moment, he moved so far away from me it was jarring, the distance he'd placed between us in just a blink.

"No."

"Erin, what are you doing? Why aren't you sharing information with me?" He fumed with wary sharpness. His professional neutrality and stoicism were nowhere in sight.

"Because it happened today."

A knock at the door interrupted the rest of my explanation, and Ms. Harp's raspy, distressed voice pierced the silence that her knock had created.

"Erin." She sounded so pitiful only a special type of monster could ignore her. As I moved to the door, fully aware that she wasn't nearly as distressed as her voice would have me believe, I still couldn't summon the hardness needed to leave her where she was.

"Yes?" I asked, opening the door. Her phone in hand, she barged into the apartment. "I can't get it to work. I don't remember anything Asher told me."

I find that highly unlikely, but please go on with your rendition of the helpless geriatric.

When her eyes cut to Mephisto, I knew my suspicions were correct.

"Do you remember what he said I should do to unlock it?"

she asked, her voice oozing helplessness and dismay. Not helping her felt like kicking a puppy. Oh, she was good.

I looked at the locked screen, vowing to call Asher and tell him to give her the flip phone back and find another way to track her.

"All you have to do is put your pin number in," I told her. "Do you remember what it is?"

Her hands clamped on each side of her face. "Oh my, I don't. Should we call Asher and see if he knows?"

I'm sure he knows it and there's no way I'm calling him.

I didn't want to give her the satisfaction of showing I was on to her. So, I stood back and enjoyed the performance like I was at *Hamilton*, while she put on her Tony award-winning act.

"No, let's try to figure it out. If we problem solve it, then we'll know the pin and we can write it down and put it in a place where we both can find it." I gave her the most innocent saccharine sweet smile I could manage without breaking character while she shoveled me her BS.

"That's a good idea. But it might take a while." She looked straight at Mephisto. His impassive eyes held steady on hers.

He had hundreds of years on her but he still nodded respectfully in her direction. "I can wait," he said.

With great effort, Ms. Harp kept on with her little show.

"Try your birthday," I suggested.

It didn't work. We tried it without the year and several more variations.

Arms crossed over his chest, Mephisto waited patiently. Periodically I'd look up from the phone to meet his amused eyes.

"Maybe he put it in wrong. He seemed so distracted when I came over here. I can't believe he had the audacity to visit you looking so unkempt. His hair was in shambles and his clothes in disarray. I've never seen him look so disheveled. I wished he would have come to see me first. I would have straightened him right up because when he answered your door, he looked like he'd just rolled out of bed." Her eyes quickly flicked in Mephisto's direction.

Keep it up, old lady.

I forced a tight-lipped smile.

"Have you used the pin before to unlock your phone?"

She nodded.

"Then the pin is right."

"This mind of mine. Getting old has its challenges." *Especially when you're full of crap.*

"Maybe I should go," Mephisto suggested.

"That would probably be best. This might take a while," Ms. Harp said without looking up from the phone.

He stepped forward, probably to give me a departing wave, shoulder touch, or something. Whatever it was, Ms. Harp wasn't having any of it. For such a short woman, she seemed to be everywhere, keeping Mephisto at a distance from me. Finally, he stepped back and simply gave me a small wave before leaving.

A few minutes passed after Mephisto had left and she took the phone from me. "Let's see." She tapped on the screen and made an excited gasp. "We fixed it."

"Uh-huh. We 'fixed' it." Giving her a sharp knowing look, I said, "How fortunate that you remembered the number."

"I know."

You're going to keep with this schtick, huh?

"I think if it wasn't for your wonderful line of questioning, my memory would have never been jogged. It's the year I retired from teaching."

"I'll remember that."

"You're such a dear to help me. I'm sorry that your friend had to leave. Maybe he'll come back." Insincerity drenched her sweet words.

"Probably, but not tonight."

"Aw, that's a shame." She started backing toward the door.

Backing. Not doing her geriatric shuffle. Not tiny steps that would make a person think she wasn't quite going to make it. No, she was walking back with the ease and grace of someone two-thirds her age. It might have been a moonwalk.

"Ms. Harp, you forgot your cane." I brought it to her. When she reached for it, I held on to it until she lifted her eyes from it to meet mine.

Before I could confront her, she said, "You know who I'd like to see you with?"

Let me guess, Asher?

"No, who?"

"Cory."

My eyes widened. "What?" I choked out.

"I really like him. He's kind, caring, and whenever he sees me, he always stops to ask me how I'm doing."

Yes, he does and the last few times he did, you pretended that the battery in your nonexistent hearing aid was on the fritz and rushed away to change it. But I'm sure you conveniently forgot that part, didn't you?

Giving her a faint smile, I said, "We're just friends and he's seeing someone."

"Well that's too bad. The good ones are always taken." She gave my apartment a considering look. Returning her attention to me, she flashed a practiced smile. "I think Asher's single, and you two get along, don't you? Seems a lot better than what's-his-face."

"His name is Mephisto," I said.

She made a disapproving scoff. "After the devil?"

"Or from Faust, I'm not sure."

"Well if that's not a red flag, I don't know what is. His name just screams 'run girl, you're in trouble,' but I'm not one to meddle in other people's business."

Really? When did that start?

"What are you doing, Ms. Harp?" I asked, a serious edge to my voice.

131

"I'm not sure what you're asking." Her voice was filled with such sincere innocence and curiosity, for a brief moment I second-guessed my own question.

"Asher and I are just friends. That's it. Nothing more."

"I know that. But just because that's the case now doesn't mean it should stay that way. He's a good man. A little bossier than he needs to be." She rolled her eyes. "He acts like his wishes aren't ever ignored or rejected. Making commands as if he expects them to be followed without question. Even if he adds a 'please,' it's still a little too auto-cratic for my liking."

"He's an Alpha. His world is almost an autocracy. It's not often that his pack disobeys his orders."

She made a face. "Well then, it's a good thing he has us. A person needs to hear that once in a while, don't you think? And you're just the person to let him know he's not the Alpha everywhere he goes."

I couldn't help but laugh. "I don't think I have enough ire in me to teach him that lesson."

"Sure you do." She tugged her cane from me. "If you were next to someone about to be hit by a speeding car, would you push them out of the way?" she asked quietly, her expression pensive.

"Of course."

Giving me a knowing look, she smiled. It was tight and expressive. "Me too." Those were her parting words and they left me in a state of contemplation. Even if she didn't shift, she had some of their instincts, and probably heightened perception. Did she see something in Mephisto that I had missed?

As I thought about Ms. Harp's comment and the events of the day, I sipped on a glass of the Chateau Léoville Las Cases that Mephisto had given me. I had received another case along with a case of Belvedere vodka, I guess in response to the cheap vodka I'd offered him. Pretentious much?

Taking another long draw from the glass, I knew I shouldn't get accustomed to drinking wine like this. Mephisto was footing the bill and there wasn't any sense in getting used to imbibing that quality of vodka and wine, since I had no intention of drinking it when it wasn't free. The cheaper stuff fit my palate just fine.

Before I could take another indulging sip, someone knocked lightly on the door. When I saw that it was Mephisto, I opened it and he hastily slipped in.

"Are you hiding from my neighbor?" I teased.

I didn't think Mephisto was capable of sheepish, but he gave me a smile that closely resembled it.

"I've not figured out if she's overly protective of you or overbearing without any sense of boundaries."

"It's about ten percent from column A, eighty from column B, and the rest can be contributed to her Asher fandom."

His expression changed and his head tilted in appraisal. "I don't think that fondness for the Alpha is just limited to your neighbor."

I shrugged. "He was worried about me," I offered.

He followed me to the living room, where I returned to my glass of wine. He smiled at the open bottle on the table.

"You're enjoying it?" he asked.

"It's an indulgence," I admitted. "One I don't think I should get used to."

His eyes trailed along the planes of my face and then my lips, where they lingered. "Some indulgences are worth it." He leaned against the wall closest to me, one leg crossed over the other, and I felt the full weight of his contemplative look. "Tell me about your visit with the demon."

"I didn't visit a demon, I visited a witch," I clarified.

"Fine, tell me about the witch who introduced you to a demon."

As I recounted the story, Mephisto had great difficulty

keeping his impassive look. It kept slipping between irritation and anger.

"Harrison tried to use you to pay a debt to the demon?"

"That's what we suspected."

"You shouldn't have stopped Cory. Harrison will try it again and the next person might not be so lucky."

"Then Cory would have killed someone in cold blood. I don't think he would have handled it well. I'll talk to Madison and she can have someone watch Harrison. If he tries it again, he'll go to the Enclave, where he belongs."

Mephisto didn't seem pleased with that course of action, but he didn't push it.

"What did he mean I'm protected by elven magic?"

"If he's correct, it might be the reason we haven't been able to remove your restriction. Witch and mage magic are the most closely aligned—"

"Good luck getting them to believe that." My words were punctuated with the same level of annoyance that rose in me every time I was confronted with the litany of *alleged* differences between the two that was spewed by either sect when people failed to see them as different.

He gave me a shrug as if he'd experienced it firsthand. "Fae magic is a variation of it. God magic works differently. Although fae, mage, and witch magic have similar properties to ours, they don't affect us and aren't nearly as strong. Elven magic is not only comparable in power but is equally different. It's the only magic that will work against us, and we can't undo or duplicate their spells. For that reason, your mother wanted them as allies. When they refused..." His lips tightened into a thin line, rage and anger casting a dark look over his face. "She handled it the way she always does. Wrathful violence. Peaceful by nature, the elves weren't prepared for her to attack while they slept and—"

"Don't finish," I requested quietly. I couldn't stomach another story about the ruthlessness of a woman who didn't follow the rules of engagement and common decency. Each recount made that flicker of hope that she would just leave me alone, be happy with her weaker state and inability to make another ruthless army, diminish even more.

"So that means?" I inquired.

"It means that if your father put a restriction on you, then he is an elf. You're a demigod, an elf/god hybrid. The first ever known. And there might be more elves."

The intense look of interest that he'd held when I was the death mage who could navigate the Veil had returned.

"Stop looking at me like that."

"I'm sorry. I knew you were an anomaly. I just didn't know to what extent." He unsheathed a dagger at his waist and handed it to me. The markings on it were similar to the ones on his sword.

"What's this?"

"One of Kai's blades. You're good with a blade. I don't think you have to worry about the Immortalis anymore, but it should work against your mother."

"Malific," I corrected. The blade didn't instill me with the level of confidence I thought it would. I'd be going up against her ruthlessness, magic, and her weapon of choice. Talk about bringing a knife to a gunfight. "What's her weapon of choice?"

"It was a saber."

Looking down at the blade again, I pursed my lips.

"Can you use a sword?" he asked.

I nodded. "I'm better with a dagger, but a sword will keep me better protected. Provide a better defense."

"Then you can have mine."

I breathed a sigh of relief, but he had something else I needed, magic. Easing closer to him, I rested my hand on his waist. As if he sensed what went through my mind, his lips kinked into a smile. "Magic. She has magic."

Threaded into my desire for magic was an actual need.

Not like before where I had conflated the two. I needed magic to protect myself not just against Malific but whoever was casting spells on me and causing me to lose time.

His lips brushed lightly against mine. "I wish I could, but now more than ever, I can't be in a weakened state." He removed the temptation by moving away from me. "We will figure out a way to remove the restriction."

I recognized the bravado and overconfidence because I'd seen it in myself when dealing with Madison and Cory. It was a tactic I used when I didn't want them to worry.

"Clayton said he hadn't seen an elf in over fifty years."

"That's how long we've been here. If your father is an elf, that means they aren't truly extinct. We will find one. We only need one to remove your spell. Or we will find your father."

The doubt must have crossed my face. He moved closer to give my hand a quick squeeze and a quick "I will." Then he just as quickly replaced the distance between us. "I'm a very resourceful man," he reminded me.

That he was.

"Speaking of resourceful, rescind your offer to the Lunar Marked coven." Taking his silence for consideration, I added, "Please."

It wasn't my polite entreaty that bothered me. It was the breathy way I delivered it. The doe eyes and the ever-so-slight lip bite that followed. I thought I'd turned the sexy on to an inferno, but based on his amused look and the laughter that twinkled in his eyes, I'd missed the mark. Did I look more like a constipated toddler than a sex kitten?

"Ah, am I about to be seduced into giving you what you want?"

If you have to ask, I'm seducing wrong.

He took slow, deliberate steps toward me, and I took him in. The powerful grace of his movement. The way the shirt molded to his body. The relaxed jeans that I was sure covered defined and well-muscled legs. Intense midnight eyes. Lightly ruffled hair that was just as dark with hints of indigo. And supple lips that looked even more enticing after he slowly ran his tongue over them.

I should be taking lessons on the art of seduction from you.

His finger hooked my chin and lifted it until my eyes met his. "Erin. My enigmatic, delectable, incorrigible demigoddess, your mere presence is a seduction." His warm breath teased my lips. "I gather no pleasure in telling you no, and yet I have to." Movements no longer slow and measured, he moved into his unsettling speed and had his hands on the door in a blink. "Our interests will not always align. It is important that you remember that," he said, and then he was gone before I could respond.

Plopping down in the chair, I shoved my hands into my hair and wondered how I was going to fix the mess with the vampires. I tried not to take on the blame. If it ended badly for the coven, it would be due to their avariciousness. It wasn't my problem. But no matter how many times I said it, the guilt still tugged at me.

"How do I fix this?"

CHAPTER 13

"*Y*ou meddler," Cory teased when I answered his video call. Him beaming at me on the screen sent relief through me.

I returned the smile. "I did good?"

"You did excellent. I'm sorry about rejecting your company. I thought I wanted to be alone, but Alex coming over helped."

Yeah, it did. I pulled my mind out of the gutter where it had sashayed.

He sighed and the smile faded. "It was embarrassing and a little scary how out of control I was. And you being there after seeing me like that wasn't something I could handle," he admitted in a somber whisper. "I reacted badly."

"If I had magic, I'd have been just as out of control as you were. Probably more. But you stopped."

"*You* stopped me." He huffed out a breath. "If the situation were reversed, who would I send to your house to comfort you?" he asked with a new liveliness to his voice. "The Alpha or the god?" His question was breezy and casual, but I knew there was true curiosity and sincerity to it.

"Neither. They both suck," I said, not caring that I

sounded like a petulant child. "Because of Asher, I'm being stalked by a geriatric." I told him about Ms. Harp's running interference the night before. Cory's fight to suppress his laughter didn't make the situation any better. And then I told him about my efforts to convince Mephisto to rescind his offer.

"Did you use your charm?"

"Yes, I did my sexy kitten face and everything." I lay back on my bed, holding up the phone so he could get a better look at me. "And I even gave him a 'please.'" I said the last part in the sexy breathy voice I used with Mephisto before flashing him my sex kitten look.

Cory's face scrunched. "Can I get you to promise to never show me that face again? That's not sexy kitten, that's suspicious mange face. Can kittens have mange? I feel like I should call the vet or animal control."

"Shut up!" I laughed. "I've blinded you with my sexy allure and hotness."

"I never denied your hotness. It's the sex kitten part I'm calling into question. If that's the look you gave him, you probably could have gotten him to rescind his offer by promising never to make that face again."

I rolled my eyes. "Whatever." My smile faded. "Should I be concerned that I use seduction on Mephisto for my job?"

"Oh honey, that face you made was more like an assault than a seduction. Your integrity is intact. The only thing you should be concerned about is actually getting a sexy face because the one you have is in desperate need of work."

"Quiet!" I lashed out playfully.

"Did you try your other charming tactic? You know, the one where you storm the castle with all your violent toys and weapons and threaten to beat everyone up? That seems to have a higher success rate."

"I don't want to fight with Mephisto because...I need him." I needed the Huntsmen and had to accept that some-

139

times our interests wouldn't align. Because of Mephisto, I had an Obitus blade and the promise of a sword with an Obitus blade. I no longer had to worry about attacks from the Immortalis. And if anyone could find an elf to lift my restrictions, Mephisto could.

I sighed. "I have to get Landon to make an offer better than Mephisto's. I need to visit him."

"Do you need me to go with you?"

"No, I have it."

I didn't. Convincing Landon to pay more when he would rather decimate the coven and be done with it was going to be a task in itself. Having an audience would only make things more difficult.

———

I shrugged the bag filled with stakes over my shoulder and had my stake-loaded crossbow with me. Part of my whip was bundled into my other hand. Landon was reluctant to take a meeting with me because he only wanted to hear that the situation had been handled. Anything other than that wasn't up for discussion. I hoped the meeting would be amicable, because once weapons come out, things get hostile quickly. The only thing that would be more difficult to deal with than a hostile vampire would be a vampire throwing a tantrum. I took Landon for one who'd throw an over-the-top-spectacu-lar-vamp-trum. Today, I didn't have the tolerance for either. Sometimes, that's what the job entailed. I was definitely sticking him with a hazard surcharge.

To make sure the Lunar Marked coven didn't become victims of their greed and stupidity, I had to coddle Landon and convince him to make an offer persuasive enough for them to reject Mephisto's offer. I cursed Mephisto for the fifth time. I was used to interests not aligning; at times they hadn't with Madison, either. But this was different. Madison and I had a conflict because my actions were selfish and in the best interest of my clients. Although this current situation was in the best interest of my clients—it was going to save a coven's life—not even that had been enough to change Mephisto's mind.

A few feet from my car, magic swirled around me. Familiar magic. Magic that had taken time from me. Dropping my bag and the whip, I spun around, pointing the crossbow in the direction I thought the magic had originated. Crossbows weren't just good for vampires. The nearly vacant parking lot didn't have any hiding places. Eyes focused, I thoroughly scanned the area, letting the scent of the magic wash over me.

Following it, I saw a figure watching me from the sidewalk of the building across the street. We were separated by the parking lot and a cross street. I slowed my advance and let the crossbow relax to my side. My pounding heart was distracting and my breaths came in ragged clips. The man wore a moss-green long-sleeve button down and tan pants. From a distance, his dark hair appeared to be graying around the temples.

I needed to get closer, to see the ears. Was he an elf? Did they really have pointed ears? Braydon, the mouthy, rambunctious teen from the Veil, commented that Elizabeth was a fae/elf hybrid. She didn't have pointed ears, and neither did I for that matter. Fighting the urge to touch my ear as I continued to move forward, I ignored the nagging feeling of apprehension and the thought of how many ways this could go terribly. I needed to do this.

I sped up, quickly eating up the space between me and the stranger when a wolf padded up to my side.

"Asher," I said, my free hand lightly running over his head. I caressed the soft fur of the massive wolf who had sly-footed his way next to me nearly unnoticed, forgetting that I was committing the faux paus of all faux pas. It was tantamount

141

to sticking your hand in front of a starving animal while he was eating. You're just asking to be bitten. Never pet a shifter.

Asher made a low growl, warning me off.

"Sorry," I whispered. The security of a massive magic-immune wolf was comforting. I was delighted to have him with me.

The stranger's head shifted to look at the wolf, and whatever it was about the stranger's guarded movement had Asher charging in his direction. I ran, too, but by the time I got to the spot where the stranger once was, it was empty.

Asher had shifted back to his human form and looked frustrated as he walked up and down the area, nose to the air, trying to find the scent. The magic was gone; not even a hint of its magical marker remained.

"Who was that?" Asher asked once we'd made our way to his car, parked close to mine. Grabbing the clothes that were stored in the backseat, he pulled up his pants with the slow ease and total lack of concern about his nudity as a man getting dressed in his bedroom rather than a half-empty parking lot.

"I don't know." I wasn't ready to put words to my suspicion that he may have been my father. Because he might have been.

"You were scared," he pointed out, buttoning the sleeves of his shirt before shrugging on his suit jacket.

"No, I wasn't," I said, going through my bag to make sure everything was there. As if someone wanted my bag of stakes and electric pellets. My bag and the whip I'd discarded were still by my car where I'd left them.

His eyes narrowed at me. "So, you just approached a stranger for no apparent reason?"

I didn't want to go into detail about me suspecting him of bespelling me or the attack the other day. "It was the magic. I was curious about it because it felt—"

"Different," he interjected. "Different than anything else I've felt. Not the witches, mages, or fae." For the first time, it seemed like being able to detect magic was one of the senses he could do without. I could imagine that on top of all the preternatural senses they enjoyed, the newness of detecting magic had to be overwhelming.

He leaned against my car and crossed his arms, his uncompromising gaze on me. Holding it was becoming increasingly difficult. Not just because of the primality of it but because of the intensity of its search.

"Doesn't seem like you're taking our agreement seriously," Asher said.

Now it was my turn to cast doubt. "Really, because *you* violated the terms."

With a sly look, his tongue slid rakishly across his lips. "How so?" he asked innocently.

Been taking lessons from Ms. Harp, have you?

"I said no more details. Instead of your shifters following me, you have a seventy-year-old spy with boundary issues tracking me," I huffed out.

"She's worried about you and so am I," he admitted. "She told me you were upset yesterday, had to pull a weapon on Mephisto—or in her words, 'the blood-covered cretin who keeps coming around.' She said he disarmed you, causing you to become upset."

"She took all the events and switched them out of order to give you a fantastical tale and make it sound a lot worse. And I'm positive her flawed retelling was on purpose. I had a situation that he helped me with." Part of that was truth.

The smile vanished from his face. "You called him first?'

"No…no." I didn't have time to deal with this. I had an arrogant vampire and greedy, inflexible witches who were terrifyingly close to being on the receiving end of Landon's wrath. Not only was that going to be a mess to deal with, but if I failed, it would be a nightmare PR situation for Madison.

My mother wanted me dead, someone was bespelling me, and I might be part of a race considered extinct. My life was quickly becoming the hottest mess of all hot messes. The last thing I needed right now was to deal with Asher and his pack.

"Technically I didn't call him either. I told you I would call the person who could help me. I did. It was Cory. But like you, Mephisto seems to think I have an open invitation policy to my home." I flashed him a smile. "When I finally move to an undisclosed location, you will know why."

His lips lifted into a wolfish smirk. "I'm sure I could find you," he said.

"Oh, well that's not creepy at all," I chided, hitching my bag of weapons farther up my shoulder.

Seeing the concern on his face, I added, "We'll talk later, okay? I'll tell you everything." Realizing he would need to hear the edited version, I amended with, "Everything I can. But for now, call off your little spy."

"You want me to tell Ms. Harp, Ms. Evelyn Harp, what to do?" he asked with incredulous amusement.

"Yes, because that's what you do."

He shrugged, backing toward his car. His slow pace and measured steps seemed to be inviting me to look at him. Because it wouldn't be Asher if he wasn't giving someone an eyeful. "As you wish," he said. "But we both know she does the opposite of what I ask. And opposes anything I suggest out of principle."

He was right.

"Leave her alone. I'll handle it."

His easy confidence remained as he got into his car. "Once you've broken that code of getting Evelyn compliant with requests, I hope you'll share the trick with me."

———

I'd just pulled up to Landon's home when my phone rang. Wendy spoke in a strained voice as soon as I answered.

"We'll accept the offer but with our previous terms," she declared with misplaced defiance. "We will not do a death oath."

Although she made an effort to sound confident, I didn't have to be a shifter to hear the desperation in her voice. Her acceptance wasn't out of any sense of fair play or altruism; she didn't have a second offer.

"*And* we will only work with you. Not him. I don't want to see him."

Landon, how many threats did you direct at her this time?

"Is there a problem?" I asked innocently. I knew the problem: Landon didn't know how to keep his thoughts to himself.

"He is not someone I want to deal with personally. I don't take his threat against me and my coven lightly."

"Was he a big meanie after you reneged on your offer?" I should have been above this, but I wasn't in a mood for taking the high road. If she hadn't pursued Mephisto, this would have been over days ago.

"No one asked for your sarcasm," she snapped.

"No worries, I offer it freely. No requests necessary."

She huffed in exasperation.

"Let's get this handled today. You'll have your money and Landon will have the Amber Crocus," I told her in a nicer tone.

And you won't have a chance to make the offer to someone else.

She wasn't likely to find another buyer anytime soon, but continuously being snarky or bitchy wasn't going to make things easier. The deal needed to be over today because I had more pressing things to do.

After my call with Wendy, I called Landon to tell him the coven had accepted his offer. I called Cory to arrange for him to get the necessary ingredients for the *evanesco* spell, so that he could perform it. I wasn't surprised to find out he didn't need anything and was familiar with it.

After all my arrangements with Cory, Landon, and Wendy, I called Mephisto. When the call went to voicemail, I sent him a text to thank him. When he didn't respond, I considered calling him again. After his speech about our interests not always aligning, I wanted to know what had changed his mind.

CHAPTER 14

$\mathcal{I}$t was easier getting two million dollars from Landon than it was telling him he had to stay home. It's astounding that he could live for a hundred years and yet still remain oblivious to basic social contracts. People you threaten with horrific violence don't tend to want to meet. And there are some four-letter words you call people that put you on the "never want to meet" list. He'd managed to do both. Granted, with enough zeros behind a number, some people might be more inclined to forgive, but Wendy wasn't one of them.

Wendy answered the door, her nose raised to the air with a level of pomposity that made my eyes roll. Stepping aside to let us in, she gave me a passing glance, then Cory, and then her attention settled on Dallas. Cory was often on the receiving end of attention and, contrary to his self-admitted good looks, people were often drawn to the deep-set dimple that was revealed at the mere hint of a smile. If not his dimple, it was his honey-brown eyes with hints of gold that projected a magnetic warmth. People were drawn to them. In an effort to keep him humble, I never pointed out how stunning they were.

Wendy and Stacey were immune to it, giving him the same sweeping look of indifference they gave me. Had they even seen the eyes? Maybe they'd seen him before or simply found them unimpressive. Whatever it was, they decided to ogle the hot vampire. Their attention stayed on him so long, I cleared my throat to pull their attention to me.

Dallas was unbothered by the intensity of their attention; he was probably used to it. Was he numb to it? The vampire aura wasn't doing him any favors, either. If witches could make a vampire aura anti-charm, they could get out of the blackmailing business. Stacey's poor attempt at a furtive glance failed miserably. At what point was a stare held so long it became gawking? She'd passed gawking and was now openly ogling the man.

I pondered if throwing in Dallas as part of the deal and getting a significant reduction in the asking price would make me a bad person. Nah, it might not make me a bad person, but it would definitely make me a pimp. That wasn't a life choice I was prepared to make.

"The *evanesco* spell," I reminded the witches, who managed to drag their eyes from Dallas. He started to give them a faint smile and I shot him a quelling look.

You keep your smiles to yourself!

They pored over the oath in the spell, taking an exceptionally long time. I suspected they were looking for loopholes they could exploit. They wouldn't find any. Cory knew the importance of the language and how essential it was that he didn't leave room for ambiguities, which is why the meeting was made later in the evening to give him time to make the spell iron clad.

The oath would be tied to the coven. It covered particulars such as name changes, addition of new members, continued binding of the oath in the events a covener left for another. It wasn't that witches were any more nefarious or amoral than any other denizen, but memories are short and greed is strong. Five years from now, they could feel that the money wasn't enough and would want to go back to the well and look for a way to do so. This wouldn't allow them. Even with the death of the caster, the oath still held.

Wendy's tight-lipped grimace confirmed that it was iron tight. "It's very thorough," she acknowledged.

It better have been after the death stare Landon gave me when I told him Cory's fee. Which led to me having to explain to him what a magical oath entailed and that his typical subpar witches, although fine for simple wards and spells, weren't good enough for performing the oath. I trusted Cory. When Landon persisted, I pointed out that the cost of his tie could cover Cory's fees and a magical oath wasn't where he wanted to start bargain shopping.

Finally, the witches gave the nod of approval. Dallas tapped a few things on his phone. "It's done," he said.

After confirming the deposit, they flashed smiles that now matched their bank account.

"Now the oath." Dallas's tone was curt enough that the witches' gaze swung in his direction and stayed.

"Then we'll show you to the Amber Crocus. You're free to do as you please with it."

"I should hope so. The vampires just paid a hefty sum to do that," Cory mumbled under his breath. It was for my ears only, but Wendy overheard and shot him a glare.

"He wants the plants destroyed and the land salted so nothing can ever grow in that area again," I told her.

The witches rolled their eyes but nodded. They'd probably assumed Landon would leave that to them, but Cory and I were tasked with destroying the earth, ensuring the land was left barren. Landon was being trivial. The oath restricted them from growing Amber Crocus, but he was preventing them from growing any ingredients for spell-casting at all.

Wendy held the coven's crest to her chest with such reverence it sparked a tinge of empathy in me. I had to remind myself that most oaths didn't come with a seven-figure reward.

Her hold on the crest tightened when Cory requested the item that represented the bond each within the coven had made to each other. A blood oath to the crest and in turn to the coven. Several beats passed, her gaze darting to Dallas as if she was expecting a stay or for Landon to exhibit clemency and revoke the requirement.

Keep waiting, it's not happening.

After several minutes, her jaw set with confidence, but her eyes were pools of regret as she dropped it into Cory's hand.

"Let's proceed," Dallas urged, his voice warm and smooth but latent with command. Severe dark eyes remained on Wendy, and she watched him carefully before inching closer to Cory.

Magic oaths were more ritualistic than most spells. After each invocation, Wendy vocalized her agreement as the oath taker. At the final oath, the paper was set alight. Patterns of bright colors danced in the air, mingling together to form a light sheath that covered the crest, sealing the oath.

"It is done," Cory said, handing the crest to Wendy, who stared at it before taking it from him.

We followed her and Stacey to the garden. Stacey gasped. Wendy gaped. Chunks of soil were scattered near holes where the plants had been pulled up by their roots. There wasn't a plant to be seen.

Dallas surveyed the garden, then his gimlet eyes snapped to the witches.

"Where is it?" he ground out.

"I don't know." Wendy's voice was tremulous. I wasn't

sure if it was from fear or anger since both emotions were warring for dominance on her face.

"You didn't have a ward around it?" Cory asked, incredulity sharpening his words.

"I did, but I had to remove it. Every time we erected one, the plants started to die."

"There's a Klipsen ward with a trigger." Stacey pointed at the trail of pods lining the perimeter. Sleeper pods that were triggered to break if the ward was broken. A Klipsen ward would prevent a person from even Wynding. Whoever stole the AC had disabled the ward without triggering the sleepers. Or they nullified them.

Dallas moved so imperceptibly fast that I didn't register the movement until he had the witches braced with thin iridium cuffs, his hands wrapped around their necks and his fangs bared.

Both were wide eyed and struggling for breath. My gun was out but I didn't have a clear shot, and neither did Cory with his magic. It twirled around his fingers each time he moved. Dallas moved, too, using the witches as a shield.

I could see the moment Wendy realized she'd underestimated the vampires. It wasn't a deficiency in her knowledge or failure to observe them. Vampires did it intentionally, luring people into a false sense of security by allowing them to only see a fraction of their speed and strength. It wasn't until moments like this, when their intent was to kill, that the person was treated to the full extent of their strength and cunning. The older the vampire, the more dangerous.

Dallas was too young to exhibit speed like that. I wasn't under any illusion that Landon wasn't aware of that fact.

"Dallas," I entreated, hoping I could reason with the angry vampire. I was now fully aware that the amiable vampire with the dazzling smile and unquenchable magnetism was nothing more than a cleaner—an assassin if needed. Every denizen had their version. The STF was often able to keep

151

things under control, but the supernatural world, like anything else, had a darker and nefarious side.

I tried to stay knowledgeable of who these cleaners were. For the vampires, it was Elon. If Landon had paired me with Elon for this job, I would have been prepared. Would have had a stake at the ready and watched him more carefully. Instead he sent Dallas, sweet, kind, unassuming Dallas. He'd caught me off guard.

"They didn't do this," I said. "But the Amber Crocus is out there. You kill them, it will be up to the vampires to find it. I won't help and you'll be too busy dealing with the STF to find it yourself. Is that what you want to do, ruin any chance of getting it off the streets?"

Fear and rage were the worst bedfellows.

"And you'll break the oath, giving them free rein to disclose how to make it," Cory added, magic still twining around his fingers as he waited for an opening.

Wendy and Stacey clawed at Dallas's hands without success as he scrutinized me and Cory. I really hoped he couldn't detect the lie Cory just told about the oath. The oath would still be in place upon the deaths of these witches, and the living witches would still be bound to it.

He lowered them more gently than I was expecting and turned them to face him, keeping them in striking distance. His dark eyes were turbulent with rage. Wendy and Stacey stood taller in defiance and met his gaze with the same ire.

Drawing back his lips, he said, "*We* trusted you. *We* paid you. *We* honored our end of the agreement. *You* didn't." The low timbre of his voice was more frightening than if he'd snarled. "This could have been resolved days ago, but you decided you'd place our lives in jeopardy to get a better deal without the restriction of an oath. If a vampire dies from this…" The threat faded into the whoosh that accompanied a vampire Wynding. It clipped the air, leaving us staring at the vacant space where the vampire once stood.

"If you know something, you need to tell me now," I urged the witches. Landon wasn't known for his patience.

They were having a difficult time focusing and kept tugging at the magic-restricting iridium braces clamped around their arms. I retrieved my picks from the car and removed the braces. I'd return them to Landon as a consolation gift after I ripped him a new one for blindsiding me with an assassin.

Cory and I inspected the area. The ward had been removed, which meant a magic wielder stronger than Wendy had done it. This reduced the number of suspects significantly. There was a privacy fence that blocked the garden from being seen, and a lock. The lock would just be a deterrent for petty thieves, but the ward should have blocked everyone else.

"How many people did you approach about the AC?" I asked.

"Just Mephisto," Wendy said, her voice hoarse. There wasn't any visible bruising, but I was sure her rough voice was from the shock of seeing anyone demonstrate the ability to brace and disable her so quickly. I wondered if she was recalling the warning I'd given her about dealing with vampires and regretting blackmailing them. It was too late for regrets.

"Wendy, I need a list of any witch or mage whose magic ability rivals yours."

She rolled her eyes at "mage." Even with her life at risk, she couldn't ignore her witch-superiority bias enough to consider them a threat.

"Put any mages you know at the top of the list. If it got out that you had the Amber Crocus or that you were blackmailing the vampires, I wouldn't put it past a mage to do this." Landon wouldn't let anyone know he was being blackmailed; his ego and reputation couldn't handle it.

Stacey and Wendy worked on the list longer than I

expected. Several times Wendy's jaw clenched at Stacey's insistence on adding certain people to the list. Stacey gravitated toward caution.

While they worked on their list, I mentally compiled mine. I didn't suspect a coven. It was probably a witch without a coven or a mage without a consortium. I'd seen Wendy in action, knew the extent of her magical ability, and knew how difficult a Klipsen ward was to disable. The thief not only disabled it but did so without setting off the trigger. The number of people who could do that was minute. I was in the presence of the few who could.

CHAPTER 15

"What the hell, Landon!" I snapped the moment he opened the door. A taunting sneer tugged at his lips and I gripped the karambit tighter at my side. I had it with me despite Cory's suggestion that showing up at Landon's home armed with a weapon would seem hostile. Damn straight it looked hostile, because among innumerable other feelings, hostility was ranking pretty high.

"I take it that things didn't go as expected," he said airily.

"You know they didn't. Who the hell is Dallas? Was he even the person who found out about the AC or simply a plant that you used?"

"Ah, he is quite unassuming, isn't he? That's the advantage of him. He's enthralling, I'd even go so far as to say breathtaking. People are so busy being beguiled by him that they underestimate his abilities. But if you are aware of them, something went wrong." Landon turned his back on me and headed down that hall. It was a slight, dismissing me as inconsequential, someone he didn't consider a threat.

Leading me into the office, he closed the door behind me. I was taking slow, measured breaths to calm myself. Knowing that Cory was in the car made it easier.

"I'm sure you know that the Amber Crocus was stolen. The witches didn't have anything to do with it. Where they held it was fenced and warded."

"That's quite unfortunate."

This was the calm before the storm, and the storm would be directed at the witches. Or maybe me. Despite the feet of distance between us, I kept a careful eye on him.

"I need a promise from you."

He scoffed, removing the distance in one sweeping movement. Just inches from my face, stormy night-dark eyes met mine. Lips slowly inched back to bare fangs.

Those look dangerous.

With all his eloquence, extravagance, and aesthetic taste, it was easy to forget Landon's penchant for violence, his adoration for the macabre, and his well-documented atrocities. Surrounding himself with beauty and his appreciation of it in the form of art made it easy to do. His return to his old ways was just one perceived betrayal, offense, or slight away. I tried not to let that overtake my thoughts, but it was nearly impossible.

Refusing to give him the satisfaction of seeing me cower, I stood taller and squared my shoulders. Taking my free hand, I placed it on his chest and nudged him back. "You're too close. Why don't you step back a few feet?"

His dark laughter reverberated throughout the large space as he stepped back. "You want a promise from me, Erin?" There were still traces of amusement in his voice. "I don't know if I should admire your gumption or pity it."

No need to be an ass.

"I want to fix this for you." I took the edge out of my voice, forcing it to become softer and imploring. Pandering to the powerful and self-entitled was my least favorite thing. It was the sordid part of my business that annoyed me. But "bite me, this is how things are going to be" didn't get the results I needed. There's some wisdom behind the bees, honey, and vinegar saying. And telling a vamp to bite me was just an invitation.

"The witches weren't involved, so promise that you'll extend some clemency to them."

He scoffed.

"Give me a week. I can find it. The witches are under my protection."

Another scoff. "Let you? No, love, this is your *obligation*. You can't possibly think I consider it a coincidence that the competing buyer was Mephisto. He conveniently withdrew the offer. I'm out of money and I don't have the Amber Crocus. I don't think the witches were involved in the theft. I think you and Mephisto were." Arrogance and violence dripped from every word.

The distance between us was ripped away in a blink of an eye. The karambit was torn from my hand and thrown into the wall across the room. My drawn Ruger was yanked from me and discarded near the karambit.

"Your death will be so devastating for Madison and Cory."

Without weapons, I had to reason my way out of this danger and bluster like I'd never blustered before.

"Who do you think has a better chance of getting the Amber Crocus, me or you?"

He still looked as if he was seconds from going for my throat.

"I had nothing to do with it being stolen. But what do you think will happen if I don't walk out of here?" I couldn't defend Mephisto's innocence with confidence because there might be some validity to Landon's accusation.

My eyes swept over the room as I tried to devise an exit strategy or a way to defend myself. Landon watched me. It was like being under the scrutiny of a viper. One strike of his fangs and I'd bleed out.

"Madison wouldn't just be devastated by my death, she'd

be vengeful. You don't want to be a target of a pissed-off Madison, I assure you. Vampires aren't immune to magic, you're just fast. You know who's good with magic? Madison and Cory. Would you prefer me to find the Amber Crocus for you, or would you rather spend your days dealing with them, while the AC is out there somewhere? Eventually it might fall into the wrong hands and my death would be in vain. The vampires' extinction would be inevitable. All because you had a murdery tantrum."

The taut muscles in Landon's neck had relaxed and he took a few steps away from me, but the anger and thirst for violence remained in his eyes.

"You have seventy-two hours to find it."

The fact that he didn't bother to issue a parting threat was scarier than if he'd gone into detail about my murder. Him quietly and methodically retrieving my weapons and handing them to me was equivalent to lunging at me with bared fangs. With great effort, I left his home with the casual breeziness of someone who wasn't marked for death.

Cory waited patiently in the passenger seat while I let out a string of curses, borrowing very heavily from Madison's Irish-Haitian lexicon.

"Landon thinks Mephisto took the AC," I eventually said. My head dropped back against the headrest. I laid my forearm over my eyes, blocking out the crescent illumination of the setting sun. It had been a long day.

Cory seemed faced with the same inability to defend Mephisto with confidence. The tension-filled silence stretched on.

"He made an offer, then rescinded it after telling you he wouldn't. He made a trip to Dante's to find some. It's possible," Cory admitted.

The stilted silence of the drive left room for both of us to do some planning. Occasionally the silence was interrupted by suggestions.

"Let me question the witches," urged Cory. "I can do an *herba* detection spell when I talk to them. That'll tell me if there's plant life in the house."

It would be positive in any witch's home since they used plants, flowers, and herbs in their spells, but it was worth a shot. Maybe under his questioning, like in a courtroom drama, they would break under the pressure and confess. It was unlikely, but a woman could hope, couldn't she?

CHAPTER 16

*I*t wasn't comforting that instead of me meeting Mephisto at his home, he'd suggested we meet at a restaurant twenty minutes from my home. The nagging feeling that this wasn't going to be a confrontation but a discovery was hard to dismiss, and I'd prefer to confront Mephisto without an audience.

Turned out it wasn't a restaurant but a posh cigar bar. It only took a cursory scan of the luxury cars in the lot, the lightly tinted windows, and the script on the building to see this place lauded exclusivity. The woman who greeted me at the door was dressed in a sheer-sleeved beige pin-tucked shirt and a high-waisted pencil skirt that gave her a vintage look befitting the classic look of the lounge. Adding to the classic appeal were chocolate leather chairs, shelves displaying a selection of cigars, and a bar to the far left complete with a bartender in a dark-brown vest, a crisp white shirt rolled to the forearms, and slacks. Across from the bartender was a built-in bookcase filled with leather-bound books; I suspected classics and first editions.

The lounge was classic elegant noir with the air of mystery that would appeal to Mephisto.

"Ms. Jensen?" the greeter asked after looking down at the tablet in her hand. "Erin Jensen?"

"Yes." She audited my appearance with a critical eye. It merited a tight-lipped look of disapproval. Her sharp gaze slowly trailed over my well-worn fitted jeans, teal Henley shirt with a light dusting of dirt that I'd missed when I brushed it off earlier after examining the garden, my high ponytail and its flyaways, and my grimace of irritation at Mephisto choosing this place to meet.

"Please follow me," she directed, escorting me to the back corner of the lounge where Mephisto was seated, secluded from the other five patrons in the room. Soft music in the background prevented conversations from being overheard. I didn't feel magic as we navigated through the room.

With the exception of Mephisto, everyone in the room was human. Dressed in his typical black suit, he'd traded the black shirt for a white one and complemented it with a multicolored gray tie. It shocked me into a halt, ignoring the seat across from him that he offered. Instead, I gaped at him as he took puffs from the cigar in his hand. The small oval window to his right filtered in some muted peach illumination from the setting sun that highlighted the hues of midnight blue and black in his hair.

The keen focus he kept on me was an undeniable reminder of who and what he was. It sparked in me the same doubt and concerns Madison had about the Huntsmen. I wanted to trust him and believe that we were on the same team, but were we?

"You look nice," he said with a sincerity that only proved he was a practiced liar.

"No, I don't. I look like I've had a crappy day, which, by the way, I have."

His eyes roved slowly over me, obviously seeing something quite differently than the greeter.

"I disagree. I like the way you look," he said. He offered

me his cigar. The smell wafted to me and I inhaled spice, pepper, creosote, and eucalyptus. I loved the smell of cigars but was convinced that people *only* liked the smell, not the taste.

I waved my hand, declining his offer.

"You know it's considered rude not to partake in a cigar bar."

"Why did we meet here?" I asked, ignoring his etiquette lesson.

"I needed to get out," he admitted.

Did that theft leave you a little fidgety?

Mephisto was a collector of all things and it wasn't unlikely that he'd stolen the Amber Crocus.

"There's something on your mind, Ms. Jensen."

Ms. Jensen? How did we get back there?

"The Amber Crocus was stolen from the Lunar Marked coven."

"That's quite unfortunate for both parties involved." His airy tepid tone wasn't doing anything to disprove my suspicions.

"And me, because Landon thinks you had something to do with it and that I colluded with you in the theft."

His brows inched together and he took another pull from the cigar.

"If he's threatening you, I suspect Madison can get the STF to intervene," he said, his cool indifference making it impossible for me to give him the benefit of the doubt.

"Tell me you didn't have anything to do with it being stolen."

"I had nothing to do with it being stolen." His tone lacked any emotion and the contours of his face went flat.

"Did Kai, Simeon, or Clayton?"

He set the cigar down and took a drink from the glass on the table next to him, inhaling it before taking a sip.

My irritation spiked.

He was dangerously close to having the drink thrown in his face.

Answer me, dammit!

"I don't believe so," he responded in the same aloof tone.

"I don't like these games."

Annoyance flickered in his dark eyes. "I don't like these accusations."

I diverted my eyes and gazed around the room as a distraction. I hoped that he wouldn't lie to me. I never would have thought that I'd ever consider Mephisto a beacon in my life. He'd brought me back to life, told me about my mother, revealed who he was, made attempts to protect me, got rid of the Immortalis—eliminating one of the many problems and complexities in my life. In a convoluted way, we were on the same team. A blatant lie meant I couldn't trust him. I wanted to trust him. I *needed* to trust him.

Returning my attention to him, I whispered, "If you did, I'll figure something out. I just…" I sighed. "I need you to be truthful with me."

Perhaps he heard the earnestness, the entreaty, or my real need for the truth because he got up and came around to my side of the table in a slow, graceful, and deceptively human way, as if it were a performance for any possible onlookers. Kneeling in front of me, his eyes lost the sharpness. They were soft and solemn.

"No, I'm not lying to you. None of us had anything to do with it. Our interests might not align, but I have no desire to hurt you, which is why I withdrew the offer. Clay is right, perhaps…" His voice trailed off, but I knew what he was referring to. Clayton believed that I was a weakness of Mephisto's and that his decision-making was compromised when it came to me. I wasn't convinced. Maybe I possessed the same weaknesses. Despite all evidence, I questioned him instead of throwing outright accusations.

Humble pie is really grainy with a hint of tang. And I had to eat a great deal of it.

There was something in his voice and in his face and in the lines of his grimace. I couldn't quite place it. Unease? Regret? Shame?

Warmth crept up my thigh where he'd placed his hand. I leaned into him, feeling his magic wash over me. When I found myself moving closer and coveting his magic, I inched back and turned away. I wasn't sure it was just his magic that I wanted.

"I think you should move."

His lips wisped over my cheek, then he moved back to his chair. Sinking back against the comfortable looking leather, he steepled his hands. "Were there any parts of the AC left?"

"Nothing. We looked."

If even a broken piece was left, we could have traced it using the chlorophyll in the plant. Anything that lived had a life source.

"Someone disabled a Klipsen ward that was protecting it," I told him.

"Who do you know that shares my interests in collections and is, due to your intervention, immune to magic?" he inquired, brow raised.

He responded to my scathing look of suspicion with a knavish smirk and picked up the cigar.

"The Alpha is no less of a collector than I am," he reminded me. "He has a reputation for accumulating things he doesn't really want or need, which is where we differ. I might not need it, but I will want it."

Were we still talking about the AC?

Scrutinizing him, I wondered if he really suspected Asher or whether he was Ms. Harp-ing him. I made her a verb, because she deserved it.

"Shifters can go through wards, but there was a trigger on

the ward. Once the ward was disturbed, the sleep pods would have broken open. Aside from the garden itself, nothing was disturbed."

Mephisto traced a finger along his lips, uncertainty in his eyes as he listened to the measures we had taken.

"Cory's questioning any witches that he believes can disarm a Klipsen ward. He'll use a *herba* detection spell to determine the existence of plant life."

"It will probably be positive in most witches' homes," Mephisto pointed out.

I nodded in agreement, but we were working with limited options and not a lot of leads. His sigh encompassed exactly how I felt. There was a long considering pause before he spoke again.

"I suppose you don't want me to intervene in this matter between you and Landon."

"No," I said too quickly. "I'll figure something out." I had been brainstorming since I'd left Landon, in the event I couldn't find the AC. I had to offer him something just as appealing.

"Is there an antidote or a counterspell to the AC?" I asked Mephisto. Nothing in my research had revealed anything.

"No, that's the draw of it. Nothing can be done to reverse it. Death is imminent."

That's what I'd figured. If there were countermeasures, Landon would have discovered them before I had.

After thanking Mephisto, I stood to leave and so did he. He laced his fingers through mine as though it was the most natural thing for him to do.

In silence we navigated through the lounge. Mephisto stopped by the host to retrieve a beautifully decorated bag bearing the lounge's name. Cigars, I was sure. When he walked me to my car, he seemed distracted.

"I need something from you," he admitted.

"What?"

He slipped his hand from mine and pressed his finger to my temple.

"My brain?" I asked, bewildered.

"No, your memory. You said that you had access to the other *Mystic Souls.*"

"I don't have access to it."

"I know. And since you're so secretive about it, I'm sure Asher is involved." He didn't even try hiding his discontent.

His hand found mine again. I indulged in the scent of his magic the way he did the cigar. I snapped myself back once I realized how close I had moved into him. It wasn't fair. Knowing that I had restricted magic and eventually I'd have it did nothing to curb the desire, and again made me question if that desire extended only to Mephisto's magic. My eyes dropped from his, not wanting him to read the complicated longing and thoughts on my face or see the malevolence that snaked through it. If I could take his magic without him stopping me, I would. Period. I wasn't proud of it.

"Yes, Clayton seems to believe the book you had might contain the spell to remove your restriction. It would have to be an archaic spell."

"We couldn't read those. Madison was the only one who really looked at them. Once Cory and I realized we couldn't decipher the language, we passed on them." But Madison hadn't. She had scanned the pages, convinced she could translate the spells.

"If she saw the pages, we can retrieve the information. Can she meet with Clay to see?"

Even memories of earlier failures with the book didn't deter me. I was that desperate. I agreed. A little too enthusiastically.

He relaxed some. Did he think I'd say no?

"Good." He didn't give me the opportunity to ask more questions before he slipped from me. "Clay will contact you."

Great. I wasn't sure how fond Madison would be of Clay rooting around in her head.

CHAPTER 17

*T*he morning after my discussion with Mephisto, the pale-yellow walls, the scent of lavender from the diffuser that inundated the air, and the peaceful hum of music coming from my speaker hadn't done anything to relax me. The bedroom that I'd converted to a meditation room had magic books sprawled around my meditation cushion. I still scoured through my magic books hoping to find something, although I was doubtful I would.

Throughout my attempt to meditate, I couldn't stop thinking about Mephisto's accusations. No matter how hard I tried to redirect my thoughts, they remained on two things: There wasn't an antidote or counterspell for Amber Crocus, and I didn't have anything to bargain with if I couldn't find it. And Asher could possibly be a player.

Alex and Landon were friends, but Asher and Landon's relationship was the strained cordiality seen between most heads of denizens. It had nothing to do with the alleged rivalry people thought existed between shifters and vamps, and everything to do with the rivalry that occurred between powerful people. I doubted being immune to magic changed Asher's propensity to acquire magical objects, even though he couldn't use them and they couldn't be used against him or his pack. Anyone who possessed the AC had an advantage, and with the shifters' speed, which closely rivaled the vamps', having the AC would make the difference between one dominating the other.

But Asher wasn't like that.

I convinced myself he wasn't. I couldn't disregard the fact that he'd double-crossed me and stole the Salem Stone right under my nose. Could he have done the same with the Amber Crocus? After five more minutes of unsuccessful attempts to meditate and trying to keep my mind from being a chaotic mess, I gave up.

In the living room I picked up my phone. I had three texts and a missed call from Clayton. Patience definitely wasn't one of his strengths. There weren't any messages from Madison, which was surprising. I'd texted her twice about meeting up with Clayton. It was unlike her to not respond to a text and definitely a call, even if it was just with an autoresponder to let me know she'd call me later. Nothing. Worry nagged at me, but I pushed it aside. She was probably busy. But I still sent another text reminding her to call me as soon as she could.

Then I held the phone, staring at it, contemplating whether to call Asher. I'd falsely accused Mephisto; did I want to do the same with Asher? Overlooking the list of things that would make Asher a likely suspect couldn't be ignored. I decided questioning him was something I should do in person.

———

Asher was waiting for me near the off-putting statues of the howling wolves in front of his building. His sharp, appraising gaze, predaceous ease of movement, and curl of his lips that wasn't quite a smirk all hinted at his cunning nature and

169

eased the apprehension I felt about overreacting by questioning him. I just didn't know what to do if he was guilty.

"Erin." My name eased from his lips in a lazy drawl and he sidled up next to me. We both seemed to appreciate the nice, breezy day, and I didn't object when Asher led me to the perimeter of the oversized building toward the back where there was a sitting area surrounded by a thicket of lush flowering trees that offered a degree of privacy. The shifters' building was ostentatious and could be seen from blocks away, but they still enjoyed their privacy, which was why there were alcoves that allowed them to be outside but secluded.

"You wanted to talk to me," he said, taking a seat on the bench. Curiosity-whetted eyes held mine. I returned his inquisitive gaze, hoping I'd be able to determine if he was lying. It was doubtful. Being able to detect lies himself made him exceptionally skilled at telling them.

"You said to come to you if I needed something and you'd be there for me," I reminded him.

"Yes, what's wrong?"

"I need you to promise to be honest with me. No lies of omission or wordplay. This is very important."

He tensed, his brows drawing together, his expression a cross between skepticism and concern. He started a nod of agreement but stopped. "Does it involve my pack?"

That question had so many layers and nuances. Asher's actions were always done in an effort to protect his pack, sometimes preemptively.

"Not really," I eased out reluctantly.

Silence ticked by as I tried to determine the right course of action. I knew that I wasn't doing a great job hiding my dilemma.

"I promise," he agreed. "*But*, depending on what it is, my actions may not change."

Asher, what did you do?

"Are you familiar with Amber Crocus?"

He frowned. "Yes. I've heard that it's a plant that can kill vampires, if they're staked with it or somehow it gets into their system. From what I've gathered, it's just a rumor or the vampires assisted in it becoming extinct," he said brusquely, giving me the impression, he believed it was one of the many baseless rumors swirling around. I couldn't determine if he thought the plant was mythical or extinct. It didn't matter; the burden that had weighed on me since we sat down lifted.

"Why are you asking?"

I shrugged. "No reason."

"Ah, so you drove all the way here to ask me about an extinct plant for no reason?" Doubt placed a hard frown on his face.

"It's not mythical. They exist, or rather someone found a way to make more."

"Half truth," Asher announced.

He could not possibly have known that. Damn, shifters are annoying.

"Your voice is always stilted when you do that. It's subtle but still detectable, if you pay attention," he told me with a shrug. Shifting his position, he relaxed back on the bench, his fingers clasped behind his head, looking straight ahead. "Let me guess. The witches learned how to make it and were blackmailing Landon. You were hired to acquire it from them. Correct?"

"Something like that," I conceded. "How did you know?"

He let out a dry, mirthless scoff. "Wolfsbane," he said.

"That doesn't kill you, it just drugs you."

"There's a particular variety that affects us worse than the rest. It dulls our senses and is the only one we can't metabolize quickly. For days, our senses, scent, hearing, and speed are impaired until it's out of our system." His face hardened. For people who relied so heavily on their preternatural abilities, losing them for days had to be its own special hell.

"When I became Alpha, I followed what was rumored to be the vampires' example and got rid of as much of it as I could. Needless to say, a coven found some and was determined to make more. I assumed to sell. It's difficult to grow and is very fragile. I discovered it and we came to an arrangement." A hint of menace lingered over his words.

"Do I want to know?"

"It was an agreement. They were compensated."

"Was the compensation along the lines of a 'give me the wolfsbane and you keep your life' sort of deal?"

Lips quirked into a sly smile as he ignored my question. "Why did you ask me about the Amber Crocus?" he asked.

"It was taken," I admitted.

His eyes were slits as they scrutinized me. In a lissome sweep of movement, he was standing. "You think I took it?" His jaw was clenched, his posture guarded.

"I didn't. But I was just covering—"

"Yeah, you did." He looked away, his features softening to something that resembled hurt, maybe disappointment.

"I'm just covering all my bases, Asher. It's not personal."

"But it should be." He shoved his hand into his pocket, his eyes finding so many things more interesting to look at than me. "If I'd heard about it, I probably would have acquired it. So, I should be a suspect." He pulled his eyes back to me. Intense, solemn gray eyes held mine. "But if I knew you were involved, I would have backed off. I owe you that much. I hate that you don't know that."

"I do."

"Lie."

"Stop doing that and let me lie in peace," I snapped.

His roar of laughter broke the tension. "I wish it was that easy. Sometimes I want to be lied to."

"For you, I'll get better at it."

"The Amber Crocus was really stolen?"

I nodded. "They disabled a Klipsen ward and didn't set off any of the triggers."

If he was shocked, he hid it well.

"Mephisto also made an offer, which he rescinded. Landon paid but thinks I had something to do with the theft. He believes I colluded with Mephisto to steal it, and I have less than forty-eight hours to find it."

He nodded slowly. "Your dealings with Mephisto always seem to have consequences, don't they? Perhaps that's a sign you should limit them."

Everyone was casting aspersions and giving unrequested advice.

At my silence, he gave a solitary blink. "Would you like me to—"

"Handle it? No," I interrupted. Whatever his and Mephisto's way of "handling it" would be, it'd probably be worse for my career and reputation than my backup plan, which was to involve the STF. But at least the shifters and Mephisto wouldn't be at war with the vampires. There was no way I could protect the witches and involve the STF without being implicated, and the moment I became known for doing that to a client, my reputation and business would be ruined. I needed to figure things out.

"You have a plan?" he asked.

"Yeah."

"Is it a good one?"

"No."

"Truth," he said softly. I was glad he didn't ask about my plan, but something in the gentle, sympathetic way he squeezed my shoulder when we departed gave me the impression he knew. Good, because it wasn't something I wanted to say aloud.

CHAPTER 18

*C*ory wasn't having any success with interviewing the witches, who surprisingly were more forthcoming than expected. All the suspects had complied with his questioning, despite him being evasive and not letting them know the specifics of the plant, just that it involved the vampires. Since most covens used the same plants and flowers, with very few deviations depending on the specialty or strength, they were more than willing to let him see their gardens. With the exception of the Lunar Marked coven, Cory got the impression that if the plant would have brought them trouble, they would quickly and willingly have given it to the vampires. Some would probably sell it, but I was sure for a lot less than the Lunar Marked coven asked for.

"What do we do next?" Cory asked through the speaker in my car after giving me the details of his conversations.

"I don't know." I blew out an exasperated breath. "The dragons," I said, grasping at the tiniest of straws. They were a trio of thieves consisting of a gifted witch and two dragons. They did more than just hoard treasures. Because of the witch's penchant for collecting expensive things, this group wasn't your typical dragon hoarders. They were thieves I'd encountered while retrieving items they'd stolen during a poker game.

"It wouldn't hurt to question them," Cory suggested. Wrong. It would hurt a great deal. The witch hated me and her dragon boyfriend tended to follow her lead, which left me with the younger of the dragons. I'd managed to ingratiate myself by giving him a Glanin's claw, which injects silver into shifters and prevents them from shifting. He and I had a better working relationship, but I didn't trust him.

"I can talk to Maddox?" I offered.

"The younger one you beat up and who now has a crush on you?"

"I didn't beat him up. I disarmed him, and the reason he likes me is because I gave them a hell of a lot of money for a magical object and let him keep the Glanin's claw. And I promised to take him to Kelsey's."

"Take him on a date—"

"Not a date, just dinner at Kelsey's."

"Whatever. Schmooze him, or whatever your version of it is, and question him. And for the love of all that's good in the world, do not show him your sex kitten face. The man will be eating. No one needs to see that face while they're eating."

I said a few choice words to him before hanging up. I'd decided to call Maddox once I got to the parking lot, but when I came to a stop, Clayton's motorcycle pulling up to the side of my car was a reminder that I hadn't heard from Madison all day.

"You haven't returned my texts," Clayton said, dismounting and securing the sling pack to him.

"I haven't heard from Madison."

"Is that typical?"

It wasn't, and him reminding me made me worry even more. Taking my phone out, I gave her another call, and when she didn't answer, I called Claire, her closest friend at the STF. She hadn't heard from or seen Madison in two days.

Claire's disclosure had me speeding toward Madison's house, recalling Landon's threats. He wouldn't be foolish or shortsighted enough to hurt her, would he? Or was it my mother? Had she found out about Madison? Was it a case of mistaken identity? My thoughts raced from the plausible to the highly implausible to the extreme, and my anxiety and fear had me driving much too fast through the streets, keeping pace with Clayton, who pushed his bike to speeds that made him just shy of a blur.

"You know where Maddie lives," I stated, shooting him a look as he flanked me while we walked to her house. I was grateful for his presence because I had no idea what to expect.

"Not in a creepy way."

"Are you sure?" I had my karambit in hand, and his hands were positioned to perform magic if needed.

"I thought it was prudent to know the potential location of The Raven."

I cringed at the name but didn't comment.

Standing at Madison's door, I cursed every gangster, espionage, and thriller movie about abduction and torture that Cory had made me watch, hailing them as "must-see" or "classics," because now they were playing out in my head in 4k images and making me paranoid.

I knocked. She didn't answer. I sent another text and waited. Nothing. I called. Nothing.

With a sigh, I pulled out my keyring that had my spare keys. I had a key to Madison's, my parents', and her parents' home.

"Madison," I called out when entering. "Maddie!" I yelled. If anything, she would have answered that just to snap at me for calling her that.

"I hear movement," Clayton said.

I did, too. Movement was bad, especially if she wasn't answering.

I ran up the stairs and followed the noise to her bedroom. I threw open the door to find Maddie dressed in shorts that displayed every inch of her toned, sinewy legs, a fitted t-shirt with nothing underneath, and over-the-ear headphones. Her hips were rocking from side to side, arm flailing out when she wasn't bringing it to her mouth to sing into her imaginary mic. She was moving in a way that would make any pop diva proud.

A pile of clothes was sprawled out on her bed. Some of them were folded, which I assumed was the chore she'd been working on.

Clayton's smile was so wide I could see all his teeth. His expression held rapt appreciation, and pleasure sparked in his eyes. He took a step forward.

"Get out." I shoved him back. It was like trying to move a truck. My hands pushed against solid, defined pec muscles that stretched his t-shirt. I made another attempt at moving the boulder. I think he forgot I was there. His eyes trailed from Madison's socked feet, her legs, her ass-flattering shorts that took a lion's share of his attention, then her shirt. Her pixie cut growing out made the natural waves of her hair noticeable.

My protective claws came out. "Stop looking at her." She'd be embarrassed to be caught like this. When I pushed his chest again, he finally gave, taking several steps back.

"Go downstairs," I ordered. Not moving immediately, he gave Madison's emphatic dancing another glance before turning, still flashing his teeth.

What is she listening to, Beyoncé?

Seeing him turn to get another look, I quickly closed the door.

"Madison," I screamed at the top of my lungs. She finally turned at the bloodcurdling sound and shuffled back, eyes gawking, lips gaping.

"How long have you been there?" she asked, pulling the

177

headphones from her ears. Loud music blasted from them before she turned off her iPod and tossed the headphones on the bed.

"You didn't answer *any* of my texts or phone calls."

"I took the day off and my phone is on silent." She scanned the room. I got the impression she wasn't entirely sure where she left it.

My face must have still looked panic-stricken because she walked to me, took two fingers, and quickly brushed them over the bridge of my nose. We did that when we wanted the person to smile. I still don't know how it became our thing... come to think of it, it was silly. The first impulse should be to frown not smile. Tweaking someone's nose is annoying, not cute or an act of endearment. But in a way it summed up our relationship.

"I needed a little break," she admitted.

"From me?"

"Yeah," she said softly.

Hey, the polite thing to say is no and come up with a good lie.

"Things are messy, Erin, and I'm scared for you and I have no idea where to begin to fix it."

"You don't have to fix it. Stop feeling like you always have to fix things. Or me."

That had been our roles in the past. I screwed up; she fixed it. I'd created the pattern. Years of being irresponsible, not getting a handle on my craving, and being reckless had left her in a position of having to clean things up. She had become my net and I let her. It sucked. She intervened more when my parents' handling of me moved from pity to frustration.

Now, knowing that I wasn't their birth child, I wondered if there were times they wished they hadn't adopted me and all the problems that came with me being their daughter. Pushing that thought away took more effort than I expected. It just took me remembering my mother's face when I told them I knew I wasn't theirs. There were no regrets, I just knew it.

Madison needing a day off from me sent a pang of guilt through me. All the bravado and optimism I'd put on had done nothing to allay her worry.

"It's my life and I'll fix it somehow. Besides, I'm the one with four gods in my corner. They want Malific dead, too," I reminded her, keeping my tone light to ease her.

"That only makes things worse. They're gods of the underworld. Have you ever considered that maybe they got that job as a punishment? Who wants to be the person who captures and guards the worst of the worst?"

"Isn't that similar to what you do? What the police do?" I countered. She considered it, one arm crossed over her chest supporting the other arm, while her fingers drummed away at her bottom lip. It was a weird nervous tick.

"Yes, but there's something different. I'm not fond of the people in the Veil. Something seems off." Maddie's lips lifted into a tight grim smile. "I'm afraid for you," she admitted.

She plopped down on her bed. "I don't want you to die. Again. It will be like losing a sister. We joke about our parents giving the middle finger to the rules of genealogy, but you are my sister. We should have grown up in the same house, not just really close by." She attempted a playful eye roll but couldn't quite pull it off. Her eyes glistened from the tears she blinked back.

"Madison, my life and all the drama that has unfolded is not your mess to fix." Guilt was making my breathing difficult and getting air nearly impossible.

I sat next to her, covering her hand with mine. "I know me telling you to stop worrying won't do anything to stop you. So, I'll say this. We're in this together. Let me share some of your burden. I'm not worried. I have a magically immune pack, gods, a kick-ass fae, and a witch on my side. Magical objects up the wazoo. Something has to work." The level of confidence in my voice surprised me. But it wasn't for me; I needed to comfort Madison.

She laughed. "You have a lot of unearned confidence," she teased.

"Hey!" I said. "It's not unearned. I've gotten out of a lot of tight things."

I could see the weight lifting from her as she sat up taller, her shoulders relaxed, and a small genuine smile of relief settled on her lips.

Good, now I can hit her with the Clayton situation.

When silence fell and she noticed me twirling a lock of hair around my fingers, her eyes narrowed on me.

"I didn't come here alone," I said hurriedly. "We heard noises and rushed up here. I had no idea you'd be here in barely there shorts getting your Beyoncé on."

She shrugged. I'd seen her in less, and although this was my first time seeing her dance with such vitality and reckless abandonment, we were well past true embarrassment.

"Clayton saw you," I admitted.

"No big deal. What, he's never seen a person dance before?"

That wasn't just dancing. With those moves you looked like you were ready to headline Coachella.

"Give me ten minutes. I'll meet you downstairs."

I tried to explain the reason for our visit, but she held up her hand to stop me, telling me she'd listen to and read my messages to catch up and then we'd discuss everything when she came downstairs. Stunned by how nonchalant she was, I kept a watchful eye on her as I backed out of her room, waiting for the freakout.

———

It was more than ten minutes before Madison emerged, dressed in the most uninspired outfit I'd ever seen her wear

180

and a stark contrast to what she had on before. Khaki pants and a crisp beige shirt buttoned to the very top. Her hair, despite her curly roots, had been straightened. Except for the slight glow on her face that increased each time she glanced in Clayton's direction, she looked drab.

Kai, a bound ball of energy, had joined us and was pacing throughout the room, taking a special interest in her bookcase. Clayton had settled on the sofa and was leafing through a book. He looked up from the book, his eyes traveling over Madison from her sensible brown slip-on shoes, her meticulously neat hair, clothes, and professionally stoic expression.

"I liked the other outfit," he teased. Madison's deep copper-colored skin made it difficult to see a blush, but it was there. Pulling her attention from Clayton, she moved it in Kai's direction, displaying the same curiosity about him as I had.

"He'll help you with recalling the information," Clayton explained.

Madison frowned. "What do you mean?"

"I can pull your memories," Kai said.

Oh, well, it's worse than I thought.

Instead of elaborating, Kai gave Madison's home another considering look. "I like your home, it's very neat." Then he shot me a look.

I'd forgotten, Kai was a neat freak with a tendency to be very vocal about telling people they were messy. My home had to give him neat attacks, assaulting his type-A sensibilities.

Madison lived by the rule that everything had a place, a belief that could be seen most profoundly in her kitchen. Despite being used frequently, it looked as if it was just for show. The remainder of her house was just as meticulously neat. Everything from the pictures on the walls to the decorative pillows on the chairs were perfectly aligned; even the blanket over the back of the sofa was folded into a perfect square. If things weren't on the floor, there were only a few dishes in the sink, and my shoes weren't blocking the pathway, I considered my place clean.

"You should have a better bookcase," Kai said. Madison looked at me and I shrugged. How do you answer that?

"It's made of plywood." That really bothered him.

"I know. It's cheap. I needed a bookcase and hadn't found one I loved enough to shell out the money for."

"I can make you one that you'll love."

Again Madison's eyes flew in my direction like I had the Kai key. I hoped my eyes conveyed "just go with it."

For several moments Madison and I engaged in a series of looks, shrugs, and attempts to read each other's lips.

"I'd love that. Thank you," she eventually said. It seemed like a reasonable way to respond.

"What type of wood do you like?"

I can answer that. The one that comes from a tree. Nailed it. Is that really something people know?

"Maple," she answered.

I stand corrected. It was the first genuine look of pleasure I'd ever seen on Kai's face. Usually his expression hovered between suppressed hyperactivity and listlessness. A slow smile eased over his lips, his tawny skin alight and his cherubic features sharpened with interest.

Call me unimaginative, but should a discussion about wood brighten anyone's day this much?

"Why maple?" he inquired, his head slightly canted. Unlike what would have happened if he had asked me, Madison didn't have the glassy look of someone who wasn't expecting a quiz about wood.

"I remember reading it's easier to stain," she told him.

That was a beam. Kai was beaming.

Clayton caught the change in Kai's demeanor. His eyes narrowed ever so slightly as Kai moved, in an effortless glide, to get closer to Madison.

My life is in peril and they're talking about wood? I looked at Clayton, Mr. You-are-a-distraction-to-Mephisto, let me intervene. *Where's the intervention now?*

Instead of stopping Kai, he just kept a careful eye on the interaction.

"It is, but"—Kai looked around the room—"mahogany, koa, and African padauk are stronger and very fitting for this room." Exhilaration and interest shone in Kai's eyes and in his words.

It's lumber. That's what gets you going?

"Kai." Clayton redirected him to the more pressing topic.

Snapping out of his state of lumber intrigue, he gave Clayton a weak smile, which Clayton returned with a fraternal affection. Kai was a bird with clipped wings, prohibited from doing what I suspected he did often in the Veil. This was his alternative.

As much as I didn't want to merge the worlds or have anything to do with it, I wanted to get him back to the Veil. An unexpected twinge shot through me. Returning him to the Veil meant the same for Mephisto. I didn't want to unpack that unexpected feeling.

"If you remember what you saw, I can recover it," Kai explained.

I imagined I held the same look of bewilderment and discomfort as Madison did.

"He has telepathic abilities. The ability to see what you see," Clayton said.

That only added to the confusion and unease. And a little panic. He could read our minds. Everything? How? There were so many questions, but "What?" was the only thing I managed to sputter out.

I found myself doing a quick inventory of everything I had ever thought in Kai's presence. It changed everything. I felt invaded and thoroughly exposed.

"It's a spell that I'm more adept at performing than the

others. It requires a great deal of concentration and is very difficult to do without participation."

"The other person must be actively involved," Clayton clarified, perhaps still sensing our apprehension.

"Do you agree?" Kai asked, easing toward Madison.

She frowned. "Whatever I think about?"

"Yes, as long as we are linked. If you only think about the book, that's all I'll see." Madison's eyes swung to Clayton, who, judging from the light in his brown eyes, was pleased by her attention. She yanked her gaze from him with a roll of her eyes and looked at me. We both attempted to ignore him biting his lips to suppress a chuckle.

The intensity of her frown relaxed once her focus was on me. "Okay," she said.

A combination of relief and guilt fell over me; the only reason she'd agreed was for me. For once, I wished she wasn't the one making the sacrifice. I mouthed a thank you and she simply shrugged as if she was saying that's what she did.

Kai lowered himself to the floor and asked Madison to join him. Once she was seated, Clayton pulled out their copy of *Mystic Souls* and a notepad from his bag. He opened the book to a page with writing that looked very similar to the spell he'd used on me, but the page was no longer blank. They'd recovered the lost spell.

Responding to my look of curiosity, he said, "I have a good memory and Kai helped me recover the rest." Then he quickly returned his attention to Kai and Madison.

Kai's voice was low and gentle as he explained the process to Madison. He reminded her that he'd be able to see everything she was thinking. It wasn't something you had to remind a person of. Tell them once and, believe me, they're going to remember you're the person who can read their mind.

He instructed her to close her eyes. When his hand

covered hers, Madison's eyes snapped back open and looked down at it.

"Sorry," he whispered, before saying an invocation that conjured a gust of magic so powerful my breath whooshed out. Madison gasped a ragged breath and her eyes fluttered under her lids. Tensing, Kai's free hand grasped her unclasped one.

A sheen of blue illumination covered Kai and expanded outward, reminding me of his wings. He continued to instruct Madison to only think of the pages from *Mystic Souls* that she couldn't read.

It took nearly an hour for Clayton to transcribe the two pages, with Kai taking several breaks to remind Madison that he was able to see everything that she was thinking about. The Cheshire grin on Clayton's face hadn't eased since Kai told Madison that Clayton was only there to take notes and interpret and to stop focusing on him. That led to a flushed Madison requesting a break before rushing out of the house for air.

She returned with more resolve that did nothing to remove Clayton's resting smirk.

Clayton had *Mystic Souls* opened and compared the pages in it with the notes he'd taken. "They're different." He scribbled more notes, deciphering the differences in the spells. After several long moments, he turned to me.

"Are you ready to try it?"

"Yes," I rushed out, without a second thought of the pain the similar spell had caused the first time.

Again, he pulled out the knife and another granite-like slab. He pricked my extended finger and started reciting the spell when the droplet touched the slab.

When the last words fell from Clayton, I winced in anticipation of the pain, the emergence of my enigmatic raven. But there wasn't anything. The granite slab was intact, my skin flushed but normal, and the raven remained concealed. It was as if a spell hadn't been cast. Clayton reviewed his work, did the comparison again, and even performed the spell again, but without success.

"Is there a way for you to get the other *Mystic Souls* again?" he asked.

The only thing I could give him was a noncommittal, disheartened, "Maybe."

Too many failures had taken away the last spark of hope and optimism in me. I was going to stay like this until I found the person who had restricted my magic.

When my thoughts went to the stranger outside my apartment, I used the need to get the *Mystic Souls* as an excuse to leave. Feeling their eyes boring into me, I turned to give them the most encouraging look I could marshal.

CHAPTER 19

The drive through the city hadn't helped. When I left Madison's home, I thought I'd set up a meeting with Asher and make arrangements to get access to his copy of *Mystic Souls*. I wasn't in any rush. I couldn't take another demoralizing failure, and the idea of accidentally doing something as cataclysmic as releasing Ian made me want to stay far away from the book.

Most of the day had dwindled away and I sat in the parking lot of my apartment, contemplating my next move. Calling Maddox seemed like another dead end but I'd do it. I wasn't sure that he'd be as forthcoming as the witches, especially if Lexi, the witch in the trio, was near. Instead of calling, I sent him a text, asking if we could meet.

Part of me wanted to be done with the whole situation. To tell the Lunar Marked coven to return the money and give Landon a "suck it up, buttercup" diatribe, return his upfront fee and even the consult fee, and walk away. Preserving my reputation didn't seem as important as saving my life from my mother.

But walking away wasn't going to be that easy. Landon thought I was involved. I might be over it, but he wouldn't be. And the Lunar Marked coven was a target. It was likely none of us were going to get out of it alive; it was just a matter of how inconspicuous he was going to be about it. The countdown clock was ticking and I wasn't any closer to finding the AC.

The cloak of impending destruction of my career was over me. Getting the Supernatural Task Force involved had to be my last resort, I decided as I got out of the car. I wouldn't get Madison involved unless absolutely necessary. If I'd discovered nothing else today, it was that she needed a reprieve.

Walking to my apartment, I tried to keep my mind on Landon and the situation, but it kept slipping to the man I'd seen earlier. My gut was telling me he was a player and that maybe… No, it was too ridiculous to even consider. I refused to give life to the words I was thinking. But it didn't stop the possibility. My father. He could be my father.

I tried to vanquish the thoughts as if they were a dark spell that needed to be cast out. They persisted. A few feet from my door I was confronted with the earthy scent of magic with hints of meadow and evergreen. I turned to find him. *Him.* Dark-brown hair with highlights of lighter hues was peppered with silver. I took him in: olive-skinned, oblong face, light eyes, sharp nose, and sharp features that mirrored my own. I squinted at his ears, looking for points, but there weren't any. I couldn't tamp down the feeling of familiarity and kinship.

His tall thin frame moved with the fluid grace of someone trained in martial arts and the confidence of a person who knew he wasn't likely to be bested. Gentle eyes. So gentle that it was difficult to keep my karambit at the ready and not relax it at my side. His eyes dropped to my weapon, but it was clear he didn't see it as a threat.

Why did I feel that way, too? No, this was the part of the movie where the viewers yell, "Run, dumbass."

I didn't run, but I did step back several feet.

"Peace," he said, in a voice so melodic it was like a lullaby. It wasn't an enchantment, just a soft gentle voice.

"Peace, daughter," he said, inching closer and closer, still with the same confidence but seemingly reticent for my benefit.

I swallowed and stayed still, allowing him to approach. My grip tightened around the karambit.

"I'm not your daughter," I snapped. I was Gene's daughter. This man, I didn't know.

I was counting the feet as he got closer. Six, five, four, three, two.

"That's close enough," I commanded.

"Of course." He kept staring at me, his eyes taking in every inch of my face, then a smile slowly emerged.

"You have a lot of features that resemble your mother's," he said. His effort to keep his voice warm and welcoming slipped. It was now tight with shades of disappointment and anger.

That's what happens when you have a child with someone! They look like both the parents, you psycho-screwing whackadoodle. The question remained, was he not seeing the same person I saw every morning? He and I looked alike. Damn, did my parents look alike and it was some weird narcissistic fetish where they were indirectly having sex with themselves? Eww.

"Your hair is dark like hers and your smile, very similar."

When did he see me smile?

"How long have you been following me?" My voice was harsh and arctic cold. I didn't mean it to come out that way, but it did and I wasn't going to apologize. It was uncomfortable having him take inventory of me.

"Years. I wanted to make sure you were safe." The corners of his lips kinked up. "You smile when you have magic. You always smile when you have magic."

"You're the reason I don't," I shot back, hoping to get confirmation of our hypothesis.

He nodded. "It was the only way to protect you."

There was no relief to be found in his answer. Clutching my karambit at my side, I waited for the anger that rampaged through me to subside and the irritation to wind down. His eyes remained gentle; I was sure mine were not, narrowed on him as they were. I closed them for a moment to stop the twitching. They snapped open when Ms. Harp's door opened and she peeked out. Instead of walking in our direction, she went to the mailbox near her door and lingered there, sorting through her mail without managing to look at it. It had to be hard to extend the sorting time of two pieces of mail.

You're not even trying to pretend.

I turned my head and locked eyes with her, and my expression said: *The jig is up, woman.*

Using her cane, surprisingly, in one of the patterns I showed her, and moving slowly, I knew I was wrong. She'd mastered the frail elderly voice and was laying it on rather thick with each small, careful step.

What was she, a drama teacher?

"Hi, I'm Evelyn. I've seen you around a few times. If I'd known you were looking for Erin, I would have let her know she had a returning guest." I'll give it to Ms. Harp, she was covert and smooth at letting me know she'd seen him around and when her eyes slipped in my direction, watching me for a response. Her intel wouldn't stop with just her; she'd relay the information to Asher. I didn't like having a spy in my building.

"Erin, would you introduce me to your friend?"

No.

"We look out for each other, so we like to know who's coming and going. You can never be too safe," she continued when I didn't respond.

Trying to read my *father's* eyes, I wasn't sure if he was buying it. The affable curl of his lips didn't change, but he didn't offer a name and I didn't put the effort into making one up.

"Thank you, Ms. Harp, for checking on me. My guest and I need to talk. Will you excuse us?" I wasn't ready to give her any more information to report. And I really wanted to talk to Daddy Dearest.

Responding to her narrowed gaze with a pleasant smile, I started for my apartment with my *father* close behind. Ms. Harp made it back to her apartment, throwing off her geriatric facade with a shrug.

"Enjoy your guest." She'd managed to keep her same sweet tone while scrutinizing us.

Enjoy your snitch call to Asher.

If I didn't know better, I would have sworn she read my thoughts because the purse of her lips profoundly said: *so*.

Opening the door, I took a brief account of my room, doing a mental sweep of where I stored my weapons and how quickly I could get to them. The magic coming off him might prove to be more than I could handle without my own magic. I kept a closer distance than I wanted between us. I could take his magic if necessary.

"Do you have a name?" I asked.

"Nolan." He paused in consideration. "You don't want to call me Father?" His genuine query stunned me into silence. Confusion, anger, frustration, fear, and sadness all roiled inside me, and sorting through them and trying to think clearly became a monumental task. I hated every minute of it.

"No. If you were my father, I'd know your name."

With a pained expression, he closed his eyes. *How could that hurt?* He didn't know me.

"I've done what I could to protect you. If people knew of your existence, you never would have been safe. In the Veil, you wouldn't have been safe. You weakened her. Those who answer to her and share her beliefs would have murdered you to restore her power."

He was wrong. The Immortalis wanted me alive long enough to serve my intended purpose—to free Malific. Those who thought I could be used to break the Omni ward probably would have wanted me dead, if they'd known of my existence.

All the questions scrolled through my mind and I tried to order them by the most pressing, but they all seemed so important.

"Why are you here now?"

That wasn't really the question I wanted to ask but it was the one that came out first.

"Malific is no longer imprisoned. I have no idea how she did it. Her abilities and cunning never cease."

For someone who had a child with her and, I'm assuming, some form of relationship—possibly sordid and dysfunctional—he seemed to hold her in contempt.

"I know."

His brows inched together in question.

"I died and it released her," I told him. Each time I said it, it got easier. Pretty soon, I'd be like, "Hey, I died, pass me the Nutella and bagel, will ya."

His eyes closed and he whispered something. A prayer? A spell? A request for forgiveness? I looked at my arm, hoping there was some indicator that the restriction had been removed.

But there wasn't. The raven hadn't appeared and there wasn't any magic coursing through me. Just the empty feeling of something missing.

"I did everything to protect you. You were left with someone I knew would take care of you. A sister I felt would do the same. I never…" He blew out a breath, his expression bleak. "I thought you would stay with them. For the two weeks I watched her with her child, I knew she'd take care of you the same way."

"She gave me to her best friend because she couldn't have children. Madison is my sister. We were raised as sisters. Always told we were."

I hated that I was relieved that my explanation offered him some comfort.

"When your identity was discovered I made sure no one ever found out."

The *incident.* He was referring to that. Everything about meeting Hudson had seemed coincidental. Two people who met at a bar, finding comfort in people watching and dancing. We weren't friends, acquaintances at best. He'd never struck me as the type of person drawn to the appeal of cheating death, or the euphoric pleasure from drifting in that liminal place between life and death, or some sadistic appeal to my magic. When I acquired a new spell book, he seemed genuine about wanting me to explore it by letting me borrow his magic.

Before I could stop myself, I'd stepped back several feet from Nolan, trying to shake off that entire day and the fallout from it. The tailspin my life devolved into. That *incident* changed my life.

"What did you do?" I hissed.

Silence ticked by and flashes of that night replayed in my head in an erratic blur: Me waking up confused, finding Hudson dead, the call to Madison, the arrest, the plea deals, my stay at the Stygian, my court-ordered appointments with Dr. Sumner, and the hateful way River looked at me each time he saw me.

I slammed Nolan into the wall, the point of my karambit at his throat. "What. Did. You. Do?" I pushed out through clenched teeth.

"I protected you," he said, lifting his head and baring his neck to me. He didn't want to do that, because my fingers ached to pierce his skin with the weapon. Every attempt I made to slow my breath failed. Shuffling back from him, I forced myself to take slower, deeper breaths or I was going to pass out.

"What did you do?" I whispered, my voice cracking.

"He was there to kill you. To restore Malific's power. I just wanted to make things right. You saw me and I—" He stopped. Pain filled his eyes before he cast them down to the floor.

"You took my memory, but you didn't protect me." A lump formed in my throat, making it difficult to speak. Karambit still in hand, I went to the kitchen, yanked open the cabinet, and pulled out the vodka Mephisto had given me. It was to be savored, not guzzled the way I was doing it. It tasted like ash and I quickly put it down.

I turned away from Nolan when the tears that welled in my eyes spilled down my cheeks. "You didn't help. You screwed things up. People thought I killed him. *I* thought I killed him. All these years, I've walked around thinking that I was capable of murder." My voice broke. No longer believing I was capable of making rational decisions when it came to preserving Nolan's life, I laid the karambit on the counter.

He eased toward me with the caution of someone approaching a potentially dangerous animal. At his approach, I stiffened.

"Once he determined you were the one marked with the raven, he would have killed you."

"Why a raven?"

His lips lifted in a half smile. "You have a small mark on your leg that looks like a raven." No, it didn't, it looked like a small splat of discoloration. His smile disappeared. "And Malific is your mother. Most see her as portentous, a prelude to death. You are her daughter," he whispered.

Unable to continue to hold his gaze, I looked away. "I never killed anyone. You did."

"Let me take that burden from you. I did it. I made it so. I thought I was protecting you. You'd be hidden where no one from the Veil could get to you. You should have been at the Enclave. I underestimated Madison. She is...impressive."

And you bungled your so-called protection by making it worse. Ineffectual and catastrophic. With protection like his, I didn't need enemies.

"If Malific is out, you will need your magic to protect yourself. I restricted it to keep you hidden, but now it will only serve as a weakness. Let me lift your restriction."

Breath expelled out of me that didn't seem like my own. I nodded.

His lips lifted in an appreciative smile as if he had been expecting me to decline.

He looked at me and said, "We need to visit my sister."

CHAPTER 20

*S*ister? *Sister.*

Was this really my life?

In silence I got out of the car and moved toward the house with Nolan next to me. We made our way toward the labyrinth of trees that existed only to create mental confusion and distort the direction to the home of the Woman in Black, the trickster. The purveyor of strong enigmatic magic. And my father's sister, Elizabeth. My aunt.

This time, a Mirra of fire didn't rise as it had when I came here with the Huntsmen. Nor did a persnickety imp confront me and Cory at the entrance only to pepper us with inane riddles to prevent us moving forward and to cheat and deny us admission by claiming the answer we gave was incorrect.

Again, out of my peripheral sight, I found myself examining my father's features, wondering which part of me was Malific. The stiff silence between us became more strained with each passing moment.

My attention was drawn to the ranch home a few feet away and the bridge that formed, allowing us passage. The dangerous-looking fish with the fang-like teeth sprang out of the water, going from one end of the bridge to the other, forcing us to stop or get smacked by them or, even worse, bitten. Not something I ever wanted to explain as a reason for an injury.

Elizabeth emerged before we could get to the door. She was dressed in the image presented to those who sought her out. Her hair was pulled back into a sleek high ponytail, her lips stained a dark wine, her eyes coated in dark liner. A black coverlet covered a half-petticoat revealing slim-fitting black pants. She contrasted the attire with an oversized man's shirt tied at the bottom. It was an eclectic combination of styles that marked her as the goth trickster, a misnomer of the Woman in Black or the Woman in the Forest.

The stern look she gave me softened at the sight of her brother. She embraced him for a long time. Sighing when she pulled away, she directed her attention back to me.

"The Raven."

"Don't call her that. She's Erin," Nolan corrected before I could.

"And Malific's daughter." Venom laced her words and hard eyes narrowed on me.

I was still grappling with everything that had transpired over the past few days regarding my mother. It made it hard to find the right words.

"You're my aunt?" I asked, my tone harsher than intended.

Stopping mid-step to her house, she took me in with a disdain she'd never shown me before. "No, I'm *his* sister," she said airily.

"Elizabeth," Nolan snapped. Then he said something in a language I didn't understand. His tone was gentle but obviously chastising. Her response to him was a sharp rebuke. I might not have known the language, but their nonverbal communication spoke volumes. He was the peacemaker of the two.

Knowing that I was there to have my restriction removed and that when I left, I'd have magic, was the only reason I continued to follow the bickering siblings. They needed a time-out.

"We're removing her restriction?" Elizabeth ground out through clenched teeth once we were in the house.

"Yes, we can't leave her defenseless." He kept his voice even despite the hostility in hers.

"We're just going to unleash Malific's daughter on the city, with magic. Malific destroys the lives of those who live within the Veil, and you'll have her daughter destroy the ones outside it. She's a *Naut*, like us, and able to move through this world and the Veil with ease. Perhaps she'll sow chaos that rivals her mother's. Will that make you happy, brother?"

"She's not Malific, she's my daughter."

"The only reason she exists is because of your foolish optimism and convoluted plan to make Malific pay. But it was foolish in its inception. To create *that*." She waved her hand in my direction, and a flurry of magic drummed into me, nudging me back a few feet.

When I got my footing but before I could think clearly, a blade was in my hand and it was pointed at her to warn her off from doing it again.

"I give you Malific's daughter. She'll slaughter me as I stand here, although I'm poised to help you give her magic. And this is what you want?" A scowl of abhorrence marred her face. I wasn't going to receive any maternal regard from her.

"You provoked her."

"How many others will provoke her? You give her magic, you're unleashing a person with both god *and* elven magic. Do you want to be responsible for that?"

"Malific is free. What should I do, leave her unable to defend herself and then—" He snapped his mouth shut and when he spoke again it was in their language.

"Your plan was for naught? You having a child with Malific for the sole purpose of weakening her and making her vulnerable so she'd be forced to live that way was foolish. If you had the chance to kill her, you should have taken it."

Nolan closed his eyes and inhaled. In that moment, the dullness of his eyes, the folds of his frown, and the furrow of his brow aged him.

"People think that the most fitting revenge is death. It isn't. It's making that person live a life they aren't likely to survive. People who need power wither when they are powerless. Dominators shatter when forced to capitulate. Those who need to lead an army are at a loss when they have no one but themselves. That is what I wanted to do to Malific. Leave her in a way that she'd live her immortal life doing the very things she hates. That was a fitting punishment for such a monster."

Elizabeth's expression softened as she turned to her brother who spoke with conviction, in a manner that couldn't deny he felt he'd done the right thing. She pressed the palm of her hand to his cheek.

"The cost of vengeance is often too high, Nolan. You paid dearly." Her eyes slipped to me. "This is the debt you will continue to carry."

The room became too crowded, shrinking to a fraction of its size. My breathing became forced and labored as I processed exactly what had taken place between Nolan and Malific. I wasn't the love child of a man with questionable taste. I was a plan.

Nothing felt more devastating than to discover my life, my very existence, was a strategic maneuver. I was a pawn. For my father, I was a tool to weaken Malific and exact his revenge. For my mother, I was a sacrificial lamb to gain her freedom and return to her life of mayhem and destruction.

I needed to get the hell out of the house and away from them.

"I'm not a *this*. I'm a person and I'm standing right here!"

Her eyes flicked in my direction and she dismissed me

just as quickly. "But you shouldn't be." Returning her attention to Nolan, she said, "Malific is free because of Erin. The Omni ward that imprisoned her was linked to Malific, and the only way it could be released was if Malific died, or Erin was magically linked to it, and died in her place." I received another wave of her pure disdain, but this time without the magical assault.

"Erin should have been discovered and killed. Never allowed to be used as a means of releasing Malific." Her voice lowered when she turned her attention to me. "How did you do it? With the Huntsmen? They discovered who you are and yet here you stand."

Seething, it took all my effort to keep the knife at my side where I'd lowered it. Going through the Mirra was her effort to expose me to the Huntsmen. I was positive she had revealed to Mephisto what my markings meant, putting in motion a means to my death.

"You revealed me in the hope that they would kill me?"

A solitary blink was the only response.

"Put your weapon away," she demanded. Eyes locked on her, I was slow to move, evoking a response of magic winding around her hands.

Anger and the need for violence rampaged through me and I was unable to rein it in. I hated her. I hated this situation. And I hated that I needed her. The strength of my emotions made my face as hot as the fury alight in me.

Nolan stepped between us. After a sharp command from him in their language, she extinguished the magic.

"Peace," he demanded, giving each one of us the full intensity of his stare. He might have requested peace, but it belied the harshness he directed at Elizabeth.

Without looking at me, she said, "You must come closer if we are to remove the *vinculum*."

Sheathing my knife took a lot of effort because I really didn't trust her. But I did it and cautiously moved closer.

Rolling up the sleeves of her shirt, she revealed the snake that gave the impression of being jewelry but that I knew was more. Leaning into it, she whispered something, magic thrummed through the room, and before I could gather what was happening, the creature struck, latching on to my arm, sinking its fangs into me, and drawing blood. It pulled from me roughly, leaving a fang trail on my arm.

"Elizabeth," Nolan warned.

She brushed off his chastisement with a shrug before extending her arm for the serpent to wrap around it.

"What are you?" I asked.

"An elf like you?" Elizabeth said.

"She's elf and fae, I'm half human. It's the reason we both were needed to put the restriction on you. We used elf magic to restrict it so that only our magic could lift it," Nolan clarified.

"And warded it with elven magic, too," I added.

His head barely moved into the nod.

He split his attention between his sister and me as she gathered things and started to mix them together. The final ingredients were the combining of the elven blood, mine and theirs.

I wasn't sure what I expected my magic would be like. A tsunami of magic racing through me, a jolt that floored me as the restricted magic surged back into me, or a metaphysical display of me levitating with arms outstretched, body glowing as magic flowed over me. I admit, I expected something spectacular. What I got was a light dusting of warmth that eased over my arm. The distinctive raven flashed before swirls of black and gold from the markings meshed together, pulled from my skin, and disappeared in a cloud of smoke. My skin was unmarred, and I didn't feel in any way different. Not even the way I felt when I borrowed magic.

The gnawing urges were gone, but they were replaced by

an overwhelming feeling of emptiness. A husk. A vacant shell.

Shouldn't I have felt something...more?

I *needed* to feel something.

For years, I had felt this nearly unquenchable thirst, only for it to be replaced by a state of nothingness, leaving me feeling unlike myself. I was positive it wasn't something I could get used to.

Nolan and Elizabeth joined hands and whispered words in their language, and a flare raced through me, forcing out a gasp. I doubled over. Tears welled in my eyes. It tore through me and I knew I couldn't function that way. I released it, magic shooting from me like a bullet, knocking over the sofa, tables, and everything else in its path.

Magic. I felt it. The heavy weight of it replaced the emptiness as it poured through every inch of my body. It was a livewire inside me, making everything I felt pale in comparison. I knew it was impossible, or just my imagination, but things seemed brighter, as if a film had been lifted. Renewed. I was no longer a shadow of myself. I wanted more than just that fleeting moment of destruction, I wanted to use it. Be one with my magic.

Elizabeth frowned at the destruction, whereas Nolan seemed pleased.

"She's powerful," Nolan acknowledged with paternal pride.

"Did you expect her to be any other way?" Elizabeth asked sharply.

Studying me with an air of judgment, she asked, "How do you and your mother do it?" Although her words were benign, the level of contempt wasn't. "Malific should have been destroyed years ago and yet she lived. The Huntsmen found out who you are, but instead of destroying you, they protect you. They aren't known for protection, quite the

202

contrary." She exhaled and shook her head, turning from me to straighten the mess I'd created.

Nolan assisted while talking to her, his voice level and entreating in direct contrast to her edgy responses.

"I'd like to know what's going on," I finally said, my patience frayed as Elizabeth continue to treat me as a nuisance. She set me up to be killed? Well, fine, I held her in equal contempt.

"He wants to teach you to use our magic. Rather, he wants me to teach you while he tries to find others of our kind. He's convinced there are more on this side of the Veil, hiding. *Now* he believes she should be killed."

"She's a mere god now, with their weaknesses, not an Archdeity. She can't create an army. You're right, it is time for her to be killed. She'll come for Erin, so Erin needs to be prepared."

"She'll come for Erin and will kill her. Her magic will be restored and things will return as they were. Your plan was shortsighted, brother. Foolish. What about her sycophants? There weren't many but they were gods. Do you think they won't join her again?"

They slipped back into their language, sniping back and forth at each other.

I didn't want any part of it. I had magic. I'd gotten what I came for.

Deciding to leave, I went to the kitchen and found myself distracted by the window view of the haughty imp traipsing toward the back of the house with a hose in hand. After seeing people garden in ratty clothes, overalls, blindingly bright floral shirts and pants, and other attire, I couldn't help but be intrigued by him doing it in vest and slacks.

In the backyard there were beds of flowers nestled along the side of the house. A small vegetable garden was to the far left and to the right of it an apple tree and vine of berries. Another small garden was a little farther away, with herbs, unfamiliar flowers, and next to it, a tree bearing a fruit that looked very similar to mango. It was highly unlikely that it was mango since it was hard to grow them in the Midwest.

Unlike the other gardens, the dirt looked freshly turned. Newly planted.

"What is that?" I asked, stepping outside, my voice so loud and commanding it startled the imp. His head jerked in my direction. Arius looked at me with aloof condescension.

"It's Amber Crocus."

"Where did you get it?"

"I'm not sure. You'll have to make your inquiry to the mistress."

He was lying and I didn't need to be a shifter to know that.

Charging back into the house, I confronted my aunt.

"Where did you get the Amber Crocus?"

"We stumbled upon it," Elizabeth said, her arms folded over her chest, a humorless smile on her face.

"You didn't stumble upon it. You stole it."

And I planned to take it back. I stormed out of the house, shoving past the imp, who looked appalled at my rudeness. Kneeling, I clawed up the dirt and pulled out each plant individually. Nolan took up position next to me, also scooping up the plants.

Elizabeth looked smug as she watched us destroy her newly planted garden.

I shot her a sharp look. "Do you know what you've done? You probably don't even care. This little stunt put my life and the coven you took it from in danger. They were supposed to sell this to the vampires, and then it was stolen."

Instead of remorse, she held a look of lofty indifference until the streak of magic from me pelted her chest. It hit harder than I expected. I would have to learn to modulate it. With it directed at my cynical aunt, though, I didn't care. My magic was comparable to the magic I'd borrowed from

Mephisto, but with subtle differences, intrinsic because it was mine. I owned it.

When she came to her feet, I shot another one in her direction, but the field she erected protected it. The reversal spell I performed shattered the field and left her glaring at me. It had been a shot in the dark; reversal spells countered spells, not destroyed protective fields. I wasn't sure what had caused me to do it, but now I knew how it worked.

"Her magic is very unique." The sneer in her voice was a massive "I told you so."

To an adulating Nolan, it didn't have any effect.

"And that's a good thing," he replied, pride in his voice.

It did nothing but fuel my anger. His admiration and satisfaction meant nothing to me. I was a pawn. Part of his stratagem. Just a tool he created for revenge. The more I thought about these to, the more livid I became.

When he spoke, it was just above a whisper. "I was foolish and wrong in what I did. My goal was to be heartless and cruel to get back at Malific." He stopped, and in my periphery, I could see him looking at me. "I worried you'd be like her. Having you locked away was to protect you from becoming like her. Watching you struggle the way you did proved that you weren't. She would have killed without remorse, given in to the urges, not cared about the consequences."

I tuned him out. Whether he meant it or not, it made things worse. With my magic unfettered and uncontrolled running through me, I felt like nothing more than magic and emotions running amok. I wanted this day to be over and everything that had unfolded over the past few days to be in my distant past.

I knelt once again, recalling the spell that Cory found that would destroy the land, preventing it from ever growing anything. Another spell that wasn't light magic and that tap danced along the lines between light and dark, good and bad.

Shoving my hand into the earth, I said the spell, and the dark, ominous feeling of death and necrosis rushed through me, moving from me into the earth. It pulled the moisture, leaving dried crumbs. The putrid smell of destruction drifted from the earth as a gray sheen covered it. Even without the discoloring patina, the land looked barren beyond repair.

"Look, your daughter has destroyed the land, one of the many things she will annihilate."

"You go to hell," I barked at my aunt, and then turned my ire on good ol' dad and his distorted and disturbing reason for making me and not being in my life. "And you can go with her."

With the AC crushed to my chest, I ignored Nolan's calls.

Tossing the plants in the back seat of my car, I closed my eyes and rested against the seat. My breathing eased and I found some remnants of calm despite the nagging feeling of remorse for telling the only people who could help me with the other aspects of my magic to go to hell. At least I didn't tell them to fuck off. I kept it nice. There had to be some bonus points for that.

CHAPTER 21

*I*t took me an hour to ease my thoughts away from Elizabeth and Nolan. The peppermint white mocha that I was sipping on when Landon called didn't have its usual appeal. Probably because I wanted—no, needed—something a little stronger.

"I have the Amber Crocus," I informed him the moment he answered the phone. There were probably only a handful of times saying five words brought me so much relief.

"Ah, did Mephisto give it to you?"

"He didn't have it."

"I'm sure you're going to tell me who stole it. Such betrayal can't be ignored."

"No, I'm not going to tell you."

"Erin, is it really necessary to have this debate? You will tell me," he asserted, defiance and entitlement coursing through his words.

"You want the AC or not?" I snapped.

Even over the phone, I could feel the cold tension. As more time passed, I looked at the phone to make sure we hadn't been disconnected.

"I will see you soon," he conceded in a huff.

I wasn't looking forward to seeing him.

Of all the unwise things I've done in life, seeing a powerful vampire when my emotions were frayed and my temper was on a short fuse was definitely topping the list. But the longer I had the Amber Crocus, the more opportunities there were for something to happen to it. Once it was in his possession, my job was complete and it became his problem.

Landon opened the door and sneered at the exposed AC poking out of my bag. He put some distance between us before waving me forward to follow him to the room I'd met him in when he hired me for this job. Taking a seat in the throne-like chair, he fixed his night-dark slits on me.

"If not Mephisto, then who?" he asked.

The answer was on the tip of my tongue. I wanted so desperately to let him take his wrath out on Elizabeth, or perhaps she'd teach him a lesson about revenge. Best-case scenario, they hurt each other in a fiery blaze. But situations like that never play out as intended and it was more likely they'd walk away unharmed but leaving innocent bystanders injured, or worse.

"I'm not going to tell you," I said. "Know that the land where it was planted was destroyed. Nothing was left behind. Unless someone finds another batch somewhere or learns to create it, you have the only AC available. The witches are still under their oath."

"Yet, I still feel dissatisfied." There was a sneer in his voice.

Suck it up, buttercup.

I cursed under my breath when Elon, the vampire's henchman, entered the room. The rigid lines of his face betrayed the effort it took him to move humanly and deceptively slowly. As the actual vampire's cleaner, he lived a clandestine existence. I knew of him because it was my business to know. And if he was here, it was either to make a point or to do his job. This wasn't going to end without bloodshed; I just hoped it wouldn't be mine.

Having magic gave me an advantage. Neither of them knowing that I had magic gave me even more of an edge. It was exactly what I needed when dealing with self-entitled asses, high on their feelings of umbrage and with a thirst for revenge and retribution.

"Erin, you have proven to be exceptional whenever I've worked with you. Impressive, but putting me and the other vampires at risk can't be tolerated. So, you will tell me who stole this," he demanded in a voice that was so hypnotic, I wondered if he was trying to compel me.

"Hmmm. Will I?"

"This doesn't have to be contentious."

"You're right. Yet here we are." I kept a cautious eye on Elon.

Play nice, Erin.

Typically, it wasn't too difficult to exhibit some diplomacy; after all it was part of my job most of the time. On any other day, I'd shrug off Landon sitting on his throne, looking like a supervillain hopped up on the drug of privilege and entitlement, as him being eccentric and overly annoying. I'd finish the job, add a surcharge for the trouble of having to deal with his eccentricities and him getting on my damn nerves, and be done with it. Today I didn't have it in me.

"You're not getting a name," I said decisively. "You have the AC, the job is over. Pay me so I can leave."

He slipped a look in Elon's direction. I dropped the electric pellets I'd slid from my pocket to his left side. The mini explosion drew their attention, giving me the time I needed to yank the stake out from the back of my pants and shove it into Landon's chest. His eyes widened and he gasped in unneeded breaths as his eyes dropped to the wood protruding from his chest.

He bared his fangs.

"Now, put those away."

White-hot anger moved over his face. The sharp gaze he leveled at me was rife with malice. With great effort, he drew his lips down into a tight line, covering the fangs.

Taking several steps back, I locked eyes with Elon while blindly reaching for the Amber Crocus. Pulling out a piece of it, I held it out at him like people did with crosses, to ward off vampires, an act that usually resulted in the vampire cackling with amusement. It was a clue that the person hadn't done their vampire research. But the Amber Crocus had Elon moving to the other room and me considering keeping a piece of it for myself. For it to work, I had to imbed it in him, but that didn't seem to matter. He retreated as if a mere touch would be his true death.

I had Amber Crocus in one hand and a blade in the other. On the long list of things I wanted Mephisto to show me how to do, moving at their eerily fast speed was one of them. Happenstance and good fortune were the only reasons this particular situation had worked out. Living by luck wasn't a good strategy because luck eventually ran out.

Splitting my attention between Elon and Landon, I addressed Landon. "You're going to have true death if I don't feed you. You've attempted to bully me, threatened me, and accused me of betraying you, which I didn't." I kept my voice low and neutral to prevent inciting more anger from them. I didn't want to fight Elon and I wasn't ready to reveal my ability to use magic. It was a tactical advantage I wanted to keep secret until I really needed it.

Landon's glare intensified as I eased toward him, twining the plant around the blade. "What's it going to be? We end this now with my face being the last thing you see before true death *and* I walk out of here with the AC and your

210

vampires still at risk. *Or* I feed you, you pay me, and I leave the AC here with you?"

If looks could kill, I'd have died a thousand times over. His eyes screwed tight. "You have my word, no harm will come to you over the AC," Landon ground out through gritted teeth. True death was starting, and watching rigor mortis set in and the putrid changes in his skin wasn't something I wanted to see again.

"No, I need your word you won't try to retaliate, either. I was just protecting myself."

After a few beats, he conceded. "You have your wish."

Even among the morally gray, promises were kept. It was a part of currency as much as money.

I yanked out the stake and extended my arm to him. He took it and with more care than I expected, bit. Landon slowly drew from me until he didn't move with the stiffness of before and his skin had returned to its pale coloring.

When he released my arm, I moved away from him, watching his tongue glide over his lips, removing the rivulets. Anger gave way to lust. Vampires tended to conflate sex and violence.

"Perhaps we should have a drink, to celebrate our resolution," he suggested, giving Elon a nod, cueing him to leave, his interest undeniably lascivious.

What is wrong with you! I just staked you and threatened you with true death and that's made you hot?

"No thank you, I'll just take payment."

His movements were devoid of his usual fluid grace and stealth as he moved to his desk. It would return once he had a proper feeding. He had taken just enough to stave off death.

"Very well." He tapped at his computer and I pulled out my phone, confirmed his payment, and smiled. He'd given me a bonus.

"Thank you."

"Thank you for not letting me die," he said, a flirty tease to his voice.

I needed to get the hell out of this house of weirdness where attempts on a life made me alluring.

"Erin, I do think we've reached a very special place in our relationship."

Not a relationship. Let your freak flag fly. It's all good but it won't be with me, you weirdo.

"You're right. If you're ever in need for another job like this, hire someone else."

I unraveled the AC from my blade and dropped it with the others. If they were too afraid to move it, I was sure Landon had someone who could help them.

Backing out of the room, I kept my blade in my hand and my guard up as I quickly made my way out of the house. I stayed on high alert until I was safely in the car. I texted Wendy to inform her that the Amber Crocus had been found. She received the same response I gave Landon when she inquired who had taken it. After I reminded her that the oath still stood, I tossed my phone aside and headed home.

CHAPTER 22

*M*s. Harp, if nothing else, you are consistent, I thought when the silver 911 Carrera started following me once I turned onto the main road leading to my apartment. I decreased my speed to a snail's pace, forcing the sports car tailing me to do the same. Checking my rearview mirror, I expected to see a look of irritation from Asher; instead, there was a smirk of comfortable arrogance. Several blocks he kept with that pace, then he moved past me and slammed on his brakes, forcing me to stop. He was out of his car and walking toward mine moments later.

His smile vanished when he saw me.

I didn't bother to let my window down; he could hear me clearly through it. "What embellished tale did Ms. Harp give you this time?"

He tapped on my window, requesting me to lower it. His expression grew severe. "There's blood on your shirt."

"It's not mine, it's Landon's."

He blew out an exasperated huff. "Erin, what happened?"

We were just a few blocks from my house, and I wanted a shower and a drink and to vent. I sighed. "Let me get home and shower, and I'll tell you everything. Okay?"

213

He nodded, got back in the car, and zoomed away. I'd probably make it to my place before him, because he was definitely getting a speeding ticket.

———

Asher hadn't gotten a ticket. He was standing next to his car, waiting on me when I pulled into the parking lot. Pulling in next to him, I got out and put my bag of weapons over my shoulder; the stake I'd used on Landon was in the other. It needed to be cleaned. When I opened my trunk to get the overnight bag, Asher grabbed it.

"I need to refill it," I explained in answer to his inquiring gaze. Typically I kept enough clothes for a couple days in the bag, but the looming feeling of being Malific's target made me think it would be wise to have at least a week's worth, if not two.

Ms. Harp's door eased open just a crack at my arrival at my door.

"Look who I found loitering," I announced to the spy. She was trying to be inconspicuous, but I refused to make that possible.

"Hi, Erin. I thought I heard noise in the hallway."

And you were going to check it out and report to Asher.

My lips spread into a wide, overly enthusiastic grin. "It's just us."

Asher greeted her with a wave. Her attention homed in on the overnight bag he was carrying, and Team Asher was unable to hide her delight.

"Good. You seem to be in better spirits, too. Earlier you looked distressed, I was worried. I'm glad to see you're okay. You two have a good night." She needed to work on her covert looks because I didn't miss the one she shot at Asher.

"I'm sure your spy told you about my visitor earlier." I

shrugged off the bag and put it next to the door. Then I toed off my shoes and took my overnight bag from Asher.

Lips curling into a wry smile, he said, "She might have mentioned that you had a guest and you seemed uneasy. Not a lot of detail."

I didn't believe that for one moment. There was detail, play-by-play detail of his description and everything that occurred during her interruption.

"Did she just mention it in passing?"

He shrugged. "Yeah, she happened to mention it."

"Then you decided to find me."

He busied himself with the knickknacks on my table, feigning indifference.

"How did you know where to find me?" I asked.

His tongue slid over his lips, I guess savoring the lie. "I'm a hunter, I hunt."

I didn't push, because I knew I'd get the same answer.

"I did have a guest and it was my dad," I told him.

He stopped playing with the little figure on my table and gave me his undivided attention. "What happened?"

I looked down at my shirt. "Shower first." I wanted to get the blood off me and sort through the information to reveal. My feelings were too raw and the newness still felt unsettling. A shower would give me a moment to sort things out and maybe get a better perspective. I grabbed my overnight bag to pack it while I was in the bedroom.

In my room, the gravity of everything finally hit me. I had magic. I. HAD. MAGIC. No more borrowing it and no more longings. My life had irrefutably changed.

The influx of emotions was hard to control. Relief. Fear. Euphoria. The culmination of them was impossible to sort. So I just let them pour into me, accepting it as my new normal.

I was sure using magic to close a door, retrieve my clothes, and turn on the shower would soon get old, but I enjoyed it. The shower had given me clarity, something I needed, although it didn't wash away the unnerving feeling I got from knowing the reason for my birth, my father's role in it, and that my aunt wanted me killed.

The smell of food had me rushing out of my room. I tossed my overnight bag in the living room and headed for the kitchen, where Asher was unpacking a takeout bag.

Becks Grill.

"I figured you probably needed to eat and this is your favorite burger place."

He pushed the container to me when I took a seat at the counter. "Medium well, just the way you like it." Disgust rang in his voice.

He hated seeing me eat my "overcooked" burger just as much as I hated seeing him eat his undercooked one. I had to look away when he took a bite.

"Why do you do that?" he asked, taking a seat next to me.

"What? Look away whenever you try to eat a raw cow in front of me?" I said, getting an eyeful of the barely cooked burger. Rare. It was the only way he'd eat his steak and his burgers. We were equally appalled by each other's meal.

He chuckled and took another big bite.

"Thank you," I said between bites. "You didn't have to do this. I have food."

"I looked in your fridge. It's cute that you're calling that food. Pizza bagels, a box of frozen macaroni, a burrito, and that salmon in your freezer looks suspect."

"I don't like to cook."

"What? I never would have guessed." He flashed me a grin.

I hadn't realized I was so hungry. After I scarfed down my burger, Asher pushed another container to me. Asher and I didn't have the same taste in burgers but we both loved our Texas cheese fries.

We picked at the fries while I shared my day, leaving out

the part about Elizabeth setting me up to be dealt with by the Huntsmen. Asher's face remained impassive throughout the retelling, except when he gave me a glimpse of surprised satisfaction when I told him about staking Landon.

"What are you *not* telling me?" he asked. Head tilted, he studied me.

"Things that I can't share," I admitted. I started chewing on my lower lip as if I feared the words would escape.

Giving me a weak smile, he returned to the fries, picking at them as if he'd lost the taste for them. He folded his arms and studied me for a long moment.

"A strange man comes to your home, tells you he's your father and has been stalking you for most of your life, asks you to go to his sister's house, and not one time did you consider bringing someone with you?" His voice was strangely neutral but his eyes were intense with frustration, irritation, and definitely anger.

"Sometimes I go with my gut," I admitted, feeling a little embarrassed by how irrational my behavior seemed.

"Until it's ripped out of you." He bit his lip and rubbed his hand along the shadow of a forming beard.

"Ouch." It wasn't just the image the words elicited but the roughness of his words.

Again, I was under his scrutiny.

"With you, I have no idea if you're overzealously brave or needlessly reckless," he whispered.

"It was my father, and something in me, maybe instinct, or the way he looked at me, made me feel"—I wanted to say "safe," but I remembered his role in me being here and I went with—"like he wouldn't hurt me."

Asher's finger lightly traced small circles on my hand. "I'm just a phone call or text away. If I can't be with you, I have hundreds of people at my command. You don't have to go at anything alone, Erin."

Before I could answer, he said, "Just remember that, okay?"

In an effort to avoid his weighted and uncompromising gaze, I moved my attention to my fries, placing an absurdly inordinate amount of concentration into making sure I had a balance of cheese, bacon, jalapenos, and fries each time I ate a bite. The fries would have continued being my top priority, except after an eddy of silence, Asher went to the fridge and took out a small to-go container.

He opened it, revealing a piece of strawberry cake.

"Who's the cake for?"

He flushed and looked away. "Evelyn," he admitted.

"No dessert for us," I teased. Kind of teased. Okay, I wasn't kidding at all. I wanted dessert.

He took out another container and handed it to me. "You don't like their strawberry cake."

I didn't like anyone's strawberry cake. Not everything should be made into a cake. I'm looking at you, carrot. Inside the container were salted dark chocolate brownie sticks and berry sauce. We'd eaten at Becks three, maybe four times. I couldn't believe he'd remembered.

"You're the best!" Despite getting magic, it had been a rough day. No matter what anyone said, brownies made it better.

He flashed me his trademark smirk. "Admitting it is the first step." Then he slipped out of the door.

While he was gone, I opened some wine, poured us both a glass, and moved them and the brownie sticks to the living room.

My kitchen stools weren't as comfortable as the couch.

"I thought you'd be gone longer," I said, when Asher returned.

"No, she was watching *Judy* and was quite insistent that I return. *But*, not before initially declining the cake and giving graphic details as to how I can use it as a form of seduction with you. Can't get that imagery out of my head or unhear anything she said," he said.

Almost everyone in this city has seen you naked because you'll change from your wolf anywhere, and this is what left you scandalized?

"I have to hear what she said," I probed.

"Not a chance."

I laughed so hard I snorted.

"Well, *that's* hot. I want to seduce the hell out of you right now, using all her strawberry cake strategies." Immediately he made a face of regret, I assumed from invoking memories of the conversation. Sinking onto the sofa next to me and grabbing the glass, he shifted his body to look at me. From the long draw he took from the glass, it seemed he hoped he would get drunk, or at the very least chase away the imagery.

Asher gave the glass an appreciative nod. I didn't usually have good wine and definitely not Léoville Las Cases quality. I didn't want to get used to it, but I was starting to appreciate it.

Setting the glass of wine on the table, he relaxed back on the sofa, clasping his fingers behind his head.

"Malific," he started out slowly, tentatively. "Do you really think she's coming after you?" Before I could answer he added, "You've read stories about her from books Mephisto provided to you." A frown beveled his lips at the mention of Mephisto's name. "And everyone's telling you how horrible and dangerous she is, but what evidence do *you* have that she is?"

"I don't know. But the Immortalis tried to abduct me in the street," I pointed out.

"Did they say they were working on her behalf? Could their actions be self-serving? Hopes that she'd be able to find a way to get them back into the Veil?"

I considered it for longer than I wanted to because there was a small flame of hope still burning that I was more to my birth parents than a pawn. I wanted my birth mother to be more than the monster in the stories.

Asher's concerned look was the last thing I needed. I busied myself with refolding the clothes I'd stuffed into my overnight bag. He seemed to recognize that I didn't want to continue in the direction the conversation was quickly devolving into. Instead, he asked about my magical abilities.

Between shoving things into the bag, I stopped. "I've only had it for a few hours and haven't been able to really delve into it. So far, I've established I can do disarming magic, and defensive and offensive magic." I walked to the front door and swept my finger over the threshold as I whispered a spell. A purplish shimmer flared, followed by an illumination that spread over the length of the entryway, creating an invisible barrier. It was a simple ward, a simple deterrent, but I was confident I could make a stronger one. I returned to Asher. "And wards. All the things that I could do when I borrowed magic from others. I haven't tried spellweaving."

He gave me in inquiring look.

"It's creating your own spell from other spells," I told him. Not all witches or mages were adept at it. Cory was a great spellweaver. "I'm an elf/god hybrid. I have no idea what my brand of magic can do."

Asher didn't bother to hide what he was thinking in the look he gave me: Should I have cut my ties with my father?

"I'm not sure what to do," I admitted, dropping into the seat next to him. My frown wouldn't relax.

"You don't have anyone else to teach you about your magic," he said.

I did when it came to my god magic; it was the elf part that was missing. I needed to figure out how to use it, especially if it was the only magic that could be used against a god.

. . .

Overnight bag shouldered, I followed Asher out to put my bag into the trunk of my car. I appreciated the companionable silence because my mind was racing, like the magic that continued to run through me. It was surreal to finally have my own.

After I put my bag in the trunk, I gave Asher a small wave.

"Goodnight," Asher said, with a pause before getting in his car. He stopped, then leaned forward and pressed a kiss on my cheek. Pulling back, his eyes grazed over my lips before kissing them. Soft and tentative. His fingers curled into my waist, the kiss becoming more fervid as warmth moved through me. He lightly nipped at my lip as he pulled away, leaving me softly panting.

"Night," I breathed out in a barely audible whisper.

Asher's movement was a lightning strike, grabbing the arrow just inches before it hit my throat. Choking out a gasp, we both scanned in the direction from where it came. We raced together toward the building where the shadowy figure of a tall and lanky person, I suspected a man, stood on the roof.

I glimpsed the odd red illumination of his eyes before they snapped to Asher, who was charging toward him. I was paces behind Asher. The shooter's attention stayed focused on Asher, who looked like he planned to use the car parked in front of the building as leverage to jump to the roof.

The streetlights were out, probably the work of the assailant, making the area dark. Asher may not have needed light, but I did. With only the soft glow of the moon, I managed to make out the man stripping off his shirt. Gathering magic into a ball, I sent it soaring at him. It smashed into him and dissipated in a wash of amber color, leaving the would-be assassin unscathed. He yanked off his pants, keeping an eye on Asher, who was making his second attempt to leap to the roof.

With a second failed attempt, Asher ran toward the back

of the building to look for another way up. I ran toward my car for my gun, only to return to see a hawk fly from the roof. It was too far away for me to hit and it quickly disappeared into the night.

"Shifter," Asher ground out angrily.

Not any shifter, one from the Veil. We didn't have bird shifters on this side.

"I think that might have disproved my theory," he admitted drily, shoving his hand through his hair and disheveling it more. He lifted his nose to the air as if he was trying to commit the smell to memory.

I nodded. Whether the hawk shifter was a follower or just a paid assassin, it was obvious that the arrow was intended to kill me. I was pretty sure who had sent him. I wrapped my arms around myself to stop the chill that ran through me, but it didn't help.

"Your heart's still racing," Asher said.

"I'm fine."

"Lie."

Neither of us looked at each other, keeping an eye on the area.

"Stay with me," Asher suggested.

"What, no dinner and wooing? Just straight to it." It was a faint and pitiful effort to try not to spiral into fear.

"You shouldn't be alone. You can either stay with me or at the pack's safehouse."

"I should be fine. I have a ward at the door that prevents people from Wynding or coming through the Veil to my home. I'll put a ward at the front door to keep all magic wielders out. No one will be able to get to me."

"Are you sure?" he asked. "Because shifters can get through wards."

"For shifters, I have a trunk full of silver knives and bullets. I'll be fine."

I felt confident and didn't think it was a lie. If Asher

believed it was one, he didn't call me on it. It took him a moment before he got into his car. Eventually he did, and as he drove off, I questioned if I was making a mistake. One attempt had been made; I couldn't be sure there wouldn't be another.

CHAPTER 23

*D*istracted by the text from Mephisto with the code to the gate of his home, I nearly face-planted over the massive wolf lying just outside my door. A mass of black fur blocked my exit. He simply looked up with disinterest and returned his large head to his equally enormous paws. When I tried to step over him, he stood. His body reached my waist. My track and field abilities had much to desire, and hurdling over him was the only way I'd be able to clear his height.

"Move," I asserted with the command of an Alpha. Or what I suspected. I'd seen Asher command his pack; it had an undertone of authority but not the bluster that I put in it.

Did that damn wolf just snicker at me?

His head butted into my hip, pushing me back when I attempted to squeeze past him.

"I said move," I demanded. *Okay, that's not working.* "On the authority of your Alpha, I command you to move."

I didn't think it would work, but it was worth a shot. A four-legged animal giving you a look of derisive amusement is more demeaning than you'd imagine. Livid, I backed away, closed the door, and yanked my phone out of my purse.

"There's a massive bear-like wolf at my door," I said as soon as Asher answered the phone.

"Erin," he greeted, casual confidence in his voice.

"Your ginormous shifter is at my door. I need him *not* to be there."

"Ah, that's Daniel. He's a Mackenzie Valley wolf. He's terrifyingly large, isn't he? Been with the pack for about a year. He's a transfer from Alaska. Speaks four languages."

"Thanks for the biography. Is English one of those languages because I told him to move and he didn't budge."

"He'll move, if instructed by me."

"Then do that."

The stretch of silence led to me pushing Asher's name through clenched teeth to get a response.

"Yesterday someone attempted to assassinate you," he said.

"I know, I was there." I made an unsuccessful attempt at keeping my voice tepid and even.

"I like having you around, so I plan to make sure you are." Then there was silence. Not a pause. Silence from him disconnecting as if the conversation was over.

The second time, he got a video call because I wanted him to see my scowl.

"Hello again." The airiness of his tone just added fodder to the flames of exasperation. The dichotomy of my feelings didn't help. It was hard not to appreciate his caring, but he was doing it wrong. He was Alpha-ing it up and I wasn't sure he knew any other way to do it.

"Asher. I appreciate your concern, and if you weren't with me yesterday, things would have been bad for me."

"You would have been dead. Things would have been bad for the people you left behind," he rebutted.

Seeing the anger pass over his face, I blew out a breath.

"I know. What's your plan? For me to be holed up in my

225

home forever? I have magic I need to explore, and I need to see Mephisto."

His teeth gripped the bottom of his lip. "Why him? What is he? I've been curious about him and I suspect you know."

Holding his intense gaze became a struggle with each beat of time. "The secrets that we have will always stay between us. I know it's difficult, but you need to extend the same consideration for others' secrets as you have for your pack."

Asher's face relaxed. "I guess I should ask him."

"Probably." *Good luck getting an answer.*

Asher raised his voice just a few decibels and told Daniel he could leave. I gave him a smile of appreciation and a thanks as my parting remarks. Despite knowing how sensitive shifter hearing was, it was still hard to imagine Daniel had heard.

He was trotting away by the time I made it to the door. He had the good manners to have his back to me as he slipped on his pants. When you live in a city heavily populated with shifters, seeing a naked ass was as common as seeing a bare arm. You learn that you're more embarrassed by it than they are.

Pulling out of the driveway, I wasn't the least bit surprised to have a tail. It was more surprising that it was only one.

Pick your battles, Erin, I encouraged myself. It was the only thing that kept me from calling Asher again.

My shifter escort followed me to Mephisto's gate, and once I drove through it, out of my rearview mirror, I saw them turn around and leave.

Walking to the door, too many thoughts and questions ran through my mind. Was I immortal now, despite being a demigod? What were my magical limitations? The previous night, instead of sleeping, I'd performed almost all the spells in my spell books, and shifted to a cat using a transformation spell. My transformation ability seemed to be just cats. I spent an hour unsuccessfully trying to transform into a hawk.

I'd also discovered I couldn't Wynd, and I was positive I didn't have Kai's ability to fly. Two hours and nearly passing out from trying to sprout wings proved that.

The many nuances and differences in magic were so vast. Cory wasn't able to Wynd, even with magic-boosting charms, but there were very few spells he couldn't cast.

For a person with cameras in his home, a space secluded from most of his neighbors, and a "Benton," I always found it odd that Mephisto left his door open so often. Met with silence when I entered the home, I called his name. The room where I usually found Benton was empty. I called for Mephisto again.

"You've seen your father." His voice came from behind me, startling me.

Hand to my chest, I spun around. "What?" I managed through my rapid breaths.

Moving in with the eerie speed that I decidedly would never get used to, his attentive eyes slowly roved over me.

"You've met your father," he repeated, his attention uncompromising.

I had no idea how he deduced that. "How do you know?"

A slow, easy smile lifted his lips. "You have magic. I can feel it coming off you."

I wondered if my magic felt the same as his did to me. Did it have a distinct allure? It felt different being around him without the ache to get closer and draw in his magic. But there was still an undeniable lure that I ignored because it had nothing to do with his magic.

"Yeah, I met my father," I confirmed.

"You have your magic," he said, stepping back to take me in as if being presented with a new person of interest.

I told him about meeting Nolan, giving him the unedited version, including why Elizabeth told them who I was and her theft of the Amber Crocus. His only response was an extended blink and an unreadable expression. His lack of denial didn't go unnoticed. He would have handled the situation differently if it were anyone other than me.

"Did he show you how to do defensive *moirus*? They're stronger than even a Klipsen or Omni ward, or the *adligatura*. I believe that's what they used to restrict your magic."

I shook my head as he peppered me with more questions about spells and depths of my elven magic that I hadn't explored with Nolan. His disappointment flashed enough for me to get a glimpse of it before it faded. A look of impassivity claimed his face, but his flat dark eyes showed something different.

"Did he share any of their spells with you? Erin, there haven't been sightings of elves in over fifty years. Knowledge of their magic isn't an opportunity that most will get. Because their magic is so different, they can cast spells similar to fae, witches, and mages, but infinitely different and they can't be countered. It gives you an advantage over most, even us."

I knew that, and for us on this side of the Veil, it had been longer than that. Elves were considered extinct.

"You've had a sighting of at least one. Elizabeth. She's a fae/elf hybrid and my father's sister."

The new information only caused him to blink once. What caused the blink, that my aunt approached them with the information about who I was? Or that she was an elf?

"She told you about The Raven, didn't she?"

He gave me a small nod.

"Are you aware of what her intentions were when she told you that?"

"She is aware of my disdain for Malific." His tone was as neutral as his face.

I moved closer to him. His long fingers stroked along the contours of my cheek.

"Malific is evil. I didn't want her to ever get out. If a person existed who had the power to release her, I would do what was necessary to prevent that," he said. "Or at least I thought I would." The dejection in his voice made me wonder if he felt he'd compromised himself by not following through.

His phone buzzing prevented further conversation. Glancing down at the phone before answering it, his expression mirrored the one Asher gave me earlier.

"Asher." Mephisto's voice was brusque and cool. "How may I help you?" Insincerity and forced politeness rang in his words. Mephisto's eyes met mine and remained there as he moved closer to me. His head bent down, the phone to his ear but positioned so I could hear. Cedar, spice, and his scent drifted under my nose.

"What are you?" Asher asked.

"I'm sorry?" Mephisto's lips brushed my skin as he spoke.

"Sorry about what? Pretending you didn't hear me the first time or that you're using your question to give you more time to make up an answer?" Asher asked coolly.

"No to either."

"I'm just curious as to why Erin had to see you. She's there now, isn't she?"

Mephisto's voice was a low husky rumble. "Yes, Erin is right here." I didn't like the implication or the innuendo in his tone.

"She told me this morning she'd be visiting you." I didn't care for it in Asher's, either.

Why don't they just shout out the length and see who wins?

Slipping away from Mephisto, I glared at him and then the phone. The phone received the glower meant for Asher. "Erin is half god, half elf and after discovering this, she comes to you. Is it safe to speculate—"

"You're welcome to speculate whatever you wish. Have a

good day, Asher." Mephisto ended the call, silenced the phone, and placed it on the table.

That's not going to go over well.

He shelved the conversation with Asher with the same ease he'd discarded his phone. It was on the tip of my tongue to remind him that Asher commanded hundreds and, thanks to me, they were immune to magic, including his.

"I didn't get a chance to talk to him very much after he removed the restriction." I felt irked by my outburst at Nolan and Elizabeth. But I had cause. I must not have hidden it well, because Mephisto looked sympathetic.

"Since you are here, perhaps you should show me your skills with the sword." He inched closer and extended his hand. I guessed that was my cue to give him Kai's blade. I took it from the sheath at my waist and handed it to him.

"Thank you. Kai will be delighted to have the set now."

"He's very particular, isn't he?"

"Yes." A fleeting look of concern skimmed over his face. The same disquieting look they all shared when it came to Kai.

He moved down the hall and I followed him to the gym where he'd sparred with Kai. He shrugged off his jacket and placed it on a hook on the other side of the room. Should I be impressed by his skills or insulted by his confidence that he could test my skills without difficulty while wearing slacks and a shirt?

I looked down at my slip-on running shoes, leggings, fitted t-shirt and then to him dressed in slate-gray pants and a button-down shirt that he'd uncuffed and rolled to his forearms.

"I feel underdressed," I mocked, giving his attire a derisive sneer.

"Ah, Ms. Jensen, is that a proposition? Shall we do this in less clothing?"

Why would he want his jiggly bits out with a sword around?

Not taking his bait, I remained silent as he walked to the wall of weapons.

"Practice sword?" he asked, fighting the smirk that played at his lips. It wasn't ego or his thinly veiled mocking. Even the best practice sword didn't replicate a sword, often being too light and not balanced enough. The recoil from hard contact with another was an odd feeling that I couldn't get used to. I'd rather practice with a blunt sword or the real thing.

"No waster swords. The real thing, or are you afraid?" I asked.

"This will be interesting."

Taking a longsword from the wall, he handed it to me. It didn't have any markings like the Obitus blade but was similarly shaped. Mephisto picked up another.

I warmed up, sweeping the sword in smooth figure eights, thrusts, and overhead diagonals to test my defense, counters, and strikes.

"Ready?" he asked.

His strikes were fast but not blurs of movement as they were with Kai. He was holding back and I didn't want that. Malific wouldn't hold back.

Each of his strikes, he pulled, giving me a chance to block. Each thrust was preceded by a slow-foot advance, alerting me of his intended move. It was barely a step above novice techniques.

Countering his strike with a block, I spun out of reach until I was behind him, then swept his foot. He crashed to the ground. A quick roll and he was back on his feet with my sword pointing at him. A dark look eclipsed his face, hints of menace rolling over his features as he stepped closer until the tip of my sword pressed into his skin. Then he moved forward slightly and it pierced his skin. As quickly as the injury occurred, it disappeared, leaving behind the blood that had welled from it, which he quickly wiped away.

"What are you, a masochist? Why did you do that?"

His weapon was in his hand and thrust at me. I shuffled back without the grace I'd demonstrated before. The thrust, which he'd pulled, stopped just short of my chest and demonstrated his mastery of skills and control. I looked down at his weapon and its location and took a step back, locking my eyes on his as I moved.

"You have to learn to use your magic to heal yourself as you fight," he said. "It won't take away the pain, but it'll stop your injuries being a disadvantage." Again I was treated to his quick movements and him just inches from me. "I suppose in some way I am a masochist... How else would I explain us? I can assure you, the last thing I want is to be in my basement just sparring with you." His eyes held undeniable yearning as he stepped away.

"How do I do that? Heal while fighting," I clarified, dragging my eyes to the wall behind him because I wasn't sure he wouldn't get his wish if I didn't.

He said several words and instructed me to repeat them. A heavy cloak of magic, uncomfortable and cumbersome, covered me, making each movement seem like I was wading through thick mud.

"You'll get used to it. But you want the ability to heal during a fight. Your deity magic will protect you, but your magical ability will be limited. It's best to learn to engage it when needed." It was a complicated process that I'm sure wasn't easily mastered.

He placed his sword against the wall, grabbed a blade from the cabinet, and returned to me.

"Let's try it," he directed.

I lowered my sword to the ground and extended my hand.

The blade barely pressed into my skin, just a nick.

I looked at my hand and scoffed. "What's that? I've gotten worse from a paper cut. I don't need magic to heal that. I give it a stern look and it might heal on its own. I need a bigger cut."

I closed my eyes and waited and nothing happened. Just him staring at me with a vacant look. He handed me the knife and stepped away.

"You do it," he suggested, putting several inches of space between us.

It was the first time I'd seen him without his bold self-assurance. Unable to hold my stare, his eyes dropped to the floor as I closed my hand around the blade, hissing from the pain. When I opened my hand I could see the stain but no visible cut.

"Like I said, it doesn't take the pain away."

I shrugged. "I'm going to go with the 'don't get injured' option and save myself the trouble," I said.

His throaty laughter filled the room, and within beats, he'd devoured the distance between us, taking the hand I'd cut. He ran his hand over it, removing the light crimson stains that remained. Then he kissed the palm of my hand.

"You are so undeniably Erin," he whispered against my ear.

"I don't know what that means."

"But you do," he replied in a low raspy growl.

The heat of his lips warmed me. I should have stepped away, but my body didn't want to. I stayed, rooted in the spot.

My fingers grasped the soft fabric of his shirt, grazing against the hardness of his abs.

His eyes trailed from my hand on his waist, over my arm, to the contours of my face, lips, and back up to meet my eyes.

"What will you use now?" he asked, his voice low and rough.

"For what?" My voice was breathy and jagged. I inhaled, taking in his masculine scent that was laced with hints of the cedar scent of his magic. It lingered and taunted my senses.

"You have magic now and no longer need to borrow mine. What will you use to justify what exists between us?" He pressed soft kisses on my lips, imploring an answer I couldn't give. It made me question too many things and dive too hard into feelings and raw attraction to this enigmatic man who had chosen the name Mephisto as his moniker, that I wasn't ready to address.

Moving my hands from his waist, I took several large steps back. He did the same but with a faster pace and a greater distance.

"How do I disengage the healing magic?"

He told me the words. I quickly repeated them, appreciating the new feeling of weightlessness I felt when I picked up my sword. "Ready?"

Seconds later, he was at the wall, weapon in hand.

"How do I move like that?" I asked, again looking at the wall behind him. He responded to my inability to look at him with a faint chuckle.

"It's not a spell, you just do it."

"Okay, Nike, what do you mean, I just do it?"

"That I can't explain. It's the way you move. Like walking, except you force your body to move faster. Try it."

"I will." It was definitely not something I wanted to do in front of an audience. I imagined me looking like a fawn learning to walk, but not nearly as adorable.

Assuming ready position, this time Mephisto didn't hold back. The clink of metal on metal filled the room. And the whoosh of our breath being pushed once our weapons had been discarded and we started to spar. He blocked a front kick directed at his chest. Grabbing my leg, he gave it a jerk, causing me to crash to the ground. Retreating back just beats, I swiped his leg again. Rolling to my feet, fatigue had set in, but I refused to give up. The pleasure of seeing signs of fatigue on him, too, tugged a smile to my lips.

Being a better defensive fighter than offensive, I waved him forward.

The shift in his appearance caught me off guard and I stopped mid-movement to take in the subtle changes. It was the reason Elizabeth questioned their identity. His short midnight hair with hues of blue was the same. His nose longer, aquiline. Lips fuller and a little wider. The lines of his jaw sharper, his cheeks broader and winged. The person in front of me looked like a distant relative of the man I knew, and if I hadn't seen the glamour fall, I would have questioned his identity as well.

With the ease and efficiency that he'd dropped it, he donned it again. Mephisto.

That moment of shock he used to his advantage. It was a sphere of magic zooming at me that caused me to erect a magical protective wall. His magic hit it and disintegrated in a puff. He moved to the wall that I'd surrounded myself with. Studying it, his mouth moved. The wall wavered but held. For several minutes he tried to disable it. Walking around it, he examined my wall, thrusting his magic into it.

"You didn't fall for the distraction. Very good," he acknowledged, his fingers gliding lightly over the barrier that separated us.

Distraction was my favorite weapon in my quiver, so I was hyperaware when it was used against me. But his dropping the glamour did distract me. I would have preferred to use offensive magic instead of hiding behind my wall of protection.

"What did you do?" he asked.

"Erected it, like I did when I borrowed magic from others."

"This isn't just a basic ward," he said, still considering my cocoon of protection. "Maybe this is *your* basic ward, when you use *your* magic." He sounded pleased. "It's uniquely Erin. I can't break it."

Which meant it was probably elven magic. Which was fine, but I needed to learn when to tap into it. The thought made me frustrated with the way I had left things with my father. It was apparent there were plenty of things I needed to learn from him. I dropped the ward and Mephisto quickly removed any space it had put between us.

"Glamours. I need to learn to do them."

He frowned.

"What?"

"I don't know if you'll be able to do them. Neither Oedeus nor Malific could. That was one of the advantages we had over them. But you will be able to do things others can't, and that will follow your bloodline." There was hesitation in his voice.

"Because I'm a demi, I'll be limited?"

"Not at all. You're a demi with elven abilities. I suspect, *my* demigoddess, the things you will be able to do will far exceed what you cannot," he whispered against my lips. "You are far from limited." There was more than his typical spark of curiosity and intrigue. His eyes were pools of desire and craving, and the heat of his body enveloped me.

Mephisto kissed me, awakening sensations I hadn't known existed. He claimed my mouth with kisses that were soft but firm, tracing them along my jaw until he made his way to my ear. His breath was warm. I shuddered from the delicate and yearning touch. How could one man be simultaneously voracious heat and gentle allure?

"What's your name?" I asked when the kiss ended. He'd shown me his true face.

A wicked smile hovered at the corners of his lips. "Mephisto."

Oh, yeah. There he is.

His lips crushed into mine as he backed me against the wall, running a delicious path from my lips to my neck. Firm, delicate hands caressed my breasts as I arched into him.

Tangling my fingers through his hair, I pulled him closer, tasting the intensity of his kiss and the hardness of his body.

His name, our history, and his history in the Veil was overshadowed by his touch. The heat that was left by his barest touch, the way he moaned my name between kisses. His raspy rough whispers calling me his demigoddess as he slipped my shirt off and nipped and licked the exposed skin, then trailed his lips back up to mine. I quickly started to unbutton his shirt, fighting the urge to rip it off him. His hand inched over my waist, kneading my skin, traveling to the edge of my panties.

A throat clearing had us pulling apart and me crossing my arms over my chest to cover my half-exposed breasts.

"Clayton, hi," I fumbled out, dropping to my knees to retrieve my shirt and quickly put it on.

Expressionless, Clayton's steps were slow and measured as he moved toward us with the same sly-footed ease that had left him undetected as he entered the room.

Heat warmed my cheeks and the bridge of my nose. I didn't embarrass easily when it came to sex. I'm pretty sure at some point in my life, I was doing it in front of an audience or at the very least had been heard. But under Clayton's appraising gaze, I felt uncomfortable. His gaze swept from me to give a look of castigation to Mephisto.

Mephisto's eyes narrowed on Clayton, and whatever passed between them in their silent communication left them glaring at each other.

"I have magic," I blurted, needing something to break the tension. Clayton didn't dislike me, but he definitely disliked me and Mephisto together.

"Yes, I can tell." His voice was soft and warm, diametrically opposed to the stern look he was still leveling at Mephisto.

"We were practicing?" I kept on. Pretty soon I'd be prattling.

"Magic?" he inquired, brows raised.

Yeah, practicing magic. Trying to make each other's clothes disappear and making the other reach the height of pleasure. Under Clayton's scrutiny, I willed the color to leave my face.

"What are you doing here?" Mephisto asked Clayton, rebuttoning his shirt.

"You've always had an open door policy, M. What's changed?" he teased.

"No, you've always *acted* as if I had an open door policy," Mephisto countered in a tight voice. It was obvious he was considering revoking any liberties he had to his house.

Clayton dragged his eyes from Mephisto. "Magic now. Your restrictions were removed by your father?" There was uncertainty in his voice.

I nodded.

"Elf?"

When I confirmed, another look passed between them. Clayton didn't question anymore but instead busied himself with putting away the weapons.

"Let me get the sword for you," Mephisto said.

I followed him upstairs, with Clayton not too far behind. I guess we had earned ourselves a chaperone.

Mephisto went to his office and returned with the sword but didn't look at our chaperone as he offered it to me. Out of my periphery, I could see Clayton watching us with a stringent look, so different than what I was used to. Irritation and curiosity piqued simultaneously, and before I could ask what his problem was with Mephisto and me, Mephisto spoke up.

"You've only had your magic for two days. Practice, and we'll meet up again and see where you are. What I need to show you."

"What *we* need to show her," Clayton said. "We still don't know the extent of her magic. Where you are weak, one of us

238

is stronger. That combination will work best for this situation."

When a knowing look passed between the two of them, I knew we weren't just talking about magic.

With everything that had taken place over the past few days, waiting a day or two to find out was fine with me. Sword in hand, I waved a hasty goodbye.

CHAPTER 24

*T*he same relief I heard in Dr. Sumner's voice when I contacted him for an appointment, after leaving Mephisto's, shone on his face.

When he got out of his car, his lips lifted into a tight-lipped smile. He was dressed in a black t-shirt with *Run DMC* across it in silver letters, a dark-blue jacket, loose-fitting jeans, and his new oversized prescription-less glasses. His beard had filled out. I couldn't force a smile; instead I looked at him, bewildered. He looked like a professor at a school I wasn't cool enough to attend.

Was I unknowingly involved in a ludicrous game of fashion chicken? Would his attire become increasingly cliched or eclectic, his beard transform from a low tidy scruff to something long and unmanageable? His slightly disheveled hair become an unruly mess? And his glasses larger and larger to distract from his light-blue eyes, angular jaw, kind resting smile, and seemingly self-loathed studious good looks?

"This is what you look like when you're resting at home?"

He shrugged. "You wanted to see me."

"It didn't have to be today." I had expected him to give me

a time the next day. I hadn't expected him to tell me to meet him at his office in an hour.

He unlocked the door, letting me in first. Once he was inside, I closed the door with a flick of my finger.

He quickly turned. "You have magic?"

"I have magic." I beamed.

Concern peeked through before he turned from me. "Have a seat. Coffee?"

"No, I'm fine."

"This isn't a tequila-type visit, is it?" His voice was tight, the humor in it forced.

"No, but things are complicated." So complicated.

"You and complicated have formed a bond and seem to have a contentious relationship," he said, preparing himself a cup of tea. Once seated, he took a long sip from his cup, placed it on the table, and grabbed his notepad and pen. "How is Erin?"

I gave him more than a casual update. The dam broke and I flooded him with information. The unabridged version. This was no longer therapy but me venting. Even my therapy was a complicated mess.

"Did the demon want you because you're a demi-elf?"

I laughed, not at his question, but at him referring to me as a demi-elf.

"Why demi-elf?" I asked.

"Why demigod?" he countered. "From what you've told me, it seems like your elven magic is the most powerful. Your wards and spells can't be broken by gods. Demi-elf seems more apropos."

Dr. Sumner was just bizarre and he leaned into it. I liked it. I smiled but kept my opinion to myself.

"No, I don't know if it had anything to do with me being a demi-elf. Harrison was indebted to the demon, and I was the acceptable currency. Never make a deal with a demon," I told him.

"I'll remember that." There was a spark of curiosity intermingled with fear.

I was reluctant to continue, until he urged me to with an expectant look.

"You were right, I wasn't responsible for the *incident*. I didn't kill him. I was set up by my father."

I told him about meeting my father, finding out the WIB was my aunt, and the reason behind my birth. He had managed to keep his face stolid up until that point, then a look of contempt and disgust hardened his features. It took time for him to usher it from his face.

Dr. Sumner placed the notepad on the table and ran his hand over his beard, seemingly having problems processing everything I'd told him.

Imagine living it.

"Your dad wasn't being malicious when he initially took your memories. He thought he was doing the right thing."

"Yet he screwed up. My life changed because of it."

"It did," he agreed. "How does that make you feel?"

I didn't call him out on his cliched question because of the sincerity in his voice and the gentle query in his eyes.

How did it make me feel?

"I feel...wrong," I admitted. "It's hard to feel any other way when you find out that to one parent, you're an instrument for revenge, and the other, an escape tool."

He leaned forward, holding my gaze, his eyes soft and comforting. "Someone else's actions can't define who you are, Erin. There's nothing wrong with you."

It was becoming increasingly hard to look at him, to be in this intense state. Not feeling bad about things didn't change the fact my mother wanted me dead.

I jerked my eyes from his and lay back on the sofa.

"Being human, learning all of this, does it bother you?" I asked.

We lapsed into a long silence. It was so long that I pulled my attention from the ceiling and turned to look at him.

He looked contemplative as he bit his bottom lip. "Let's continue discussing you."

My diversion effort had either failed or he didn't want to admit that it did. I suspected a combination of the two.

My emotional well was dry, and I didn't want to discuss things anymore. "There's not much more to say," I told him. What more was there to report other than my life was a hot mess and I needed to fix it?

"What do you plan to do about your mother?"

That was an excellent question; what do I do about a woman who had already sent an assassin for me?

"I don't know." I shrugged. "Try not to get killed by her." I glanced at the clock on my phone. I'd been talking for nearly an hour and a half. "I should go."

"You don't have to," he offered. I knew if I felt depleted from talking about it, he had to feel that way from hearing it. But he looked earnest.

"No, I should go. I really need to figure things out," I told him as I stood up. "Thank you for seeing me today."

He nodded. "No problem." There was another stretch of silence. I took that as my cue to leave. Before I could make it to the door, he said, "I'm sending my release orders tomorrow. You will not be court ordered to see me any longer."

The breath that I sucked in caught in the lump that formed in my throat.

"You don't want to see me again," I croaked out, turning to face him. Why did this hurt? It shouldn't hurt. I'd spent a greater part of my time with him trying to get away, and now I felt like my visits with him were one of the few existing tendrils that linked me to my former life. And he'd just snapped it. I blinked, but my vision still blurred.

"No, not at all." He came to his feet moving humanly slow,

making me appreciate the normalcy of typical human grace and speed. Nothing preternatural about him.

He placed his hand on my shoulder and gave it a squeeze. "You can see me whenever you need me. I'm here. It just won't be court ordered. You were seeing me for something you were never guilty of."

I blew out the breath I hadn't realized I'd been holding.

"Will you tell them that?"

He shook his head. "I think the fewer people who know what you are the better."

I nodded, speaking still more difficult than it should be. He wasn't wrong. How would humans deal with the new information: elves, gods, the Huntsmen, the Abyssus, and me, the elf/god hybrid?

"Thank you for keeping my secret, and I'll keep yours."

He furrowed his brow. "What secret?"

"By day you're a mild-mannered therapist hiding behind his eclectic glasses, and at night you take them off and fight crime."

Chuckling, he pushed them farther up his nose. "Nothing that exciting. At night I teach a class twice a week," he said. "Not as interesting as hearing about the day in the life of a demi-elf."

"You're committed to demi-elf?"

Studying me, it seemed like he was determining how I felt about it. Perhaps payback for all the jokes about his glasses. "See you next week, Erin."

I gave him a quick wave. As I headed to my car, a tinge of dread snaked around me at the thought that if it was up to my mother, that would never happen.

CHAPTER 25

Sitting in my apartment under the withering gaze of Madison and Cory, saying my plans out loud, did make me seem reckless and dangerously irresponsible rather than proactive. My conversation with Dr. Sumner made me realize I needed to go on the offensive and not wait around for another attack.

"So," Madison started out slowly, "you want to use your magic to track your mother the way she would have used it to track you?"

Madison's eyes followed Cory as he buzzed around the house straightening things.

I nodded. "I just need to see her." Frustrated, I shoved my hands through my hair. Meet her, kill her, imprison her again. One of those things. There wasn't a concrete end goal. I'd do whatever would make me safe.

"You're being reckless. There, I said it," Cory griped, crossing his arms over his chest and plopping down on the sofa next to Madison. The purse of her lips indicated she agreed.

"I'd rather be the hunter than the hunted. That's what she's doing right now."

"She killed her own brother, who was an Arch-deity and you're—"

"A demigod, and a quarter elf," Cory interrupted. "Because your mother is a god, and your father is half human and half elf. *And* are you even sure you can do elven spells? You were able to do elven spell with Elizabeth and your father's help to lift your restriction. But can you do them alone? And I know you said your ward stopped Mephisto, but that's all you seem to have so far. One magic experience with your sociopathic aunt and your absentee father. So, do you just plan to wing the elven magic part?" Cory was on his feet again, running his fingertips along the slats of the blinds.

"I'm not being reckless. What options do I have?"

Cory blew out an exasperated breath before washing his hands over his face. "Are you sure it was her who sent the shifter-hawk after you?"

"Who else? I don't have a lot of enemies."

Cory and Madison looked at each other then me.

"What?"

"Are you sure about that?" Cory worked at a smile that didn't quite make it to his eyes. "You are rather"—he stopped to search for the right word—"well, you're like an M-80 when people are expecting a little sparkler."

I shot him a dirty look.

"I like that you're a mini bomb," he went on, "storming into places like you own them, guns blazing, wreaking havoc when needed, stabbing vampire Masters, which you did the day before yesterday. Did you forget you did that? Maybe it wasn't Malific, it was him."

He didn't think it was Landon any more than I did. It would be easy to fight the threat we knew about rather than the one we didn't. No matter how difficult, Landon could be handled. Malific was a wild card.

"It wasn't Landon," I confirmed. "We don't have hawk-shifters here and I'm pretty sure he has no knowledge of the Veil."

Cory plumped a cushion vigorously. "I know. An Arch-deity weakened is...what? She can't create people, but there are a lot of levels below that that still might make a force you can't beat."

"I don't need to beat her, I just need to imprison her again."

The situation had to be handled but I didn't want to kill my mother. I didn't want her to kill me, either.

"We know four gods," Cory said. I glared at him. "Fine, we know four gods and an 'Erin.' What's the plan? Lure her somewhere where the Omni ward can be placed?"

I nodded. "But first we need to find her. I don't plan to confront her yet. I just want to know what I'm up against. All I have are secondhand accounts. I want to find her, see her—"

"And then be killed by her," Madison interjected. Worry made her sound harsher than she intended. That's what I hoped, anyway.

"I think you need to make amends with your father. You have abilities that no one other than you, Elizabeth, and Nolan have. Elven magic. Only two people were able to remove the restriction on your magic. If you want to stop her, find a way to imprison her in a manner that's linked to your elven magic. I don't think your ward will be enough. Find something that's bound to you only. That only you can control." Madison paused. "Or kill her." She revealed that last option with such cool indifference that Cory and I both snapped our eyes in her direction.

We lapsed into an uncomfortable silence.

Madison chewed her bottom lip, putting a great deal of effort into biting back what she wanted to say. A fight she apparently lost because she eventually said, "Actually, I think killing her should be plan A. Forget everything else."

Cory didn't blink for a long time, just stared at her with his lips slightly parted.

"She might be right," he added finally, joining Team Kill Malific. "She killed her brother, she attacked and killed shifters during a full moon in the middle of their change, she wiped out a race of people, and she's trying to kill you. I think she's beyond redemption, mercy, or being given any benefit of the doubt. Get rid of her and her sycophants and she's no longer a problem. If there are any of her followers left, they won't have her to follow."

"No, but they could dedicate their lives to avenging her," I countered.

From the looks they gave me, I got the impression they'd endorse the same approach for the avenging followers, too.

"I want you to be safe," Madison admitted. "The potential wrath of followers should be the least of your concerns. You safe. That should be your number one focus. And you won't be safe until she's dead."

Killing Malific still wasn't plan A for me, but I definitely wanted to imprison her. And I needed to do it sooner rather than later before there was another attempt on my life.

"I need to go see my aunt."

———

When Madison, Cory, and I got out of the car at Elizabeth's home, Cory shot me a disapproving look as I checked my weapons: sword sheathed at my back, small pouch of shurikens, knife sheathed at my waist. I considered my gun but returned it to the glove compartment.

"Nothing says 'let's make amends' like showing up heavily armed," Cory said.

I looked down at my weapons.

"They aren't gods, so why are you bringing the sword?" he said.

Madison remained quiet but only because her lips were pressed so firmly together words couldn't escape.

I removed the sword and placed it on the backseat and then tugged my shirt to conceal the knife and my pouch. Palming the necklace with the small push knife on it, I started to debate if I was being cautious or paranoid to the point of absurdity.

"Someone tried to kill me, and if it wasn't for Asher, they might have succeeded," I said. It was enough of an explanation to deter any further comment or judgmental looks as we made our way along the path to Elizabeth's home. We needed to talk to her, and my father if he was there. If he wasn't, I hoped she would give me a way to get in touch with him.

After dealing with the forest of misdirection, our advance was blocked by the imperious imp who took gratuitous pleasure at looking down his nose at us, over his glasses.

"Erin and company," he said, with even more formality to his patrician English. He straightened his striped tie before giving his dark-blue vest a tug to neaten it. "I assume you are here to see the mistress of the house."

"Yes, I'm here to see Elizabeth, and Nolan, if he's still here."

He turned his nose up at the annoyance in my voice.

"I seem to remember that your parting words were for them to go to hell. Am I to believe you changed your mind?" he asked.

Jaw set, I gave him back the same look of derisive judgment he was giving us.

"We suspected you'd be back once you'd had your little outburst. I suggested we have a binky prepared for you the next time you have one of your fits of pique."

I pressed my tongue to my teeth to keep from telling him what he could do with the binky.

"Please, follow me."

"That was easy, no riddle, no fire Mirra, just a short conversation with a judgmental imp," Cory whispered.

When the imp turned, I thought it was to respond to Cory, but instead he started to change. His body morphed. His red leathery skin stretched as his body grew to the massive creature who had tossed us off the property on our first visit. His small horns extended and curved. Machete-sharp claws replaced his smaller ones.

Just as his transformation finished, an arrow hit him in the chest and another went into his shoulder. He stumbled back. Magic spun around Cory's hand with a turbulent force and he tossed it into the chest of the tall, lanky man just a few feet away, who was definitely my attacker. Cory's magic blanketed him without any effect.

The shifter wielded his weapon with an assassin's determination, shifting from his initial target of Arius to Cory, who dove out of the way. The arrow missed his head but embedded in his shoulder. He gritted his teeth to suppress the cry of pain.

Madison used magic to rip branches from the trees. They whipped and whirled in front of the shifter, obstructing his view. Undeterred, he continued his determined stalk toward us. A swift change of direction sent an arrow in Madison's direction. A wave of her hand sent it off course. The knife he sent would have hit her if I hadn't lunged at her and knocked her to the ground. We rolled away, out from the arrows coming at us rapid fire.

As he got closer, Madison relentlessly used her magic, frustrated at its failure.

"It's a shifter from the Veil, the one from yesterday," I warned her. From my angle, it looked as if he had eight, maybe nine more arrows. I was his target. I stood and ran to the left, distracting him, watching out of my periphery as Cory came to his feet with a wince. Blood stained his shirt and he grimaced with movement. Cory ran toward the shifter. With single-minded focus, the shifter sacrificed protecting himself to get off the shot that would have hit me in the neck if I hadn't dropped to the ground.

Cory careened into the shifter with the force of his body, knocking the bow out of his hand. The shifter's hard strike to Cory's jaw made his hand jerk back from the impact. Another hard hit and I thought I heard bones crack. The shifter was stronger and faster. As they exchanged vicious blows, Cory attempted to fend off the punches as they rolled on the ground. The shifter was twisting his body at an awkward angle. I quickly realized that he was going for a knife.

Yanking out my own knife, I raced toward them, looking briefly away when Nolan yelled my name. He was rushing toward me with Elizabeth close behind him. Her attention wasn't on me but on Arius, who was lying on the ground, taking short ragged breaths, making unsuccessful attempts to dislodge the arrows.

"Erin!" Nolan called my name with more urgency, but I ignored him. The shifter had gotten the advantage and was on top of Cory, who was trying to ward off the shifter's strikes. The shifter risked a look at me and a scan of the area. I sped up, seeing his plan to exit. I shoved the knife into his side, stepped back, positioned my hands, and stuck magic into the hilt, breaking it off and leaving him with no way to pull out the silver blade. He wouldn't be able to heal or shift.

Cory shoved him to the ground as the shifter clawed at his side, trying to remove the embedded blade.

"Back, Erin!" Nolan demanded, tugging at my clothes. "You too," he commanded Cory just as I saw what had put him in such a panic.

The dark-haired woman approaching us had Nolan scrambling to get us safely away from her. Just as I knew when I first saw Nolan, I knew who the dark-haired woman was. She was flanked by another woman and a man. Their rote movements made magic pulse through the air. Nolan pulled something from his pocket and tossed it up. Grainy particles fluttered and floated to the ground. A wave of magic shoved us behind a diaphanous wall stretching over the property and securing us behind it. Magic from the Immortalis slammed into it, causing it to undulate, but the wall held.

We didn't have the woman's attention; she was observing the shifter, who was still grappling at his side, trying to pull out the blade. The lines of the woman's overly angular face softened as she watched him. Warm, sympathetic chestnut-colored eyes appraised him.

"You're hurt," she acknowledged, her voice mellifluous and her demeanor mild in contradiction to her infamous reputation. Mild people didn't send assassins after their children.

"I can't get this fucking knife out of my side," he ground out between the hisses that squeezed through his clenched teeth. He looked at me, his eyes full of his intention to complete his job, just to make me pay.

As she bent to examine him, the sun illuminated the deep red and browns in the French braid that extended to the middle of her back.

"Move your hand. Let me see." She inched in closer. "This is easy enough." Waving her hand as if it was an afterthought, the wedged blade was extracted. It floated in the air while she studied it. "Clever, clever. My daughter is clever." Her eyes flicked to me. Something in them made it apparent that my cleverness wasn't appreciated.

The hawk-shifter's face relaxed. Raising his shirt, he looked at the rapidly healing wound.

"You failed twice," she said in a low, even voice.

She didn't even give him the courtesy of a look before

plunging the floating blade into his throat. I cringed at the gargled sound he made. With casual indifference she pulled out her sword and with one strike finished the job. His body slumped to the ground; I averted my eyes from where the other part of him went.

Sheathing her sword, she advanced to the diaphanous wall that separated us and studied it. "Nolan, you were always full of little tricks, weren't you?"

"And you're still a malicious bitch."

The hatred between them was raging, rampant. His contempt and anger seemed to be woven from years of festering. How the hell did they tolerate each other long enough to have sex? Or had this hate worsened over the twenty-six years of my life? I was a result of this hate. The thought put a heavy weight on me.

"Hi, sweetheart." All the warmth she had extended to the shifter had drained from her. There wasn't anything mild or kind about what she directed at me. She didn't possess any parental adoration or even affinity. I was nothing more than a target.

Her gaze was dagger sharp and arctic cold, making me shudder at the intensity of the hatred she held. Cowering wasn't in me, but I'd never experienced such unadulterated loathing before. I had to look at Nolan to see how close he was to me, hoping her venom was a culmination of the hate she had for the two of us.

When she pressed her hand against the wall that separated us, her mouth moved and the wall rippled and wavered but held. "I. Hate. You," she said, her fiery anger solely directed at Nolan.

"He stole you from me," she whispered to me. At least she had the good manners to appear to be hurt by it. It didn't diminish the offence I took at her assuming she could fool me.

"He's not going to live," Malific said. Although she kept

her eyes on me, she was addressing Elizabeth, who was standing over Arius holding the arrows and examining them. "The tips are missing, aren't they?" she asked with satisfaction. She shrugged. "Fifty years, I picked up some things. You don't know Erin, but how long has Arius been with you? Let the wall down, and I will agree to an oath to help him. If I don't, he will die."

Nolan swiped his hand through the air and fire blazed in front of Malific. She stepped through it. Blocked by the protective wall, she was unable to get to the other side. Fire licked at her skin. She trembled once, then eased into a placid expression that gave way to something that wasn't quite pleasure or acceptance of the pain. No, it was defiance. A rejection of letting the pain subdue her or deter her from her goal. At that moment, I realized every story about her was true.

Fear settled in my chest like an anchor.

"Elizabeth." Malific finally pulled her cold eyes from me to look at Elizabeth. "Choose. Arius or Erin." She pushed out my name with a level of resentment that caused me to take a small step back.

As she moved from the fire, Nolan let it fall. Arctic, hateful eyes moved in my direction, then to Elizabeth. A diamond-shaped piece of metal appeared between Malific's fingers. She jabbed it into the ground and whispered a spell, and it sparked a metallic blue and hummed with magic that could be felt through the ward.

"Elizabeth, if you want to contact me, just use this. Call my name and it'll lead you to me."

Malific's unyielding gaze remained on me as she backed away. The malicious smile that spread over her face and claimed her eyes said one thing: It was going to be me or her.

I felt the same way.

"Who's going to be the one who ends you, your mother or

your aunt?" Her ominous laughter resounded even after I could no longer see her.

We all looked at Elizabeth casting spell after spell, trying to save a dying Arius. When she looked up, I had a feeling it was going to be my aunt.

MESSAGE TO THE READER

———

Thank you for choosing *Nightsoul* from the many titles available to you. My goal is to create an engaging world, compelling characters, and an interesting experience for you. I hope I've accomplished that. Reviews are very important to authors and help other readers discover our books. Please take a moment to leave a review. I'd love to know your thoughts about the book.

For notifications about new releases, *exclusive* contests and giveaways, and cover reveals, please sign up for my mailing list at McKenzieHunter.com.

Made in the USA
Monee, IL
26 June 2021